AF279303

*After this, Jesus
traveled about from
one town and village to
another, proclaiming the good
news of the kingdom of God. The
Twelve were with him, and also some
women who had been cured of evil
spirits and diseases: Mary (called
Magdalene) from whom seven demons
had come out; Joanna the wife of
Chuza, the manager of Herod's
household; Susanna; and many others.
These women were helping to support
them out of their own means.*

—LUKE 8:1–3 (NIV)

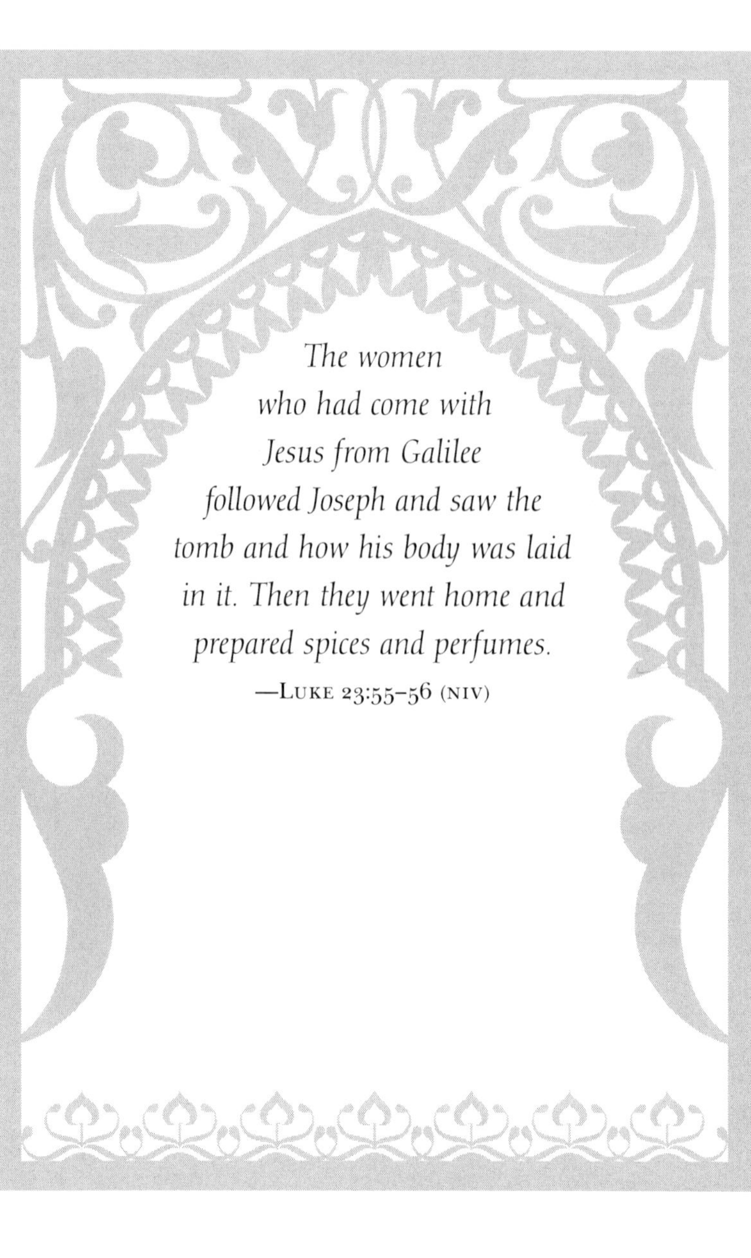
The women
who had come with
Jesus from Galilee
followed Joseph and saw the
tomb and how his body was laid
in it. Then they went home and
prepared spices and perfumes.

—LUKE 23:55–56 (NIV)

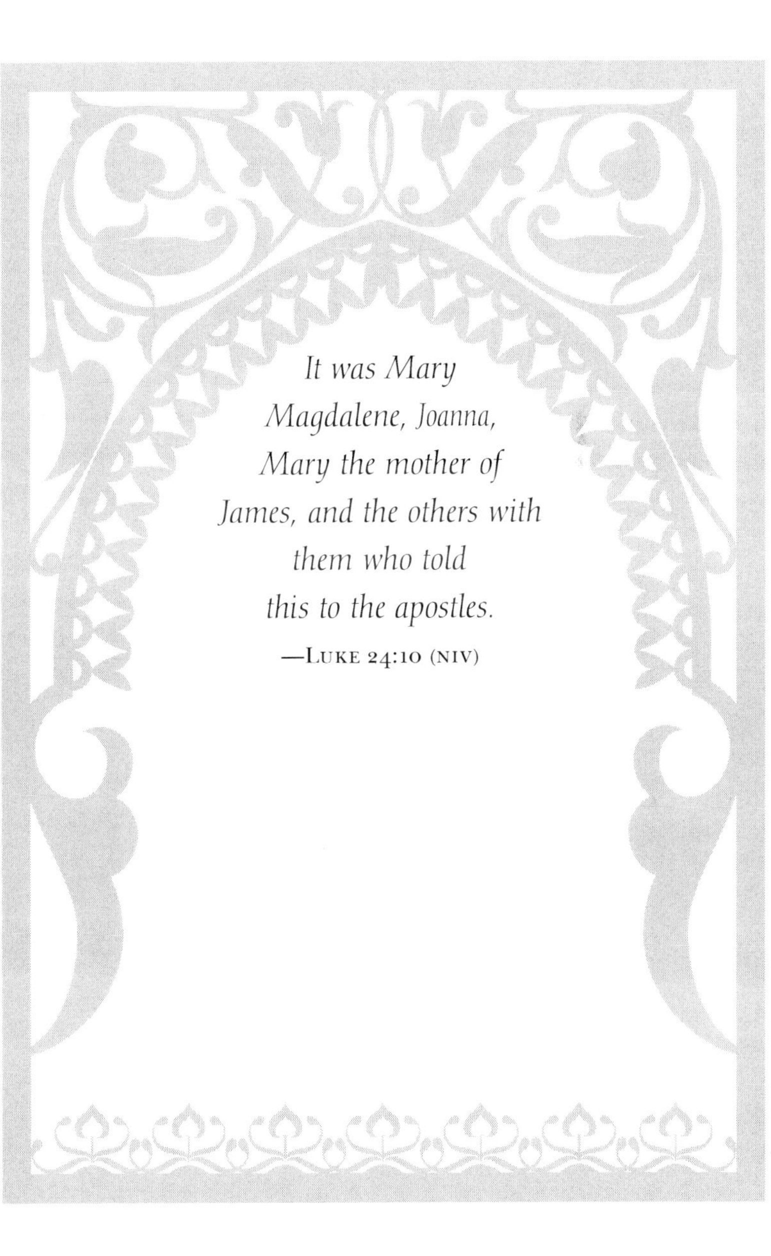

It was Mary
Magdalene, Joanna,
Mary the mother of
James, and the others with
them who told
this to the apostles.
—LUKE 24:10 (NIV)

Ordinary Women of the BIBLE

AN UNLIKELY WITNESS

JOANNA'S STORY

GINGER GARRETT

Published by Guideposts
100 Reserve Road, Suite E200
Danbury, CT 06810
Guideposts.org

Cover and interior design by Müllerhaus

Cover illustration by Brian Call and nonfiction illustrations by Nathalie Beauvois, both represented by Illustration Online LLC.

Typeset by Aptara, Inc.

ISBN 978-1-961251-25-0 (hardcover)
ISBN 978-1-961251-26-7 (softcover)
ISBN 978-1-961251-27-4 (epub)

Printed and bound in the United States of America

Ordinary Women of the BIBLE

AN UNLIKELY WITNESS

JOANNA'S STORY

CHAPTER ONE

Alone with Chuza in his chamber, Joanna watched her husband pack for the journey. Misery clutched at her heart.

"You were patient with me in the beginning," she reminded Chuza. "Kind."

"I delighted in you." He sighed. The words lingered in the air between them. They were true words. Chuza had delighted in her, but those days were over.

"When will you return?" She sat upon a bench next to the dressing table. A servant watched the couple from lowered eyes, pretending not to listen. Joanna didn't care any longer. It was hard to hold on to dignity in Herod Antipas's palace. It was hard to hold on to anything.

"A month, maybe more," he answered.

She winced. She knew why he had chosen this date to leave. Shaking her head to clear her mind, she decided she would have to think about that later. Perhaps she would walk in the gardens tomorrow morning after he left.

"You travel to Rome? For a festival?" The Roman calendar, different of course from the Jewish calendar, held several festivals at this time of year…none of which she had ever wanted to attend. For good reason.

"This is not good sailing weather." He looked away. "Herod wants me to prepare the Black Fortress."

She gasped. "Machaerus? Does he anticipate war?" Machaerus was a military fortress, known also as the Black Fortress, elevated high in the mountains on the eastern edge of the Dead Sea. On a clear day, you could see the cities vital to defense, including Masada, Jerusalem, even Cypros and Alexandrium. In good weather, if you looked to the northeast, smoke from the fires at the temple in Jerusalem were a gray blur against the blue sky.

No one vacationed at Machaerus, though. It was built by Herod the Great for defense of the kingdom.

"John the Baptizer has been spotted in that region," Chuza murmured, as if that were an explanation.

This man named John had been stirring the people up, especially her own people, the Jews.

Chuza walked to a table to review a collection of scrolls. He lifted one at a time, inspecting the seals. "Herod will travel there with the court. He very much wants to hear this man speak."

Why did not Herod command John to appear in Tiberius, then? It made no sense. Joanna started to protest. A sudden, terrible idea occurred. "Do you go to see a woman?"

He shook his head, but his back was turned. She had no way to read his expression.

"Go, then," she said softly. "I have no way to secure you."

"You did not need a way, once." Regret colored his voice.

"You did not seek to leave me, once." She gathered her frightened, exhausted thoughts and found the courage to press him for the truth. "Is it because you do not love me anymore? Or is it because you have grown tired of me? Of my infirmity?"

"No!" He turned and crossed the room, his hands extended as if to take her in his arms again.

Her breath caught in her chest. He stopped just before he reached her, dropping his hands to his sides, looking away.

"The shame is too great," he whispered. "If I lost my place at Herod's side, we would both be lost, Joanna. You cannot go back to your family. I cannot provide for us without Herod. But I have to prove that I am a man worthy of my title."

Chuza got people what they wanted. Chuza was the palace steward for Herod Antipas, in charge of all financial operations and procurements. He was good at it too. If Herod wanted building supplies, a rare wood, or the purest gold, Chuza got it. If a nobleman needed safe passage to another country for a private trade, Chuza made it happen. The world was an open market to Chuza. Nothing was denied him, and Herod took pains to be sure Chuza was well rewarded. Chuza could have anything in the world, and he could usually arrange to have it delivered too. No one said no to him. No one could.

Joanna smiled wistfully at the bitter irony. She too had never said no to him. Yet she could not give him what he most wanted, what he needed as a noble in this palace: a child.

The next morning Joanna sought refuge outside the palace walls. She emerged from the shadows into the bright sun, intent on stealing a few moments alone in the royal gardens of Herod Antipas. To walk in the quiet gardens offered something neither Rome nor ruler could grant: peace.

The gardens here in Tiberius had become a refuge for her. She had been raised in a busy village, so she wondered why the quiet gardens held such a special place in her heart. She had also been raised a Jew and should have yearned for the temple courts in Jerusalem, perhaps. In her family, however, religion was used for enhancing social position, not plumbing spiritual depths. So her love of gardens really made no sense at all, but this was a pleasant mystery she had no plans to solve.

The bright sun warmed her skin as she paused at the garden's entrance, relishing the warm light. Chuza had left the palace early this morning.

Sighing, she tilted her face to the sun, letting the rays caress her cheeks as she reminisced on ten years of marriage. She reminisced alone, as was fitting. Barren, she had been unable to give her husband what he most wanted—a child. Ambitious, he had been unable to give her what she most wanted—love.

Inhaling deeply, she caught the scent of a storm moving in. She needed to hurry, or she might miss her few moments of stolen peace. She walked down the path, grateful to be free of the thick incense of Herodias's chambers. The woman would be bitter company today. Herodias expected less important women to share entertaining gossip or information useful to the rich and powerful. Joanna trafficked in neither.

Joanna knew this was seen as a character flaw, even though Herodias was a Jew, and the women should have shared the same values. Herodias was not just a Jew, though. She was a royal, a princess from the Hasmonean line. Herodias was also married to Herod Antipas, son of Herod the Great. Herod Antipas's marriage to Herodias gave him a distinct political edge over his brothers. He married into royalty. He should naturally, then, rule over the majority of their father's kingdom. After all, Rome liked keeping the Jewish citizens content. A Jewish princess certainly could help do that.

But any hope of Herodias becoming a queen had been dashed by that cruel old tyrant, Herod the Great. Thirty-three years ago, as death drew near to the gates for Herod the Great, the venom that ran in the old king's veins spewed out onto his sons. Just before his death, he executed his firstborn son, and by the time his body was cold, his kingdom had been divided among three of his remaining sons.

Now Herod Antipas ruled over a land that was merely one-fourth the size of his father's original kingdom. Herod Antipas was only a tetrarch, "a ruler of a quarter," and not a king. His brother, Archelaus, had ruled over half, until he'd been exiled because the Jews hated him. A man named Pontius Pilate ruled in his place, appointed by Rome.

A second brother, Philip, also ruled over one-quarter. Augustus Caesar supervised both remaining brothers and reminded them regularly that their power ultimately came from Rome.

And so, Herod Antipas did not get what he most wanted, and neither did Herodias. He was not a king and so Herodias was not a queen. She was just one more woman who had married for power and woke up with a bureaucracy.

Just ahead, a grove of almond trees lined the path. Spring was not quite here, but winter had loosened its grip. This month, the month of Adar, was a month of unpredictable swings in the weather. The almond trees were heavy with white and pink blooms. Storms could destroy them in an instant, but Joanna hoped the month would be gentle. In the month of Adar, she was always tempted to count the blooms when she walked in the gardens. She wanted to protect each one, somehow, from the harsh storms that could descend in an instant. She wanted every blossom to become a thick cluster of almonds.

She didn't believe in magic, though Herod Antipas had plenty of court magicians. She believed in the one true God the rabbis spoke of. She just wished this God wasn't so cold, so stern and hard to please, because when she walked in the gardens she wanted more than anything to clap her hands and exclaim that He had done a marvelous trick, turning flowers into almonds, right under her nose!

Of course, if she could talk to God, she would have other things to discuss.

On her right, guards straightened their posture as she approached. She nodded and smiled. They visibly relaxed and nodded back.

A gardener emerged from a row of trees, carrying a basket of twine. He was accustomed to her daily strolls in the garden and nodded in greeting. Perhaps she should have insisted on more formal greetings from the staff, but she was not a royal. She was only a wife. Her sole job was childbearing. Her father's dowry had bought her into this palace, and she had failed in the one thing she had to do to stay.

Ten years married now and no children. Why did her thoughts come back to that problem, always? She had meant to enjoy a moment of peace out here and could think of only her troubles.

She'd done all that the royal physicians, here and in Rome, had recommended. She'd eaten pomegranates until her fingers were stained red, she'd drunk strange herbs until her head swam with visions, she'd bathed in rivers and prayed in the three watches of the night. Just to be sure, she'd prayed again on other nights in the four watches of the Romans. As a Jew, she marked time differently than the Roman Empire did. Rome hated that, just as Rome hated that Jews used a different calendar and celebrated different festivals. Rome preferred one calendar, one way of telling time. Which was efficient, and Chuza approved of the idea. But efficient was not to be confused with moral, and Rome was not confused about morals. It had none.

After ten years, she was so tired of hearing so much disdain from Rome about her God that she finally decided to offer up a few prayers to their gods, using one of their sundials to mark time. If a Roman official tried to offer Chuza advice about childbearing, at least Chuza could say that the Roman gods had been appeased. Even if none of the officials knew which god was on duty or when.

She shook her head. This line of thinking had to stop. This was an afternoon to be enjoyed. A rare moment of peace in a palace of strife. A storm was coming, and she would be driven back inside, trapped with Herodias for hours.

After walking along the manicured path that led through the gardens, she ducked behind an almond tree and removed her slippers. The dirt here was combed daily so that not even a stone could harm Herod. She loved the feel of the cool earth under her feet, sensing the gentle slope of a tree root beneath the ground, the tree searching for water in the darkness. Overhead, the branches sprang to life with delicate white blossoms, each with a pool of bright pinkish red at the center. No human hand could paint thousands of blossoms like this without smudging or ruining at least one. The capacity for repetition, for perfection and beauty, was a marvel. She walked along the path, watching the sunlight filter through the branches and the light play upon her skin. Soon the blossoms would fall, to be replaced with the fruit that would be the almond. She would miss the colors, though. Each season brought such beauty.

A rumble of thunder caught her attention. She reached out to touch a soft petal, hoping the storm would not shake too many free.

Rabbis taught that the blooms symbolized that God was always watching to see His Word fulfilled, yet as Joanna surveyed the Jews walking along dusty roads beneath the palace, she wondered if God saw what she did. Herod Antipas was not a friend of the Jews. Indeed, he was a friend to no one, only because he tried so hard to be a friend to everyone. His father, Herod the Great, had been so notoriously evil that his son Herod Antipas had wanted to be known for something else entirely. And he was. Herod Antipas was known for marrying his half brother's wife, who was also Antipas's niece.

The Herods were a complicated, immoral bunch. Both father and son had wanted to be thought of as Jewish leaders, but in their hearts, they were Romans. They served under a Roman caesar, and in Rome's name they ruled.

At least the son had tried to undo some of the damage his father had done to the Jews. Herod Antipas had dedicated his life to building cities, not tearing them apart. His great building project, the city of Tiberius, had started as a disaster, however, another casualty of not quite understanding the Jews.

He had chosen to build the city on top of an ancient Jewish settlement, which included a cemetery. No Jew wanted to break ground over the dead bodies of their ancestors. To do so would violate the law of cleanliness. Herod had paid dearly with imported laborers and bribes before the city had begun to take shape. She didn't know—perhaps no one did—what he had done with the bodies. Perhaps they were still in the ground.

Joanna watched the people trudging along the roads beneath the palace gardens. How many of them knew the truth about this city, this palace, this ruler?

Would God intervene one day to set things right for them? For her? She still waited for an answer to her prayers, just as they did. All the Jews waited for a rumored Savior who had never arrived. Centuries ago, the birth of a great king, the King of the Jews, had been foretold. A few decades ago, Herod the Great had commanded that every male child under two meet with the sword. He was determined to thwart the prophecy of a Savior born to the people.

Apparently, he had succeeded. No one had arisen to save the Jews. No government had formed to challenge Rome. Herod the Great had died old, fat, and wealthy. They said it was a mysterious disease that claimed his life.

Joanna scoffed at the idea. Herod had cheated death hundreds of times, perhaps thousands. There was no mystery in his death, only that such an evil man had been allowed to live and prosper, undisturbed, for so many years.

So many mothers had wept for sons lost, maybe some of these same women walking the roads in the city below. In the beginning of the construction work, there hadn't been any Jews in the city, but now they traded here freely.

Below, a lone woman paused and seemed to cast a dark glance up at the palace. Joanna wondered what the woman had lost. The palace cast a shadow over the city, the homes, the stalls at the market, and everyone's lives. The palace took a portion of everyone's earnings, even children's, and they could not refuse to pay the tax.

Nothing had ever been denied to the men who wore the crown and the seal of Herod.

Her breath caught in her throat; a quick movement among the trees caught her eye. She stilled herself, holding her breath, listening for a clue as to who else was in the garden with her.

After a moment, whispers reached her ears. She heard a man's voice, harsh and low. He was angry. Next, she heard a girl's voice, high and breathless, answering him when he paused long enough for her to reply.

After several moments, Joanna gathered the hem of her robe in her hand and checked to be sure her shawl was draped correctly with its brooch identifying her as the wife of an important official. She walked down the center of the path, searching for the couple.

Though Joanna only saw his back, the man's rank was easy enough to identify. The straps from the bronze chest piece and his thick leather belt made it clear he was a palace guard, probably a hired Gentile mercenary.

The soldier had a young servant girl cornered and cowering against a tree. The girl's face was red from tears.

"I did not mean to make a promise." The girl wept.

"You will honor your word, or I will make sure you have no honor left!" he snapped.

"What goes on here?" Joanna demanded.

CHAPTER TWO

The girl's eyes widened, and then she immediately lowered them as if ashamed. The guard spun around, his jaw clenched. His eyes swept over Joanna for an instant too long, and a shade too dismissively. But of course, at twenty-six, Joanna was past her prime, and her political power in the palace was known to be waning too. The servants and guards spoke of these things, she knew, entertaining themselves in the long watches of the night with such gossip.

Joanna met his eye and did not flinch. Her power might not be what it once was, but her husband was as powerful as ever. *Steward* was a humble title for a man who held so much power. Chuza was a doorkeeper, a gateway, the man who managed all of Herod's financial, romantic, and logistic affairs. Anyone who sought an audience with the king went through Chuza. Chuza had grown fantastically rich from bribes. He kept their secrets too. Every noble in the kingdom owed him a debt.

After a moment, the guard seemed to remember that as well and lowered his head.

"I did not know you were there," he said. "How may I be of assistance?"

"I believe I may be of assistance to you," Joanna replied, then turned to the girl. "You are a servant in the court of Herodias, are you not?"

The girl nodded, her eyes still downcast. Poor girl. Herodias was never happy when the court didn't have any visitors from Rome. Herodias was at her best when she was scheming to impress a Roman official.

"You are not in any trouble from me, little sister," Joanna said, her voice kind. She knew the look of terror she had seen on the girl's face. This guard had used his authority, size, and gender to bully the poor thing. Even if the girl was guilty of some petty crime, the guard was wrong to frighten her so.

The girl lifted her gaze and wiped her cheeks. A flicker of a grateful smile passed over her mouth.

Joanna turned back to the guard. "Was this some great matter of security? Has this child threatened to harm Herod?"

"No."

"She threatened Herodias, his wife?"

"No."

"Oh, I see. Then who was threatened? Why did you drag her out here, alone, to deal with the matter immediately, and without counsel?" Herod was a Roman ruler, and Roman law was very strict in procedure. The thought of accusing someone, and trying to obtain justice like this, was inexcusable.

"It is a matter of the heart!" The raw pain in his voice startled Joanna. Perhaps she had misread the situation, or assumed the worst based on her own experiences.

"Aresh promised herself to me," he said, not waiting for Joanna's permission to continue. "And I found her flirting with an officer of the guard. I know I'm just a foot soldier. I never had anything to offer her. If she wanted to marry another, I would have let her break our agreement."

Joanna looked from girl to guard then back again. How had she walked—literally—right into this? She had been attempting to escape the palace and its dramas. She wanted to see the green hillsides and peer out to the horizon of the Sea of Galilee. It was supposed to be a clear day, after all. She should have been able to see it. Instead, she had been swept back into this. And a storm was rolling in, stealing any hope for the afternoon.

The thick smoke of incense wafted through the trees. Above them, in the palace, Herodias was at her afternoon rituals. The incense was not for prayers, though. Herodias wasn't a prayerful woman. The incense would burn until a cloud of perfume thick enough to choke a camel had settled over her chamber, and then Herodias would soak in the vapors. The woman reeked of a burnt world.

Joanna cleared her throat, trying to dislodge the taste. Extending a hand to the girl, she nodded toward the entrance to the palace.

"Herodias will be needing you," Joanna said to Aresh. "Go on."

"Thank you," Aresh said. She started to walk past, then paused. "I am indebted to you."

"You can repay me by being more careful with your heart, or at least your words," Joanna whispered, then motioned the girl on.

The guard watched her go. Joanna recognized the pain in his eyes. She had felt this same agony just hours ago, watching Chuza leave.

"You love her."

Sighing, he turned away, as if to end the conversation. He walked back toward the guard's post at the garden's edge.

"Wait," Joanna called. He stopped. She wanted to say something, to try to offer the comfort that she had longed for just hours ago.

"You are both so young. She did not mean to hurt you. You will find another bride, and you will be happy."

He turned and looked over his shoulder at her. "And how do you know this?"

She smiled wryly. "Someone in this palace has to be happy. It might as well be you. Now go back to your post and try to forget her."

She wished Chuza could have witnessed this. He would have been impressed with her deft handling of a delicate situation. But losing her husband was doubly hard when he had also been her closest friend. He had been her only friend.

The guard left. Joanna knew it would take him a few weeks to mend his heart and his pride, but she knew that in time, he would mend. Time could do that. Time was a remedy for many wounds, the one medicine rich and poor alike could buy freely.

Time had not mended her wounds, however. Time *was* the wound. Ten years since her marriage, and no child. Not even a miscarriage. How odd to envy another woman's greatest grief! But Joanna had never even conceived, never felt the quickening of life, never known what it was to give life. *There is no greater rejection than to be denied the natural use of your own body*, she thought.

Living in the shadow of Rome made it more complicated. She had to obey Roman law but tried in her heart to follow Jewish law. What if this angered her God?

Was her infertility a punishment from God for living off of Herod's gold? His gold had come from his father, who had slaughtered the firstborn of the Jews. Yet both Herods claimed to be Jews and to honor the Jews. What a tangled mess.

Who could answer these questions? Who could live with them?

Not she. Not anymore. A cloud appeared on the horizon as purple tinged the edges of the sky. The storm was coming in too close, too fast. But of course, it was Adar, the month of storms and sunshine. It was time to go back inside and wait for this new storm to pass.

Her skin crawled, and she glanced up. Herodias stood in the window, looking down at her. "I wondered where you were," she called. "The incense bowls are smoking. When I am done you can use them. A man cannot resist a woman who perfumes herself well. Perhaps Chuza needs encouragement to call you to his chambers." Herodias loved to interfere where she didn't belong. She often made a barbed comment, then her eyes would brighten as she watched Joanna's face for a reaction.

Joanna shook her head, careful to maintain her composure. "You are gracious, but I must decline. Chuza is gone, and I have projects to tend to." She wanted to kick herself. That reply left her open to ridicule. Why was she so slow-footed when dealing with Herodias? The woman was as fast as a garden snake. She would have made an excellent queen.

"Projects?" Herodias laughed. "Without a husband or child, what could you possibly have to occupy your time? Anyway, come away from those trees. You are skinny enough to be mistaken for one, and a storm is coming." Herodias disappeared back inside.

Joanna bit back the harsh reply she so desperately wanted to give. Her weight was another source of humiliation. But, as usual, the sting of Herodias's words carried a bitter rub of truth. She was too thin. Chuza did need encouragement to call her to his chambers. And yes, a storm was coming, and no one should stand in a grove of trees during a storm. Joanna walked back toward the palace.

With a glance over her shoulder, she wondered…

Would the storm she faced ever pass?

As if in reply, lightning split the sky, and a growl of thunder shook the ground under her feet. She walked into the palace, the beautiful prison that had claimed her life.

Ten years prior
Summer, 19 CE
The Village of Gilgal

Joanna's entire village arrived before dawn and stood cheering outside her home. Of course, the people of Gilgal loved to celebrate. Gilgal had a bright and noble history—even its very name meant that the dark past had been rolled away. When Joshua had led the Israelites across the Jordan River, they had stopped to make camp. After they had honored the Lord, the Almighty said to Joshua, "Today I have rolled away the shame of your slavery in Egypt." That was why the village was named Gilgal. Gilgal sounded very much like the Hebrew word *galgal,* "to roll."

A fresh roar of approval went up from the crowd, making Joanna's mother jump. Joanna reached out to steady her mother's arm as she finished working with the heated stone to make curls in Joanna's hair. A maid called down from the roof, "Herod's chariots approach! The crowd is wild with happiness!"

Joanna was going to marry Herod's chief steward, Chuza. Chuza had picked a good month for the marriage, practically speaking. The grapes, figs, and olives were ripe and on tables everywhere, travel was easy, and people were too busy threshing grain to bother with highway robberies. To a laborer, the month of Av meant plenty of food and work. To a Jew, however, the month of Av meant something more. Jews called it "Menachem Av," or "Consoling Father." It was in Av that the Temple was destroyed, and the Jews sent into the Babylonian exile, as prophesied by Jeremiah.

Her father had forbidden any talk of that. Menachem Av would be Joanna's wedding month, nothing more.

Now, Joanna and her mother, her younger sisters, and aunts all gathered round. Joanna was the oldest sister and the first to marry, as was proper. Together, they formed a circle and grasped hands, though no one spoke. Next to her, Joanna's youngest sister sniffled, and her chin trembled. Joanna looked down and squeezed her hand, not trusting herself to speak without crying. *I'm not ready to leave.*

How Father had arranged this marriage, she never knew. Her dowry could not have been that large. And she was not that beautiful. She was only a girl from Gilgal, the town most known for a battle that had been waged long, long ago. The warriors of that age were dead now. There were no more heroes in the land. *I cannot do this.*

Her mother broke the circle first, reaching out to stroke her cheek. "You are scared."

Joanna nodded, eyes downcast. "He could have picked any-one, Mother."

Her mother kissed the top of her head as her aunt draped a richly pigmented red linen shawl over her head. As the aunt stepped back to adjust it, her mother gestured toward the door. "Do not keep him waiting."

One of the aunts supplied a thick rope of gold beads, and her mother attached this across the front of the shawl across her forehead, like a veil of golden pearls. Already Joanna fought the urge to let her head fall forward—the weight of such wealth was too much for her. Her mother clucked and lifted Joanna's chin with one finger.

Cosmetics and perfume had been applied hours before, and her hair had been set in thick curls. Joanna stood, ready. Her father swung the front door open wide, and a roar went up from the village once more.

When she stepped into the chariot, alone, she looked down at her family from a new height. She wanted to say something, especially to her mother, and tell her how much she loved her, but the noise from the crowd was too great, and the palace servants were dispensing coins as gifts.

She never saw her family again. On the heels of Joanna's successful marriage, her father married off her three sisters in rapid succession. They moved away to live with their husbands' families in distant villages. The following spring, her parents were attacked on the open road by thieves after making a pilgrimage to Jerusalem. They died where they fell.

Joanna still wished she had told her mother she loved her. But Joanna had left for her new life with the words still stuck in her throat.

Hours later, exhausted from the formalities and the feast that Herod required, she retired at last to a new bedroom with her new husband. The bedroom was huge, larger than her entire family's home. The bed itself could have fit her and her sisters. She stifled a giggle at the thought and was seized with a sudden homesickness. She had never felt so alone, yet she was surrounded by a palace filled with people.

Chuza had been kind and attentive to her all evening. At dinner he presented a wedding gift to her, a beautiful alabaster jar of perfume, the fragrance an intoxicating blend of jasmine and frankincense. She had the feeling she was a possession acquired, a deal that had been struck. The ceremony, perhaps, was the reason that she felt this way. The rite had been performed by a rabbi in the palace courtyard. Her father had been in attendance but said little, his eyes roving over the wealth surrounding them. Herodias had not been there, still angry that her own marriage had been snubbed by the religious rulers.

Herodias had married her own uncle, Herod II. He had been nicknamed "The Herod Who Does Not Have Any Land." He wasn't expected to become an important figure in the Roman government, and Herodias was a beautiful girl who felt importance was her birthright. So when Herod Antipas met her, the two claimed to be instantly lovestruck.

It made no difference that Herod Antipas and Herod II were half brothers. Or that Herod Antipas was also married at the moment. A divorce for each was quickly arranged, and a new marriage ensued.

And somehow, Herodias didn't understand why the Pharisees took issue with it all.

That evening, at Joanna's wedding feast, Herod Antipas had seemed distracted, uneasy by the brewing storm of his wife's temper. So, in reality Joanna's wedding had been a rushed affair, somber, in the presence of a rabbi she had never met and her father. A simple exchange of vows, a shared cup of wine, and she passed from maiden to wife. Her father had kissed her cheek before leaving, and she noted that his eyes were dry. But then, her father had always wanted a son. Sons were all that mattered to a man. She knew that. She had always known that, and somehow, she had been determined not to fail her own husband the way her mother had failed her father.

"Would you like me to stay?" Chuza asked.

Startled, she struggled to find a reply. She wished her mother had prepared her for what to expect. "Stay?"

His expression remained polite but dispassionate. "In your chambers. If you are afraid, or uncomfortable, you may desire company for a little while."

"These are my chambers?" She wanted to kick herself. Her first private conversation with the man she had just married, and she had done nothing so far but repeat his words.

"Yes," Chuza replied slowly, "and mine are not far from here. Would you like to see them?"

"Oh, n-no," she stammered. "That would be…"

"Inappropriate?" he suggested, a slight smile tugging at the corners of his mouth. "I agree. Oh, no. Wait. I believe we got married a few hours ago."

She laughed, and tension lifted from her like a weight. "I am sorry. I do not know how to be a bride. I have never been one before." She cringed inside, thinking how silly that sounded.

"Your father may have mentioned that." Chuza nodded solemnly, making her laugh all over again. "Still, despite your complete lack of experience, I think you did quite well today."

"It was not what I expected," she confessed. Her chin trembled. *Oh no,* she thought, *not now. Please do not start crying!* She was exhausted, though, and wounded by her father's reaction.

He laughed. "It was exactly what I expected. Very businesslike. Still, Herod paid for a splendid feast. And the musicians were lovely."

"No one seemed to enjoy the food," she ventured. "Everyone was so busy whispering."

"Of course. Welcome to palace life. Feasts are a chance to make deals and pass gossip."

Chuza moved to the bed and sat down. He removed his sandals, tossed them on the floor, stretched his legs straight out, then arched his back.

She took a step back, panicking. He had sat down on the bed! What did that mean? Was this a signal? Was she required to do or say something? Her mother had left her woefully unprepared for marriage, perhaps, but her mother had not married into a royal palace. Her mother wouldn't know the protocol here either. She had not even known how to keep a common man happy.

"These all-day affairs wear me out," he confessed. "Some kings hunt. Some fight. Herod likes to party. I would probably enjoy it all so much more if I did not know how much everything cost. Even you were quite expensive. But then, I think you are beautiful."

Joanna smiled, uncertain of him. He glanced up and tilted his head to one side, that wry smile returning to his mouth again. He wasn't a bad-looking man at all, Joanna thought. He was tall and well built, with a square jawline that made him look resolute despite the brown curls cascading down his neck. Flecks of gray adorned his temples, so she guessed him to be in his thirties.

"I make you nervous," he said. It was not a question.

"Marriage makes me nervous," she replied. For the second time, he laughed. It was the most wonderful sound in the whole world, she thought. To earn a laugh from a serious man was a treasure. She found the courage to step closer.

He patted the bed beside him. "Come and sit. Let us talk for a moment."

She obeyed. After she sat, he took her hands in his, turning his body to face her.

"Joanna, my dear. There are many kinds of men in this city. Some are cruel, and some are violent. You will meet foolish men and silly men. But your husband? Ah, he is a good man." He lifted her hands to his mouth and kissed them gently. "You do not have to be afraid of me. Ever."

She should have thanked him or complimented him. She should have pledged fidelity perhaps.

Instead, she nodded, tears stinging her eyes. What a day it had been. Saying goodbye to her mother and sisters this morning had been like a punch thrown to her stomach, and she had not expected that. It was still hard to breathe when she thought about it. And now this?

"Why me?" she asked. The question slipped out before she could censor herself. She had only met him once, when he supervised a shipment of lumber from her father's business. She hadn't even spoken to him that day.

Chuza reached one finger to her cheek and wiped a tear away. "Because from the first moment I saw you, I was enchanted. In a palace of vanity, I have the only truly beautiful woman."

Joanna blushed, and before she could look away, he leaned forward. His lips softly brushed hers.

He had been right about one thing only, she thought, even all these years later. She had never had to fear him. She feared his decisions these days but never his hand. What she wouldn't give to go back to that first night, to rewrite her vows, to promise him a child and somehow make it happen.

She would give anything, her very soul if it were possible, to rewrite the story of her life. Ten years later, and the precious gift she had been given in this man had been squandered.

Joanna sighed. How many words of love would die with her, trapped inside? Why had she left so many soft words unspoken? Now, in the hard years of life, it seemed too late.

CHAPTER THREE

Chuza smiled at Joanna, but he looked away immediately. Did he regret spending last night with her? Machaerus had such limited space that he had been forced to share a tiny room with her. She had not seen him in two months and had been relieved to find him thinner and wearied from hard work. Joanna found no evidence of any other woman.

Grateful to be reconciled, if only here in this outpost, she did not mind being denied a seat at the *triclinium*. Built across from the courtyard, the triclinium was where Herod took his meals. Featuring three couches around a low table, plus a roof overhead to shelter the diners from the elements, it was luxury on a small scale. There was only enough seating for Herod and a handful of people he deemed worthy.

He had not deemed Joanna worthy.

No matter. Machaerus lacked space, and that was a great advantage to her. Besides, spring was almost here, offering the loveliest weather. With warm breezes and cool evenings, starlit skies and dew-soaked mornings, spring in Israel was a brief dream that she always hoped would last.

Herod's court assembled in the courtyard. Positioning herself behind a pillar where she would not be noticed, she surveyed the crowd that milled around Herod's raised platform. Soldiers stood on the northern bastion that overlooked the courtyard, eager to hear from the guest. More soldiers milled in the overflow courtyard that spilled out by the storerooms.

It was easy enough to spot the one they called John. His robes were frayed at the hem. All the other men were nobles and Pharisees, and they wore their best robes to the palace. Why did John have such contempt for power? Was it for all power, or just Herod's?

Herod sat on his throne, his robes draped in layers of color: first the gold, then blue, then the red outer robe. In one hand he held a long scepter, and the rings on his fingers caught the light, as did the thick band of gold on his head. Even his beard was oiled and glistening.

Herodias sat beside him, her own crown tall and beaded with delicate gold and red silks raining down from it in cascades of color. She sat very still, her eyes alive and glittering. Her stillness reminded Joanna of a predator's stilled, calm freeze, just before the strike.

Joanna gently chided herself for being ungenerous. In truth, she knew, the crown was so heavy and so precarious upon the head that Herodias had to remain that still or the crown would tumble down and she'd be made a fool. Alas, but that would never happen. Herodias had one thing in this world that no man, no fate could ever bewitch away from her—her pride.

Joanna noted that the servants had applied extra thick kohl around Herodias's eyes today, accenting the color of her irises. Her eyes were green flames. Why did Herodias take such care with her appearance just to listen to a Jewish man? A Jewish man who was rumored to be rather odd too. Why come to Machaerus to hear him?

"Come forth." Herod lifted one hand and beckoned John. Herodias looked away as if already bored. Birds flitted overhead, landing on the towers in dark clusters.

John approached and stood before them both. "Greetings. I come, as always, in peace. I would like to speak to you alone, please, Herod."

Herodias sat stiffly, her eyes cutting to her husband.

So John had spoken to Herod before? Joanna wondered what had transpired. Herodias had not been pleased by it, that was plain.

"If this is a formality to please the Pharisees"—Herod waved a hand around the court—"then do not mind them. We do not observe strictest Jewish tradition here."

Joanna heard several muffled laughs.

"Whatever you want to say to me in private, say here, in the presence of my wife."

"I say again, you must repent, Herod," John said, squaring his shoulders. "The kingdom of God is near. It is nearer than you know. Even now, time is running short."

Herod smiled broadly. "I am a builder, John. No one knows how short time is better than a builder. But I have done nothing wrong."

Herod was crafty, but he was likable. Joanna was probably a fool, she knew, but she wanted to like him despite his flaws.

"You don't understand," John began again. "When you married your brother's wife, it was a sin. You sinned against God and against the Jews. Repent."

"I am a Jew!" Herod exclaimed. "We can argue the Jewish law all day. I can find a hundred teachers who will tell you I did nothing wrong." An uncomfortable silence fell over the court as everyone seemed to wait for the most obvious lie to fade and pass. Herod was not a Jew. His father had observed Jewish practices and holidays while brutally slaughtering any Jew who stood in his way. This was Herod Antipas's introduction to the Jewish faith, a mixture of ambition and hollow tradition. Jews despised the Herods and for good reasons.

"Besides, Philip was not a brother," Herod continued. "He was my half brother. Jewish law does not mention what is right between half brothers. And why do you focus on that one thing I did? You never focus on all I do that is good and right! Unlike my father, I have not murdered thousands of Jewish boys because of some ridiculous prophecy. I even pay for offerings to be made in my name at the temple in Jerusalem. If I am not a Jew by lineage, well, then at least I am a friend to the Jews! And do not forget my prize."

He reached for his wife's hand. "Herodias is a Jewish royal. Her lineage is beyond questioning. You should be honored that she represents us before Caesar Augustus."

Joanna watched John, waiting for his rebuttal. Instead, he only stared at the couple with what looked like grief etched across his face.

Whatever he felt for them, she knew, it was so much more than condemnation. "But is Herodias your wife? Is she truly yours and yours alone?" John ran his hands down his face then sighed. "Time is short, Herod. You listen, but you do not hear."

"You find fault with your king?" Herodias asked. She rested a hand lightly on Herod's arm, as if to restrain his temper. *She is so tricky,* Joanna thought.

Herod cleared his throat and leaned forward.

Joanna's stomach tightened at the confrontation. Herod wasn't a true king, he was a tetrarch, but if John pointed out the truth, he could be imprisoned, or worse.

"How can I find fault with Herod," John asked, with a gentle smile, "when he will not speak freely with me?"

Joanna breathed a sigh of relief. Chuza appeared at her side. Joanna's heart lifted to have him so near—she couldn't help it.

He nudged her and pointed to the guards along the walls in the back. A large crowd of nobles had pushed to the edge of the entrance of the courtyard to hear John. Joanna nodded to acknowledge her husband's worry.

"John is making trouble for himself," Chuza whispered.

John is making trouble for you, husband, Joanna thought. Chances were good that none of the noblemen at the entrance had sought an audience with Herod today. None of them had bribed Chuza either, so Chuza had no money for the day's work plus no way to prepare if Herod called one of them forward. Chuza would sound foolish.

"They're behaving like children," he muttered to her. "In the common areas, everyone gossips about John and his strange habits, his strange speeches. They also like to see Herodias get riled. Somehow, John manages to accuse Herod and his wife of the basest immorality, but they have yet to find a way to get rid of him. I think it is Herodias who will see it done."

"She was married to Herod's half brother," Joanna whispered. "That *is* base immorality."

"Keep your voice down," Chuza chided. "Remember your place. And remember that people in power have different ideas about morality. We had better support their ideas if we want to stay in this palace. Besides, the half brother lives a comfortable life as a citizen of the Roman Empire. He no longer has any territory to manage, and he has a healthy allowance." His voice had a weary tone. Joanna decided not to add to his burdens by arguing. She returned her attention to the court.

"I will leave now, Herod," John said. "But think on my words. I may not be able to return."

"You will return if your king commands it," Herodias snapped.

Herodias had referred to her husband as a king twice now. No one flinched, though everyone surely noted her choice of words.

John paused, his back turned. Slowly, he faced Herodias. The court fell silent as the two stared at each other, locked in unspoken combat. Joanna felt the air in the room change.

"You misunderstand my intention," John said steadily. "The ancient prophecy has come to pass. The Messiah is here. What was set in motion at the beginning of time has now swept us up in its path. My destiny is no longer my own."

He bowed and turned for the exit. Herodias leaped to her feet, her mouth falling open, her breath coming in ragged gasps. The crown fell with a crash, drawing cries from the spectators. Herod pushed farther back on his throne with one hand over his mouth, clearly in shock. The guards looked one to another, as if awaiting instructions to capture or kill John, but for what? The real threat was in the idea of a messiah, not John.

Joanna was aware of her heart beating, the sound like hoofbeats in her ears, as if something strong and relentless was now moving toward her. Toward her, toward the palace, toward them all. She gripped the pillar she still hid behind and tried to calm her own breath.

The Messiah?

"It cannot be," Chuza whispered. "His generation was wiped out. Not a boy left alive."

Herod the Great had killed every male under the age of two to prevent this prophecy from coming to pass. All those little lives ended. And he had failed to stop a future revolt, the prophesied King who would topple the throne? The injustice was unimaginable if that was true!

"Stop!" Herod rose from the throne.

No one moved, save John, who was at the end of the courtyard. He turned, a quizzical expression on his face.

"You say the Messiah survived, and that he is here, among my people. Not in Rome?"

John shook his head. Herod's face drained of color. Would Rome hold Herod accountable and remove him from power? He'd already lost the right to rule once. News of this Messiah, if it reached Rome, could mean exile or worse.

"How can you be sure?" Herod demanded.

"I've seen Him." John shrugged. "And soon, so will the world."

A small gasp escaped Herodias. Joanna kept her head lowered, not daring to catch her eye while she was so alarmed.

Herod the Great had rebuilt a temple for the Jews and remodeled the world for himself. But he had also shattered the hope of the Jews for a messiah. He wanted the Jews to forget everything they knew and remember only one name—his.

He had ordered the killing of all male children of the Jews, but that was thirty years ago. Where had this future King been hiding? Who had hidden Him from Herod's sons, from Rome and Caesar?

Joanna leaned forward, trying to get a deep, clean breath. A conspiracy this complex, and so well hidden for so long, could only mean one thing—whoever He was, He didn't just want one throne. He wouldn't be satisfied with just one country. He would claim nothing less than the entire world.

CHAPTER FOUR

The steps of the servants grew less frequent on the path outside Joanna's chambers. In Machaerus, the tiny chambers she shared with Chuza had an exterior door that opened to a path within the fortress. Machaerus was not built for long-term living but strategizing in times of war. Still, as always, there was a flurry of activity at day's end in the center of the fortress near Herodias's chambers. Herodias should be preparing to retire for the evening. She had to be undressed, oiled and perfumed, redressed, her hair combed and teeth cleaned, her chambers made comfortable, and the altar in her room prepared with fresh fruit or offerings to the Roman goddesses she favored.

Herodias had a fondness for the more extravagant gods she had been exposed to while in Rome. She liked the pageantry, the wars between gods, the long tales of vengeance and eternal longing.

Joanna, however, hated those Roman gods and stories. Who wanted a petulant god? What could a god like that create except chaos? Humanity created that easily enough. How had Herodias abandoned the faith of her childhood so effortlessly?

Of course, Joanna couldn't say any of this to Herodias, or Chuza, and certainly not her own maids. A maid was just a lazy method of communication. Whatever Joanna said was always repeated to Herodias. She'd learned that the hard way.

Joanna heard the shattering of glass and Herodias screaming at a servant. Her heart pounding, she moved to the doorway to listen for another noise. Moments later, a weeping servant came scampering down the path.

Herodias had been in a rage since John's visit. Herod had retreated to his chambers with Chuza and a handful of advisers.

Joanna stepped outside. The moon was a sliver. In Jerusalem, the rabbis would be celebrating the new month. A sudden longing for the familiar, for her people, seized her.

A young boy carrying a leather satchel jogged down the path. Holding out one hand, she stopped him.

"You need to be careful!" she said. "Without light, the trails here are treacherous. We are not in Tiberius."

The boy was no more than nine or ten. She noticed that the satchel held the royal seal of Herod.

"Where is he sending you?" she whispered.

"To Jerusalem," he said. "A message for the temple council." A moth flew near his head, and he swatted it away.

"No one will notify Rome?" she asked. "Or even Pilate?"

The boy shook his head. "Herod says this is a Jewish matter, not a matter for the government."

She took a step closer. "What is the message?"

The boy looked pale as his eyes grew wide.

"I am the wife of Chuza," she said, "the steward. Tell me."

The boy lowered his head and whispered. "Herod sends word that the problem of John will be handled here at Machaerus, where there are no Roman courts to interfere."

She pressed a coin into his hand, sending him on his way. Leaning against the doorway, she caught her breath. What did Herod mean, *the problem of John*?

With the storm raging in Herodias's chambers, and Chuza busy attending to Herod, no one would be looking for Joanna. If she was going to find out the truth about this prophecy, she had to do it tonight.

As she wrapped the linen shawl around her shoulders, a breeze from the window brought a chill from the night air and the scent of woodsmoke. Far below the fortress, in the sparse and poor villages, fires were burning for supper. She wondered what they had to eat. The Black Fortress was a desolate place near the Dead Sea.

She brought the shawl higher, draping it over her hair, letting the end fall over one shoulder, then tugging at the front edge to lower the fabric across her forehead. She did not want to be recognized.

Was she really going to do this? *Yes. I must know.* For all the fear and blunder happening in the chambers down the hall at the moment, Joanna remembered the prophecy too. She'd heard it enough times in her childhood to know the stories. Joanna remembered that this King of the Jews would be much more than a great king. Faithful Jews believed He would have the power to work miracles. He would be like a second Elijah.

She didn't care about the politics of the kingdom. She was terrible at those games anyway. She was being driven mad by emptiness. What she wanted, only God could give her. Or the Messiah, if He was here. That's what she had to find out. She would tell Chuza the truth, no matter what she found out. She would never betray him.

She would return immediately to the fortress and have something of great value to offer Chuza. Perhaps she would know the Messiah was here. She would know there was a chance to have her womb opened. Chuza could have the son he'd always wanted, the heir that his position demanded. Or she would return and confess that her spying had revealed the news from John to be nothing more than reckless rumors. She would be rewarded for the bravery of discovering the truth and helping to put Herod's court at ease. Chuza would be proud to be her husband.

She smiled. Maybe she wasn't terrible at politics. Maybe she was just a late bloomer.

By the early morning hours, Joanna knew one absolute truth—her sandals were too thin for the rough stones along the trails leading down from Machaerus. Jerusalem and Rome had streets where the stones had been beaten to nothing but dust. Rome excelled at making good roads. A toddler could walk on those streets without falling. But here, the stones were dreadfully sharp and loose too.

If her servants saw her bruised feet tomorrow, there would be talk. She bit her lip, trying to think of a lie. She was terrible at lying. She was terrible at life in court. She didn't think fast enough. She didn't think far enough ahead.

How was she going to find John? He couldn't have gone far since last night. She sat down by an aqueduct cut into the mountain for channeling rainwater into a cistern. Exhausted, she removed her sandals to rub her feet.

Twice already Herodias had offered her healing charms or spells from her court physicians. Twice, Joanna had declined. Herodias had even offered to send Joanna to Rome, to see the oracle there, even though this was an outrage against Jewish law and custom. Of course, everyone in the world agreed that infertility was a judgment from God. But Roman gods were subject to whimsy, and therefore could be bribed or persuaded. Seeing the oracle might provide insight into what the god wanted.

Joanna wondered why Herodias failed to see the logical flaw in this plan. A god that had no control over his or her emotions might be easy to bribe but would be just as easy to offend. Given that Joanna stumbled about so clumsily in court politics, she did not think it wise to take chances like that. Besides, she was a Jew in her heart, even if this court was not.

The sky turned pink at the edges as dawn broke, and the workers walked through the streets to their jobs.

But if her mission today failed, what option would she have but to accept? Chuza would be furious that she had left the palace like this, alone and in search of this supposed King...but only until he held his newborn son.

Voices carried on the morning wind. Lifting her head, Joanna looked around. Below her, near the opening to a cistern, locals were drawing water for their sparse flocks of sheep. Several people had left their sheep to graze and were clustered around one man.

John!

His voice rang out clear in the morning hush. "The kingdom of God is at hand!"

Chattering rose about his words, about what they could mean. Their voices rang with hope and excitement. What a contrast to Herod and Herodias, she thought, who took his words as a sour warning. She paused, considering the scene. John was sincere. He seemed to believe that the prophecy of the Messiah had been fulfilled. Hope was alive.

"Repent!" John called. "Whatever you have done that stands in the way of loving God and loving your brother, repent now! Let nothing stand in the way!"

His clear voice rang out above the clamor of the market. He was a strong man, rumored to have survived in the desert on locusts and honey. Yet he was the picture of health and vitality, and not a few of the women in the crowd seemed to admire rather than listen.

Joanna walked down to the edge of the crowd and pulled her cloak lower around her face, hoping to obscure her features as much as possible. More people walked up the path to hear John.

"The kingdom of God is at hand," he called.

This was the same message he had delivered to Herod, one of the most important men in the world. John gave the same message to common people. Either he was crazy, or he was telling the truth. He certainly wasn't angling for political gain.

Joanna's heart soared. John was not a charlatan or leading a rebellion. He really believed the Messiah was here. Had the age of miracles really arrived?

A woman in plain, threadbare robes stepped back, right onto Joanna's foot. Joanna cried out and pushed the woman aside, trying to free her foot from being crushed.

"Careful!" the woman snapped, whirling around. Several women at the edge of the crowd stopped listening to John, turning their attention instead to Joanna and this woman.

"You were on my foot!" Joanna exclaimed. Without even thinking, she took a deep breath and corrected her posture, holding herself erect. She was a wealthy woman who carried her husband's honor with great dignity. That was her only job, and it was no less noble—or exhausting—than carrying water or selling fish.

The other woman didn't seem to see it that way. She reached out and touched the edge of Joanna's cloak, a look of disdain on her face. "From Herod's court, I suppose? Out here without a guard or chaperone? Are you here to spy on us? Why do women like you always think what we have is yours? You have no right to slink around trying to pretend to be one of us. If you want to hear John, call him to court. Servants have their place, and so do the likes of you!"

Stunned, Joanna could make no reply. The other women glared at her, and they pulled the offended sister into their group, clucking and fussing over her. Joanna's foot throbbed.

The woman might have broken one of her toes, plus Joanna had the bruises from the road, and now this? The women rebuked her because of her station.

Shouting caught her attention. At the center of the men nearest John a scuffle had broken out. Men were yelling, and several were throwing punches. Joanna's hand flew to her mouth. Combat was for sport, for the arena, not for the streets! This was shameful behavior. And what was the fight over? She craned her neck, hoping to see.

Instead she was roughly pushed aside by one of Herod's guards. Joanna ducked her head, but she was too late. The guard saw her, but she could not be certain he recognized her. She was woefully out of place. Hopefully he was too distracted to remember her face or mention it to his commander.

John was served the arrest warrant in Herod's name. Men spat on the ground when they said the tetrarch's name. The women in the crowd turned to glare at Joanna, their eyes narrowing to slits.

Joanna picked up the edge of her robe and moved as quickly as she could through the crowd, desperate to make it back to the fortress before the crowd turned violent.

The following evening

"Herodias would like to see you in her chambers." Aresh, the maid Joanna had saved from a guard's affections, stood in her doorway.

Joanna's breath caught in her throat. Who else knew of her absence? And most importantly, did anyone know where she had gone?

She grabbed her outer robe and tied it quickly at the waist, then walked with Aresh along the darkened path. Aresh said nothing, focused on holding the oil lamp steady as she navigated the rocky path.

Joanna tried to think clearly. If anyone suspected what she had done, they would not have sent Aresh to fetch her to Herodias. A guard would be leading her to Herod.

Still, Joanna wanted to pinch herself for being so clumsy, so foolish. The entire outing had been a disaster. She walked carefully, trying to disguise her stiffness. The soles of her feet were tender and the muscles of her calves sore.

Aresh paused at the chamber door. "Good luck," she whispered.

Seconds later, Joanna bowed in the presence of Herodias. Herodias was at her cosmetics table, watching as another maid chose an eye palette for the evening. Herodias favored the glitter bought from the Egyptians. Made from crushed beetle wings, it caught the changing lights from torches, reflecting bronze and green as she turned her head side to side.

"Use a heavy hand with the kohl tonight," Herodias commanded the maid. "We have something to celebrate."

"What is that?" Joanna ventured. *John's arrest?*

"I thought you knew," Herodias replied. "We leave for Tiberius in the morning. I am anxious to return to my usual accommodations."

The maid moistened an ivory stick in a pot of clear liquid, then dipped it in a jar of kohl. Herodias closed her eyes, and the girl carefully traced arching lines along the eyelids.

Herodias turned on the carved stool and looked at Joanna.

Pausing, Joanna considered how she must look to Herodias. The robe was the same one she had worn yesterday. The hem was torn at the bottom, only slightly, but nothing escaped Herodias's eyes. One toe peeked out from a sandal, and it was the one that had been stepped on. The bruise was beginning to show itself, in a dark purple around the nail. Joanna withdrew her foot immediately, but it was too late.

"Do you know what I hate?" Herodias asked.

Joanna was afraid to look her in the eye. "No," she replied. Leaving the fortress to hear John had been a betrayal of Herod. Herod was not a man who liked being betrayed.

"I hate missing all the fun," Herodias said.

Joanna concealed her surprise.

Herodias watched her closely, leaning toward her. "Unlike you, I have no time for adventures. Being a dutiful wife takes all my time."

Joanna nodded, swallowing her anger at the insult.

"I just want to know," Herodias said, lowering her voice, "did John call down curses on Herod? Do or say anything that would compromise him?"

"No. I heard nothing like that."

"Do you know why my husband's brother, Archelaus, lost his right to rule? Remember, Caesar Augustus let him rule half of the kingdom, while my Herod only got one-quarter. But now

Archelaus lives in exile and Pontius Pilate rules in his place. Do you know why?" Herodias paused, studying her fingernails.

Joanna's face grew hot. She hoped she didn't turn red too. Herodias would relish her discomfort too much. "No. I do not know."

"Because of *our* people, Joanna! The Jews!" Herodias yelled, standing, knocking her chair to one side. "The Jews complained to Rome about Archelaus! The Jews complained so much that Rome took the kingdom away from him! Do you want that to happen to us?"

Joanna took a step back, her knees trembling. "Of course not!"

The maid slipped forward and put the chair back in its place.

"Then why would you leave the palace to find John? To ask about the so-called Messiah he is spreading lies about? You do not realize what he is doing?"

"No," Joanna said, feeling as foolish as a child.

"He's whipping our people into discontent. Rome will have no choice but to remove Herod, and then who will rule us? Rome. And while you may not believe that Herod and I are Jews, I can promise you this: Rome is certainly not." Herodias sat back down with a huff.

So many questions swam in Joanna's mind at once. First, how did Herodias know where she had been?

"It's a dangerous time to be naive, Joanna," Herodias said sweetly. "I know you would never betray your husband, not intentionally. But listening to an enemy of Herod, mixing with a crowd as they spoke of rebellion…the penalty for crimes against Rome is death."

Fear rose in Joanna's throat, constricting it.

"I can help you," Herodias said. "I have been called many things, but naive is not one of them."

Joanna nodded uncertainly.

"If anyone asks," Herodias said, "tell them you went on an errand for me."

"Why would you protect me?" Joanna asked, surprised she found the courage to speak.

"I'm selfish, Joanna. Or do you not listen to John?" Herodias sighed, a sneer playing at the corner of her mouth. She motioned for her maid to draw near and resume the application of cosmetics. "I want to see you prosper. Your husband is a reflection of my husband. Chuza needs to be successful because he is second in command only to Herod Antipas. I will tolerate no display of weakness in my court."

Herodias turned, looking over her shoulder, her eyes meeting Joanna's. The message was clear. Joanna's infertility would no longer be tolerated.

"How did you know I went to hear him?"

"You're a smart girl, Joanna. There are only two possibilities."

Joanna exhaled softly, trying to compose herself and hide her growing frustration. "Either you had me followed, or you have spies in the market."

Herodias chuckled. "I have spies everywhere."

Joanna walked to the window. The sun had sunk nearer to the Dead Sea. Sparkles from the water at the edge of the horizon beckoned to her. The world looked enchanted from this distance. Up close, Joanna thought, it was often something less than beautiful.

Joanna stole a sideways glance at Herodias. The light was unkind to Herodias's face. Ridges and furrows wrinkled her brow, and her mouth had deep lines etched all around. Although Herodias wore more and more makeup every year, it did nothing to recapture the glow of youth. Joanna had done the math, though. Surely Herodias was only ten years or so older than Joanna. Why did she look even older than that?

The real Herodias, the woman with the darkened heart, floated just beneath, peering out from heavily painted eyes.

"John has spoken against my marriage many times," Herodias said, not looking at Joanna. "He claims it is impure, that it does not please God. Think about that. That old tyrant, Herod the Great, wiped out an entire generation of Jewish boys, then he betrayed his own son, my husband. My husband has been fair to the Jews. He allows them to prosper, to work and worship. And yet John thinks my husband is the sinner? He wants my Herod to publicly repent. To cast me aside. I was born a Jew! A royal princess, no less. How could marrying me be a sin?"

Her voice became shrill, and Joanna knew the questions were not meant to be answered.

"I want John executed," Herodias said flatly. "Herod had John arrested instead. It was a compromise. A good marriage is based on them, you know."

Joanna swallowed nervously. A sparrow flew past the window and came to rest in an olive tree below. Its song was sweet, and Joanna longed to fly free of this room and join it.

Herodias turned and clapped her hands at the maid, who scurried from the room. Returning a brief second later, she held a clay jar in front of her body like it was an offering. She approached the women and lowered her eyes.

"Go on." Herodias nodded to Joanna.

Joanna looked from the jar back to Herodias. What was inside? Jars such as this could contain a snake or any kind of small live animal for sacrifice.

"Go on. Open it."

Joanna's breath grew shallow as her heart ticked to a faster rhythm. Reaching out, she willed her hand not to tremble. *Do not dishonor me,* she wanted to tell her body, *not again, not here. Not in front of my persecutor.*

She lifted the lid, still holding her breath. Nothing inside stirred. With a quick look at the maid, who nodded just a tiny degree for encouragement, Joanna leaned forward. Inside was a necklace with an ornate filigree ornament.

She lifted it out and held it to the light. It was in the image of a beautiful, ornate basket, and in the center was a deep purple stone. The stone was uncut, and its edges were opaque and jagged.

"A fertility charm," Herodias said, stepping to stand close beside Joanna. Her voice was thick with admiration. "From a sorcerer who serves the court in Rome. I purchased it at great expense, just for you."

"Thank you," Joanna replied. Her mind was scattered with so many thoughts, and the weight of the necklace made her arm heavy. A tremor of some light feeling, perhaps hope or perhaps fear, shot through her heart.

"I know that you desire a child, Joanna. With my help, you will have a child. Remember, in this court, our fates are tied together. Never again seek help from this so-called Messiah, and I promise that you and Chuza will have a bright future."

Joanna replaced the necklace in the box. The weight had felt unnatural in her hands.

"Put it on," Herodias urged. "Wear this as an offering to the Roman gods."

"I do not care for the Roman gods."

"Herod rules at the pleasure of Rome. It is Rome we must please. No one else."

"But I am a Jew. I cannot change what I am."

Herodias took a step closer, so close that Joanna could feel the heat radiating from her cheeks as the woman stared into her eyes.

"But I can," Herodias snapped. "I can make you something so much less than a wife." Her voice was cold as it dripped each word out.

With trembling hands, Joanna picked up the necklace and slipped it over her head. Herodias held all the power in this palace; if she wanted to get rid of Joanna, she could. Making an offering to a Roman god was unthinkable, but so was being thrown out from the palace for refusing to wear a necklace. The amulet landed with a dull thud against her heart. Excusing herself immediately, she then returned to her room with the excuse of packing for the journey home.

Blinding sunlight pierced the empty room. A headache clutched the base of her skull, its knifelike fingers wrapping around her head. Instinctively, her fingers went to the charm that hung around her neck. Scooping her fingers underneath, she began to lift it off, wanting to be free of it, wanting to draw a clean pure breath, but then stopped. Herodias would watch to be sure she wore it, and she had spies everywhere.

Knowing she was caught in a trap, Joanna let the necklace slip back down around her neck. The only escape was to give Chuza a child. *But then, who knows,* she thought, resting her forehead against the doorframe in sudden weariness. *Herodias might find a way to claim that for herself too.* Joanna had to face the truth. This way of life was how she would live and how she would die.

Even if there was a Savior, there was no salvation from Herod's court. In her soul, she felt a thousand doors slamming shut. With growing dread, she wondered if making an offering to a Roman god had opened a door best left closed.

CHAPTER FIVE

Spring, 30 CE
On the plains of lower Galilee

Joanna patted her horse, whispering encouragement to him as he picked his way around the dead volcano. A donkey would have been a better choice for this terrain, but of course, she was from the royal palace. Image was everything to Herod, because image was everything to Herodias.

The poor beast kept stumbling over the sharp rocks. The strong winds that swept past without warning did not help. The caravan had left Tiberius and was now approaching the Horns of Hattin. Once a fearsome volcano, now all that remained were two hills with a deep, treacherous ravine between them. Birds loved to nest in the ravine by the thousands.

Herod nodded to a guard, who loosed an arrow into the ravine below. Hundreds or perhaps a thousand or more birds scattered and took flight, making the traveling party laugh. To Joanna, the white birds looked like a cloud lifting from the depths.

The court was traveling to Jerusalem to celebrate Passover. Pontius Pilate would be ready to receive the party at Herod the Great's palace, and together they would send offerings to the great Jewish temple there. Pontius Pilate traveled frequently in his governance of the region, but he spent much of his time in Jerusalem. The city would be alive with visitors and pilgrims, the pious and the common criminals, those who wished to repent and those who wished to make a quick bit of coin.

Rubbing her temples, Joanna wondered if there would be a healer in the court at Jerusalem, one who might be persuaded, privately, to prescribe something for her headaches. She did not want to ask Herodias for help in finding a solution. The woman might offer more magic, not medicine.

Her horse stumbled again. Joanna started to snap at it, then caught herself and felt remorse. Looking up to see who had witnessed her weakness, she caught Chuza watching her, a scowl on his face. He had bade her to come to his bedchamber last night, but she had been sorely ill. He had taken one look at her and sent her away. She didn't want to tell anyone, but over the past year, she'd been plagued with headaches and terrible dreams.

Her nerves were stretched thin, that was all, she told herself. Riding a frightened, unsteady animal didn't help. If only there was a way to calm the poor beast.

"If only Herod had taken the King's Highway," a girl's voice said. Joanna looked up and saw that the girl she had saved in the palace gardens, Aresh, now rode beside her. Aresh rode a donkey, and that animal had no problem with the terrain. Joanna's horse fell in step with the other animal, seeming to be soothed by its presence and confidence.

"The King's Highway runs true north and south," Aresh continued. "We would not have all the switchbacks or ravines for the men to amuse themselves with. Travel is faster and easier for everyone."

Joanna's shoulders loosened as her horse settled into a steady rhythm. *Thank You, God.*

"I've never been on the King's Highway," she confessed.

"Never?" Aresh's eyebrows shot up. "I've taken many trips on it. My father was a trader. But I'm happy to serve in the palace. It's a good job for a girl." She shrugged, looking at Joanna with wide eyes, perhaps expecting confirmation of this fact.

Joanna peered at her. Aresh seemed to be telling the truth. Perhaps Aresh was the kind of girl who enjoyed everything. Maybe too much? That guard had been so hurt by her betrayal. Or the misunderstanding, whichever it was.

"You do not mind the gossip?" Joanna asked. "The backstabbing?"

Aresh laughed. "I don't pay it any mind at all." She cocked her head, as if willing Joanna to catch her meaning, but she didn't.

"If it's not about me, I ignore it," Aresh explained. "I'm lucky to be here. Half my friends are already married off to broken old men who needed a nurse. The other half are married off to men who wanted slaves, not women. Can you imagine? At least here I'm free."

"Free?" Joanna scoffed. "I mean no offense, but Herodias yells at you night and day."

"Maybe someday I will find happier arrangements." Aresh's voice trembled slightly, and Joanna wondered why. Aresh had to know she would never be anything but a servant.

"Aresh!" Herodias called. "I require water."

The girl ducked and reined her donkey back. "You could ask for me," Aresh whispered. "Ask me to serve you instead. Herodias does not yell because I am a bad servant. She yells at everyone. Please! I'm a hard worker. And you like me, I can tell."

Joanna laughed out loud at the impertinence. Aresh laughed too then circled her animal.

"If your horse has trouble, call to me," Aresh said. "I know how to make myself useful in bad situations."

True, Joanna's horse seemed steadier now. But Aresh was asking to be rescued for a second time. Was that due to circumstances or character? Chuza would counsel Joanna not to strike a deal if a flaw had revealed itself so early.

Joanna sighed, wishing Chuza still had any interest in counseling her in this matter, or any other.

Two days later

The sky was a flawless blue mirror, stretching endlessly before her. The limestone gates of Jerusalem stood in warm welcome. Joanna's back and shoulders ached from the two-day journey. Chuza liked for her to sit tall and proud, which was wonderful to look at and murder on the shoulder muscles after the fourth hour.

Still, she loved entering the old city, the jewel, Jerusalem.

When they entered by the road that led down from Caesarea, her horse had perked up at the smells and sounds of a city in full preparation mode for the Passover observation. Pack animals from every trade route carried exotic goods; merchants sold herbs and spices that could only be bought here; the markets were in full swing.

The clop of hooves of Herod Antipas's party was quickly overshadowed by the songs of children in the streets. Performing for coins, the children played lyres and lutes and sang psalms that King David had written. A few girls danced, and Joanna noticed how Salome, Herodias's daughter from her first marriage, leaned out from the litter to watch them closely. The girl loved music, Joanna knew, but most of all, Salome loved to dance. It was a pure love for the girl, not born from a hope to manipulate men or win favor. Salome had always tapped her feet and wiggled in her chair during entertainments. The little girl who loved to move had become a young woman who loved an art.

A boy ran toward Joanna and bowed low. "I have a dried fig for your horse if you have a coin," he called.

She laughed and reached into the bag on her saddle. The exchange was quick, the boy eager to see the coin in his own hand. He fed the horse and petted it on the nose before rushing off to join the others.

The Jewish boys, with their clean robes and bright sashes, left the temple after morning lessons, walking solemnly through the streets. She watched the sunlight illumine their innocent, unlined faces. Daughters of the merchants peeked out from behind stalls, watching the boys too. The young girls, tending the stalls, wore brightly colored robes, their hair loose and cascading down their backs. Joanna smiled wistfully at the sight. These girls were the true treasures in the market, and these children the wealth of Jerusalem. Joanna wished them long and happy lives.

Making their way through the newer section of the city, they passed the armory on the right, and Joanna lowered her head in respect for the soldiers on duty. Rows of shields glinted in the sun. Young boys sat at polishing wheels, sharpening the swords, while at the back of the fortress a fire burned. The dark smoke signaled that a blacksmith was at work, making repairs to armor. Of course, there had been no wars in years. Wars were only stories, passed on from grandfathers.

Herod the Great had thought he could protect his throne by ending the life of the promised Savior. She assumed— everyone assumed—that this meant the threat of war was over.

Guilt gnawed at the edges of her conscience. Had she benefited, even a little, from the death of that generation?

She passed by the temple of Herod on the left as she made the final approach for the palace. The limestone buildings, tan and warm, had passed, and now stood harsh white stone, blinding in the afternoon light. The palace walls stretched higher, trapping every whisper and careless word.

Joanna sucked in her breath, straightening in the saddle. It was time once more to play the part of a dutiful wife. A group of servants carrying water jugs stepped to the side to let the caravan through. Joanna felt the women's eyes settle on her as she passed.

And with that, she entered the gate leading into the palace of Herod the Great. Chuza rode ahead of her with Herod Antipas. The tension of these visits extended far beyond the failed hopes of two brothers. Everyone in the traveling party felt it. A brother offended was a bitter enemy, even if that brother was only a half brother and was no longer in residence at the palace. Herod Antipas rode into the palace seeking honor for all the sons: the one his father had killed, the one that Rome had exiled, and the two tetrarchs, one of which was, of course, himself.

Herod the Great had destroyed many families in order to secure his legacy. No one should have been surprised that the last family destroyed would be his own.

Overhead, a thin band of gray stretched across the sky, like a long string.

Now Herod Antipas returned to the palace that he had once been promised. They would all be guests where they should have ruled.

Joanna cleared her mind, pausing before the great wooden doors that opened to the receiving courtyard.

The string of gray grew thick, its edges fraying into smoky tendrils filling in the listless blue sky. She sniffed the air—it hinted at a coming storm.

Her head still lifted to test the air, the enormity of the palace impressed her, as it always did. Herod the Great had built the exterior with white marble, each square stone as huge as a chariot. All the stones fit so closely together that there was no visible seam between them, not unless she peered closely.

And when enchanted with anything of beauty in Herod's palace, it was always best not to peer closely.

She urged her horse forward, into the throng of people waiting for the visitors. At once she was struck with the din of voices, languages of several empires, servants from lands she had never visited. There were more servants in the receiving area than in Antipas's entire palace at Tiberius.

Herodias stopped her litter in this first courtyard. Servants ran forward to help her out. She stood in the center of the courtyard, her icy glare surveying everyone and everything. At once, she was offered a bowl of water to refresh herself. Another servant dropped to his knees, extending his hands as if in prayer. Herodias looked away, and with a flick of her hand dismissed the man. Joanna knew that Herodias did not trust Pontius Pilate, and certainly did not trust his servants. Herodias would only allow her own servants to attend her, especially here.

Chuza stepped down next and directed the servants to unload the scrolls he had brought. The two rulers had building plans to discuss. Herod Antipas stepped down from his litter, brushing aside any attempt at help by the servants. Pilate waited in an upper chamber to receive Herod in private. Herod strode in that direction without speaking to anyone. It was as if he owned the place, Joanna thought ruefully.

A fat raindrop splattered at her feet.

Perhaps, if Pilate failed in his duties, Herod would own the palace. On the other hand, if anything happened to Herod Antipas, Pilate would probably get his lands to rule. Whatever else happened between the men, she thought, if everyone made it out of that chamber alive, the visit would be considered a success. They were known to dislike each other.

More raindrops fell, swollen and cold, driving people to hurry inside quickly. Pleasantries were rushed or skipped altogether. Joanna blinked rapidly to keep the rain from her eyes.

In a matter of moments, the important people had gone, disappeared through the second grand set of double doors that led to another courtyard. Shielding her face with one hand, she scanned the courtyard for a servant, any servant, who might be assigned to her.

A girl, no more than twelve years of age, ran forward and bowed before her, offering to show her to the prepared guest room. Weary from the journey, anxious to wash the grit from her hair, Joanna followed. She had to—Herod's palace had hundreds of guest rooms. This palace could swallow her up, and no one would even know she had been lost.

The next morning

"Wake up! Joanna, wake!"

Aresh stood over her bed, hands clenched.

Joanna bolted upright. "What is it?"

"The rumors, the Savior? He is here!"

"In the palace?" Joanna swung her legs off the low bed and pushed to stand up. Aresh reached for a shawl and handed it to her. The storm from last night had passed, leaving the air crisp and clean.

"Yes! Well, no. I mean to say, He is in Jerusalem for the Passover. The servants have been whispering about Him all morning."

"Oh, Aresh," Joanna groaned. "I thought you did not listen to gossip. And you should not wake me to repeat gossip. I needed another hour, at least. How can you not be bone weary from the journey?"

Aresh's face turned a bright shade of pink, and she shrugged.

"Ah, yes," Joanna replied, realizing what Aresh would not say. "You are younger than I am. Of course."

"It's not because I'm younger," Aresh said. "I'm just stronger." She flashed a bright and entirely innocent smile. "Besides, Herodias is still asleep, and I needed something to do. I'm making myself useful."

Joanna rubbed her temples. It was too early in the morning to deal with Aresh. She took a moment to stretch, trying to get warmth and flexibility into her back. Her muscles ached from the long ride. Even after taking a bath last night in the women's bathhouse, her muscles were still a tangle of knots. Two little spots on her backside were still on fire from the saddle and the bumpy roads. Today she felt as if she'd been in a street fight.

I suppose I was, she thought. *With a horse. And the horse won.*

Aresh looked around the chamber, muttering under her breath.

"What is it, Aresh?"

Aresh sat on the bed with a sigh. Joanna really had to teach the girl manners. It was no wonder that Herodias had a harsh tone with her. Aresh did not remember her place.

"The servants here. Have you seen their robes? Or their jewelry?"

Joanna nodded, pointing to the pitcher of water on the nightstand.

Aresh glanced at it but did not move, intent on talking. "These girls have the best of everything," she continued. "And they're educated. More than I. They get respect. Some of them even have their own servants. Can you imagine? Having a servant?"

Joanna pointed again to the pitcher of water. "At the moment, I am struggling with that."

Aresh paused, looking perplexed. "Oh! Sorry. Do you want me to call your servant?"

"No, Aresh. Let everyone sleep. But since you are awake," Joanna said, smiling a bit, "why don't you make yourself useful?"

Aresh nodded with a giggle and leaped to her feet. She poured the water for Joanna's morning washing. Next, she turned to choose a robe and shawl for Joanna, and already her eye was on the small collection of jewelry on the bed table.

After a nod of approval from Joanna, Aresh began with the washing of Joanna's face and then moisturizing her skin. She frowned as she worked, in total concentration. She applied a light touch of rouge and dabbed the red pigment at the center of Joanna's lips, then followed up with a line of kohl across the eyelids. Joanna marveled at how steady her hand was.

"Not too much," Joanna said. "Chuza does not like a lot of cosmetics."

"Do not worry. I know exactly what will appeal to him," Aresh replied. "I watch everyone in the court very closely. There is not much entertainment for servants."

Joanna sighed. Aresh was a force of nature. And like any force of nature, her energies needed to be harnessed wisely.

Joanna wondered what jobs she could give Aresh to do. Without children or official job duties, she had little need for a servant.

Aresh brushed Joanna's hair out, first with deliberate strokes to unravel any tangles, then with softer strokes to smooth and shine. Only after Joanna's hair was soft and light did Aresh create braids, binding them on top of her head.

The jewelry was last. Aresh picked gold hoops for Joanna's ears to complement the heavy amethyst necklace. Joanna touched the rough edges of the amulet. Something ugly had taken root in her heart when she had slipped it on over a year ago. Not that the amulet itself was cursed, she thought. Curses were part of the superstitions and magic of other religions, not hers. But since she had compromised to avoid conflict, an even greater conflict rooted deeply in her heart, one that she didn't know how to confront.

Accepting the amulet and all it represented made her feel vulnerable in a way she'd never felt before, plagued by doubts and fears. Why had such a little concession to her enemy made such ripples through her heart?

Aresh stood back, closed one eye, and tilted her head, then repeated the gesture with her other eye. At last she smiled. "I'm finished."

Looking into a mirror of brightest polished bronze, Joanna smiled.

Aresh stood behind her, looking at her reflection beside Joanna.

"Will you ask Herodias to send me into your service?" Aresh asked.

"Promise me one thing," Joanna said. "No early-morning interruptions to share gossip."

Aresh quickly agreed.

"I know you have dreams," Joanna said. "Dreams that seem impossible for a servant. If you serve me to the best of your ability, though, I promise to help you any way I can."

CHAPTER SIX

The night was surprisingly warm and dry. Pilate held the welcome feast in the garden, under the shadow of the three towers at the northern end of the palace. Joanna sat among olive and fig trees with their lush green leaves, surrounded by flowers and herbs, with mints that released their crisp scent when crushed underfoot by the scurrying servants. The torches flickered in golden light, and musicians softly strummed along the edges of the garden as the feast was brought out and laid upon the tables. She feasted with her eyes first upon the roasted meats, fruits, both dried and fresh, skeins of wines, browned breads, raisin cakes, fish of all kinds salted, roasted, and dried.

Was this feast meant to impress or provoke?

In the morning, they would go to the temple for Passover. Joanna tried to eavesdrop as much as she could from where she sat. Herod and Herodias sat with Pilate and his wife, Procla. The seating arrangement was more Roman than Jewish. Jews liked to separate the sexes at mealtime, and not because of serving duties. The women's table was the center of refreshment and laughter. Equally, the men reveled in the meal with only brothers and friends at their side.

Next to them were their stewards, Chuza and Arius. Joanna and Arius's wife were seated below them. She could see where their gazes fell and where they lingered. They could easily sweep over the attendees, but everyone in attendance was seated so they could only look up to see the face of the rulers.

Chuza looked handsome in a freshly washed robe with a dark red sash over one shoulder. She yearned for his company, for his approving glance. He glanced at her only briefly, and she thought she saw approval in his eyes. Aresh had done a good job preparing her for the feast.

"I have collected a great deal of intelligence on the matter at hand," Pilate said.

Joanna noted how Herod shifted his weight as he sat. He was uneasy that Pilate had spies in Galilee.

"We have identified the one we believe or, more importantly, that the people believe may be the rumored Savior," Pilate said, popping a piece of bread in his mouth. "I do not think you have much to worry about. The man is none other than John's cousin."

"Cousin?" Herodias laughed out loud, her wine spilling over the edge of her goblet.

"Yes, a cousin. John used this old prophecy to stir up fear and hysteria in your court." Arrogance colored Pilate's voice. "He named his own cousin, a rather unremarkable-looking fellow from Nazareth, as the long-awaited Messiah."

Several people, including a few servants, chuckled.

"The man does not look like he could lead a revolt or topple the government," Pilate continued. "Besides, can anything good come from Nazareth?"

The table around him erupted into laughter. Pilate raised his voice to talk over them. "My spies say he does not look like he can topple a milking stool."

More laughter erupted. Procla dabbed at her eyes with the sleeve of her robe as she sighed after laughing.

"John is angry about my marriage," Herod said, dismissing the matter with a stiff shrug.

"Even if this man, Jesus, is the Messiah," Pilate said, "he is already at least thirty years old."

Thirty? Men were often dead by thirty. No one had heard of starting a revolution at that age.

"Thirty years old and how many followers?" Pilate asked, as if trying a case before a Roman court. "Four. Four fishermen. No social skills. No skills at war or governing. Their only skill was fishing, but they've sold off their boats and nets, so now they just wander around with Jesus."

By this time, the banquet attendees were at full attention, hanging on Pilate's every word. The story was too outrageous to be truth. Pilate leaned forward. "And there is one rumor far too silly to repeat."

Herodias stopped laughing, and Herod leaned forward.

"Please do repeat it," Herod said.

"He attended a wedding, this man of ours with the great powers, and he…changed water into wine. Gallons of it, apparently."

Herod threw his hands up in mock resignation. "Well, we are in trouble. If he offers to do that for every household, you and I are out of a job. We cannot offer the people a better miracle than that."

The men collapsed against each other, as if giving up in despair.

"What will his next miracle be?" Herodias cried out in mock despair. "Straw into gold?"

Moments later, Herod stood and departed with Pilate, and the musicians struck up a faster song. People rose from the tables to dance and refill their wine cups. Chuza made his way from the upper table to Joanna's, and she held her breath.

"My lord," she said, casting her eyes down, trying to remember how to be demure. It felt like foolishness. He either desired her or he didn't.

"Did you enjoy the feast?" he asked. He sounded rather formal. Perhaps it was because Aresh stood so close, and their love-talk would be overheard by this servant.

"I did. And you?" she replied, taking a step away.

"Did you not sense the pain that Herod is in?" Chuza asked, raising the volume of his voice slightly, as if to compensate. "Did you not see the agony on his face?"

Puzzled, Joanna shook her head. "I am sorry. I do not understand." She cast her eyes down, not wanting to offend him with her slowness of mind.

"His life," Chuza said. "What it means for him to sit up there."

She glanced up at him, but he was not looking at her. He was looking right at Aresh. Joanna had not told Chuza that she had arranged for a new servant, so perhaps Chuza was surprised at the new face. Aresh blushed furiously, ducking behind Joanna. Aresh was used to serving in the women's quarters. Surely Chuza and his authority made her nervous.

"He walks these grounds," Chuza said, "and he knows that they should have belonged to him. The life he could have had, the life he should have had, was stolen. Now he is forced to walk these paths, to see the life that can never be his."

Joanna looked at him, and the room seemed to shrink in size. The walls closed in. She knew exactly what Chuza talked about. The torment that Herod felt? Didn't she feel that every day of her life too? She knew what Herod felt.

But what did Chuza feel? She wanted to ask but couldn't, not with Aresh in the room.

"Come to my chambers tonight," Chuza said.

"I will," Joanna blurted, then chastised herself for sounding so desperate. To win her husband's affections, she needed to hide her unsteady emotions.

Wasn't that how this game was played?

The next morning
At the temple in Jerusalem

The thick cloud of incense from the sacrifices nearly choked Joanna. She coughed and waved a hand in front of her eyes. Passing through the Eastern Gate of the temple, her sandals padded quietly along the stones at her feet. She forced herself to look up; the dizzying array of colors in the stones was too much. Unfortunately, the colors were repeated everywhere, giant blocks of green, red, and yellow. Everything Herod the Great had done demanded attention. Even in death, he expected no less than complete focus from all who came within his kingdom.

Briefly, she wondered where he was, if there was such a thing as the afterlife. The Egyptians thought so. The Jews were divided. Sadducees said there was no afterlife. Pharisees insisted there was.

The cacophony of the Gentile market overtook her, and her senses drowned in the experience of the temple. To worship meant to pass through the gate into the Gentile market, and only then could a woman pass on to the court of women.

The outer court, which was the location for this Gentile market, was separated from the inner courts by a wall about her height. The wall didn't keep invaders out. It kept the Gentiles from coming any closer to the Holy of Holies, the God of the Jews.

Priests in white robes with wide red sashes milled through the crowd on their way to and from the inner gates. None would meet her eye. She was a woman and not even one of noble birth. She drew her shawl closer around her body.

A young boy offered her a small wooden cage of doves. He pleaded in a language she did not know, but she shook her head. She fished in her robes for a coin then sent him on his way. He offered her the birds once more, a confused frown on his face, but she merely shook her head once again.

The merchants were loud. Too loud. Her head pounded from another headache. Her new ailments were strange ones: headaches, despair, certainty that she had failed in life, yet she could not name her particular sin. How could she feel so ashamed of who she was, when she had done so little to be ashamed of?

A woman urged her to buy a clay bowl of incense. The thick wrinkled skin on the woman's hands frightened Joanna, and she stepped away.

Would she become like that? Wrinkled and coarse?

The woman caught her eye and smiled broadly. Joanna noted that her two front teeth were missing, and probably several were missing behind her sunken lower lip. How then could this woman smile?

Joanna stopped, all her fears, all her dread, descending upon her in an instant. She would die alone, some awful voice seemed to whisper to her. She would die alone, used up, worn out by life and poverty. If she didn't please Chuza, if she didn't give him a son before she turned thirty, this poor woman's fate would be her own.

"Sister?"

Joanna looked up, shocked to find that the woman had addressed her directly. That simply was not done. Did the woman not see her palace robes, her fine jewelry?

"I do not need incense, thank you," Joanna replied, picking up the hem of her robe to walk on.

The woman held a hand up. The palm was wrinkled too, Joanna noted, and yet suddenly a peace enveloped her. It was as if the woman had stopped the horrible cloud of thoughts that had so suddenly descended.

Joanna glanced above. The turquoise sky shimmered in beauty as a flock of sparrows flitted past. Strange how a woman so coarse could possess something Joanna did not.

"You seemed troubled," the woman persisted.

"I—no, I am fine, but thank you," Joanna said, nodding to signal an end to the conversation. The woman stepped away from her booth.

"You have to come to see Him, haven't you?" the woman whispered.

Joanna froze. Her eyes searched the woman's. The woman had such luminous brown eyes, like the color of a stallion's mane. Her face radiated kindness, and Joanna felt the muscles in her shoulders relax as she took a deep breath. It was a mystery how some people could instantly, silently, signal to her that they were allies and friends. Joanna frowned, wondering how that could be. They had nothing in common, after all.

Aresh came bounding up. "Herodias arrives! Prepare!"

Joanna thanked the woman, who smiled wryly and went back to her merchant's table. Turning to the side, Joanna watched as Herodias entered through the outer gate. The merchants quieted to a respectful din and clamor. Herodias was dressed in a long white robe with a red shawl on top and a purple sash at her waist.

Joanna glanced at the priest guarding the steps leading to the Corinthian Gate. He appeared not to have noticed. Or perhaps he was just that well trained not to take the royal bait.

Herodias strutted to the center of the women's court, her imperious gaze sweeping over the women and Gentiles milling about. Spying Joanna, she crooked a finger, beckoning her over.

Joanna obeyed, and seconds later bowed before Herodias.

"Have you seen this Jesus?" Herodias demanded. "Have you confirmed the rumors?"

"No. A merchant hinted that He is here. I know nothing else."

"John, of course, says nothing helpful," Herodias said, nearly spitting the words. "Herod will not let my men near him, even though I promised my men are skilled enough not to leave any marks."

Joanna flinched then caught herself and tried to smile.

"You hardly understand the danger. It is a good thing you don't have a position that matters." Herodias rolled her eyes. "John is more worried about saving Herod's soul than his kingdom."

"Well," Joanna said, stung once more by this queen of hornets, "then we can pray that both are saved. We are at the temple, after all."

Herodias looked at her as if seeing her for the first time, blinking heavily. "Oh, yes, the prayers here." She snapped her fingers, and a servant approached with a small leather sack. "Buy a nice animal for me, won't you? Pay for the sacrifices we make at this festival. I want to get some shopping done while I am in Jerusalem, and I do not plan to spend my time at this market with its cheap incense and half-starved birds."

With that, Herodias turned and left. Joanna heard her complaining as she walked away, "Masada. We could have gone to Masada. The swimming pool there is a delight. Or Caesarea Maritima palace. I love the gardens there. This whole visit is such a waste, except of course for the information about this so-called messiah."

Joanna held the leather sack, the weight of it substantial in her hand. The crowds closed in behind Herodias, and the noise level reached its previous pitch.

Turning, Joanna handed the satchel to the old woman at the incense table. "With compliments of Herodias," she said. The woman clutched at her heart, tears filling her eyes as she reached with her other hand for the gift.

Joanna stopped just short of handing it over, and leaned in.

"He's really here? The rumors are true?" she asked.

The woman grinned. "Yes. God bless you, sister. You'll find Him, I know. The truth is, He has a funny way of finding you when you need Him, I'll say that." Wiggling her eyebrows, she lifted the hem of her robe just a tad, showing Joanna a perfectly normal foot.

Joanna shrugged, completely unimpressed. The woman burst into laughter, throwing her head back with delight. Finally, Joanna laughed at the extravagance of the woman's mirth. All over a plain, everyday-looking foot. These common people were so unusual.

"It's the first time I've ever been able to stretch out my leg, you see," the woman whispered, tears filling her eyes once more and now spilling down her cheeks. "I was crippled as a child. A chariot ran over my leg. My leg was a wasted, twisted mess. My whole life was, really. Then I met *Him*."

Joanna's mouth fell open.

"He told me not to tell a soul yet, but I figured it was safe to tell you," the woman continued. "I've got a feeling you're missing something too. Something you need Him for, something only He can give you."

"Thank you," Joanna whispered. The woman turned to attend to a customer, and Joanna drew a breath for courage. She looked around at the boxes set out to collect offerings and temple taxes, but there was no sign of the rumored Savior.

What would He look like? Would He wear a crown? A royal sash? How did people find and identify Him?

Walking through the crowd, she searched every face for a sign of this Savior. Approaching the Corinthian Gate, she was once more awed by the sheer size of the temple. The gates were bronze and reached higher than any gate she had ever seen. If she tilted her head back to see all the way to the top, she'd surely fall over on her backside. Flanking the bronze gates were the pillars of white marble overlaid with gold.

She slowly walked the fifteen steps up to the bronze gates. Some of the people called these gates by another name—the Beautiful Gates. All the other gates at the temple that Herod had built had been overlaid with gold and silver. They were like giant works of jewelry, fit for the invisible God, and the artistry of each showed off the best that men were capable of. And Herod had talented and terrified prisoners, so his men had been capable of much.

But these gates? No, these had not been overlaid with gold or silver. No one knew why, except what the rumors, begun long ago, had said. It must have been during the construction, the earliest years, while the gates were being constructed and before they were hung. The legend told that in this spot a miracle had happened, inexplicably. Without warning or precedent or explanation. A crippled beggar had been suddenly healed and made whole on this very spot. The glory of God had pierced through to this place and worked a wonder. Herod had not wanted to adorn the gate with man-made artistry. Here, God's work was on display.

And when the morning sun rose and the light hit the unfinished bronze doors, the doors burst into red and orange flames of light.

A man brushed past her, without making an apology. She lowered her head and stepped aside but followed him with her eyes. He approached the gate, and as the doors opened, she glimpsed what she had been denied by being born a woman. The man walked into another world, a world of gold. A world where men met their God.

Joanna sighed. What would it be like to throw open those doors, to run in to the Holy of Holies? To see the face of God? Why couldn't God come out to her? Why didn't God come to the court of the women?

Above the merchants' cries, she heard the hard shout of the construction foreman from somewhere beyond the wall surrounding her court. The temple was still, after all, under construction, although Herod Antipas said Pilate was very close to completing it.

"Joanna, it is time to prepare for dinner." Aresh stood at her side, having appeared out of nowhere. Joanna smiled and patted her arm, grateful for the interruption to her brooding.

Why should she have such longing for a God she had never seen?

Together they left the temple, Aresh pulling Joanna's hand and taking the lead through the crowd, which Joanna quickly realized was a mistake. As they exited the main gate they were thrust into a churning crowd of people. The people wore clothes pocked with holes, and dirt lined the crevices in their necks.

"Aresh," she scolded under her breath, making sure no one else heard, "it is not safe to be among these people without an escort."

Aresh frowned and froze where she was. She looked at Joanna as if she'd never seen her before.

"I meant we are obviously from the palace. Our dress gives us away." Joanna tried to soften her words. "And these people have so little, and they are not even washed."

"*These* people have morals too," Aresh stiffly replied. "And poverty is not contagious."

Joanna waved her hands. "Oh, you misunderstand—"

"I was only trying to help," Aresh said. "I know what you came to Jerusalem looking for. Or whom, I should say. But I didn't realize that you disliked poor people so much." Her voice was thin and high, and she wouldn't look at Joanna.

Joanna swung her head to the front of the crowd then back to Aresh. "How did you—" He was here? The Savior? She grabbed Aresh's hand. "We will discuss this misunderstanding later. Right now, just take me to Him."

Aresh nodded, still avoiding all eye contact, and pulled her through the crowd again. With every step, Joanna felt the blood rush from her head, and her courage evaporated from her body like the morning dew. Her steps became more difficult. Every time she took a step it was like pulling her foot free of mud. Pushing herself forward, she felt as if she was made of cold marble, and her body resisted all movement. Why was her flesh resisting this chance to meet the Savior? She clutched the necklace.

Suddenly Aresh stopped and moved to the side.

Joanna stood before the Savior. She knew it was Him. All sense, all words and thought left her at that moment. Deep in her being, she recognized Him the way her skin knew the touch of the sun. He was the Savior, the promised one, the healer and worker of miracles.

He was outside the temple gates, ministering to the poorest of the poor. They clung to His words. Joanna gasped at what she saw—they clung to Him too! He allowed everyone to touch Him, even the women, even those with obvious ailments.

No, that was wrong. But even as her mind protested, her heart leaped to life. Her eyes drank Him in, feasting on every detail like a starved woman finally allowed to sit before a banquet. Joanna realized she was not breathing, but she did not need air. He was what she needed. How was this possible? How was it possible to have such a strong reaction to a perfect stranger?

He paused His teaching to the crowd and returned her gaze.

"It is You!" she cried, startled to hear her voice above the crowd. "I found You!"

He laughed, and she blushed to think what a silly expression of surprise must be on her face. The necklace from Herodias pinched the back of her neck, and she reached up to shift it out of the way.

"Call me Jesus," He said. "I'm so glad to see you, Joanna." He looked side to side. "Where is Aresh?"

Joanna, still speechless, looked around. Aresh was gone. With her eyes off Jesus, suddenly thoughts came crashing into her mind. John's arrest. The necklace from Herodias with a pagan charm. Chuza's disappointment in her. Her failure to do the one basic thing all women do—give her husband a child. Her total uselessness to Chuza. To the palace. To the world.

"Joanna."

She looked into His eyes, and the thoughts were vanquished. Her heart thundered in her ears. She wanted to ask, right then, if He really could heal. If He could, He could open her womb.

But nothing about Him made sense. For instance, how did He know her name? A Savior of a nation who knew your name? A King who healed bodies?

This was outrageously…not wrong, exactly. Just wildly unexpected.

Jesus continued on His way up through the main gate of the temple. Joanna watched Him go, eyes wide in wonder at His kindness. A Savior long awaited, whose arrival was prophesied four hundred years ago or more, and yet He was completely unexpected.

And then she heard the first scream.

CHAPTER SEVEN

The next evening

D id you hear Him say He would destroy the temple?" Chuza demanded. "Did you hear Him say it?"

"Again, no." Joanna wiped a tear from her eye. She stood at the window watching the sun set, feeling her hopes pass away with it. Jesus had been her one last hope for a miracle. Now all chances of seeking His healing were gone. The palace hated and feared Him more than ever.

"He claimed that if we destroyed the temple, he could raise it again in three days. Three days!" Chuza snapped, pacing in her chambers. He had been too angry to even wait while she had been brought to his chambers. Instead he had barged into her chambers just moments after she had returned from her visit with Herodias. "I had hoped there was a chance to get John released from prison, but his cousin had made that impossible."

"He seemed like a kind man," Joanna said weakly.

Chuza stopped pacing and turned to glare at her. "You still do not understand, do you? You prance around in your fancy dresses, delighting in the gossip of Herodias, never giving a thought to what it takes to run this palace. You do not think of anyone but yourself."

Joanna's heart nearly collapsed from the sting of his words. "That is not true!"

"Herod is not prepared for war! The people already hate Rome for the never-ending taxes. If Herod asks Rome to send soldiers to quash a rebellion, the people will revolt against him. If he does nothing and Jesus wins the people over, Herod will lose his throne. Why can you not understand? If this Jesus challenges him for the right to rule, Herod has no way to win."

"Why am I held accountable for Jesus?" Joanna asked. "Herodias already demanded to know everything I have seen and heard. Now you think I want to see Herod thrown out of his own palace. All I did was seek out this Jesus. Why did that cause so much upheaval?"

"Because this family kills their enemies, you little fool!" Chuza snapped. He ran a hand through his hair and sighed. "You're a Jew, Joanna, even if the court requires you to live more like a Roman. The name Herod should strike fear in your heart. Why would you do anything to displease him?"

Chuza folded his arms. He looked older than his years, she thought. While Herod feasted and grew rich, Chuza spent long nights balancing the books and keeping the kingdom running. He was stretched thin, and the lines on his face bore the signs.

"Tell me the truth. Why did you seek him out?" His voice was soft but held a dangerous edge. Was he challenging her, or questioning her?

"I needed to know who He was." Joanna could not look at her husband. "I needed to know if He could give me what I needed."

"And tell me, wife, in this palace of excess and wonder, what could you possibly need that a stranger would provide?"

"A miracle." Her voice was as thin as a water reed. "I know you want a son, Chuza. I have done everything I can think of. I have tried every remedy possible. Now I am grasping for miracles."

She walked around him and sat on the bed, exhausted.

"The amulet," he said. His eyes were focused on it. Had he never seen it before? She realized he had not looked closely at her since Herodias had given it to her. Shame made her cheeks burn. "It is not Jewish practice to wear fertility charms, is it?"

She shook her head.

He paused, rubbing his chin with one hand. "It is warm weather."

She tilted her head, confused.

"I've been a patient man and a good husband, but the arrival of this Jesus changes everything," Chuza said. "If Herod loses his rule, where would I be? Without a job. Without a home. Time is a luxury you do not have any longer."

"What are you saying?"

He turned, smiling, as if suddenly relieved. "Summer is still a way off. You can safely travel by ship to Rome until early fall. After that, of course, it's impossible. Really, I should not put you on a ship after the hottest month. Good weather could give us extra time to travel."

Chuza's words ran together too quickly. She still did not comprehend.

"Rome?" Joanna pushed farther back on the bed, instinctively wanting to be against a wall, to brace herself. "Why would you send me to Rome?"

"The festival of Lupercalia."

"No!"

He crossed the room, hands held up to stop her from standing and bolting into the hallway. "But you are wearing that amulet. Surely trying the festival could only help. You cannot claim to be a strict observer of the law."

Her heart was thundering in her ears. Was it shame or horror that made it beat rabbit-fast? "I will not consent to being stripped in the street and beaten by Roman priests!"

The festival was a well-known fertility rite practiced in Rome in late winter, just before spring. Animal sacrifices were followed by women running through the streets, stripped. Priests whipped them with pelts from the sacrifices, all in the name of invoking a blessing from fertility gods. Lupercalia was a wild, shameful festival, Joanna thought. *What god would rejoice to see any woman so degraded?*

She swallowed before speaking. "I cannot. I will not."

"You do not have any choice," he said flatly. "If your God will not give you a child, maybe the Roman gods will. I do not care who you offer prayers to, Joanna. But if you are not pregnant by the time the last ship to Rome sails before summer's end, you will certainly be one of its passengers."

The next evening, Joanna went to Chuza's chambers unannounced. Her breathing was fast and shallow, and she was certain her heartbeat could be heard echoing from the plaster walls of the corridor.

"I have a counteroffer," she said.

Chuza, sitting at his table, turned and stared at her, seeming to weigh her like she was a transaction he was considering at a market. She blinked, finding it hard to meet his calculating gaze. Where had he gone, her kind and charming husband?

"I am a Jew, and the prophecy about a messiah comes from my people. Send me out, with accompaniment from the palace, of course, in search of Jesus. Aresh tells me that He travels in the region. I will find Him, listen to His teachings, learn what He tells the people."

Chuza set the scroll that was in his hand down on the table. His eyes were narrow. "You are going to spy on a fellow Jew? For Herod?"

"I am not doing this for Herod. I need a miracle. If Jesus cannot provide one, then at least I will have earned your goodwill. And that, it seems, would be another miracle."

"Herod would like to get news that does not come from Pilate," Chuza murmured. He bit his lip, his foot tapping under the table. "One month. I can send a guard with you who knows the region. When you return from the trip, you sail for Rome."

Joanna nodded in agreement and left. She had much planning to do before returning to the palace in Tiberius. When she left the palace for this one-month trip, she did not know if she would return.

Summer, 30 CE
In the region of Capernaum, Galilee

Simon Peter's mother-in-law, Annat, cleared a spot at the heavy cedar table. Chuza had arranged the introduction, as he knew all the best fishermen in the region. Of course he would—he bought only the finest for Herod. Joanna was unused to traveling, though, and uncertain that her plan would work.

She wasn't known for being an astute player in the political games of court. That was why no one would suspect that she had intentionally planned this. Joanna had no intention of returning in two weeks' time. She was going to miss the window of safe travel to Rome. When she returned, she would have much news of Jesus, and hopefully, a miracle of healing. If not, at least she would have a safe home for the winter and be spared the indignities of Lupercalia.

Joanna sat on a cushion that Annat offered, and breathed in. Something about this humble home seemed delightful in a way she had never experienced. The deep sense of comfort was almost otherworldly. The sunlight hitting the table released a fragrance of the mountains, rich and tangy and sweet.

Annat laughed. "The table was a marriage gift from my husband. To remind me of my home, in the north. In the months of rain, though, I fear I never will feel the sun. Of course, in this month I wish we could feel it a little less." The heat during the month of fruit harvest was extreme and often unrelieved by rain or cloud.

Joanna laughed, and was surprised to remember the feeling of easy companionship. How long had it been since she had met a friend? And this was an unlikely friend, the wife of a fisherman. The woman was surprisingly vigorous. A villager had told Joanna that only last night this same woman had been quite ill with a fever. The villager had been wrong, Joanna decided. Annat's cheeks bloomed with health, and her brown eyes sparkled.

"Yes, Adar especially wears on me," Joanna confessed. "I do not like storms."

"Ah, but we are always in a storm, my daughter," Annat said, setting a plate of bread before Joanna. Tears sprang to Joanna's eyes.

Annat patted her shoulder. "I don't mind. If you'll feel better, my dear, then please do cry. At my age, I cry over nothing and everything. My husband passed years ago, and so now my son-in-law, Simon Peter, runs the business for us. It is a good life, but it is not the life I wanted."

Joanna sniffled, trying not to cry.

The palace guard standing outside the entrance of the house cleared his throat. The guard sent with her on this trip was a sour, unmovable man. Joanna held back her tears.

Her hostess watched her with a kindness in her eyes that Joanna hadn't seen in many years, and tears caught in her throat again. Annat set a cluster of ripe figs down in front of Joanna and then sat across from her at the table.

"Let us enjoy what this day has brought us. The fig tree outside our home has ripened before the others." She touched her chin thoughtfully. "Isn't that a blessing?"

Joanna reached for a fig then stopped as she watched Annat pick one up and offer it toward the heavens.

"To our great and mighty Yahweh, we give thanks for the storms that watered the earth. For the roots that ran deep and soaked up the rain. For the sun that burnished the leaves. And for the hands that picked this fruit, for people whose lives have touched our own, in invisible ways."

Joanna sat wide eyed. She'd never considered any of that. Food appeared on a platter, and she'd never given thanks for the people who plucked it. She'd certainly never given thanks for the storms or relentless sun. Even as a young girl, her parents had sheltered her from all realities except one. Marriage was her purpose, and honor would be her family's reward.

Tucked inside her home, and then the palace, she had not realized that she too was in the community of life, of giving and receiving.

"But I only take," she blurted.

Annat raised her eyebrows. "What do you mean?"

"Even now, I am trying to find Jesus because I need something from Him. My husband wants something from Him. Herod wants something from Him. And I just realized that never, not even once, have I thought about giving to others."

Annat bit into her fig and smiled. "I doubt that's true. Things are not often so neatly divided."

Joanna shook her head, then realized why she was here. "I am so sorry. This is not what I came to you for. I came to you for information about Jesus. I heard that your son has knowledge of His whereabouts."

Annat laughed. "Daughter, maybe the two things are one and the same. Have you thought of that? You seek Jesus for one reason, all the while you need Him for another. Don't be surprised when you set out to find something if something sets out to find you too."

Joanna bit into her fig, and the rich flavors overwhelmed her. A fresh fig, hours from the tree, was a wonderful experience.

Annat smiled, the wrinkles around her eyes dancing. "Tell me. Why do you seek Jesus?" She reached across the table and poured a bit of fresh olive oil onto a dish for the bread.

Joanna finished chewing her fig. She studied the plate before her, suddenly embarrassed. But she owed this woman the truth. Annat had been so gracious to welcome her. And there was something about this home, something different in the air.

"I need to bear a son for my husband. And I have heard the rumors. Some say that Jesus can work miracles."

Annat threw her head back, laughing. Placing a hand over her heart, she caught herself and sighed. "Forgive me, child. Rumors? My goodness. If you had been here only hours ago…"

Joanna sat up straighter and leaned in. Suddenly she took in the details of the home that she had glossed over earlier when she had arrived: sleeping mats stacked in a corner, too many for a widow, empty water crocks by the front door, plates stacked by the low smoldering fire. She had had guests.

"He was here?" Joanna asked, her voice barely above a whisper.

"My daughter has been away all day, telling the story." Annat nodded, settling back onto her cushion. "Only hours ago. I was upstairs, and though the sun was fierce I could not get warm. My fever made my very bones ache with cold. A maid brought a cool cloth to drape across my forehead, but my fever was so high it turned warm in seconds. She could not keep up with the constant need to refresh the water. I closed my eyes and asked God to relieve my suffering. I wanted to die."

"But you did not."

"But I wanted to!" Annat exclaimed, throwing her hands in the air. "This life was not the one I wanted. I asked God to give me, just this one time, what I most wanted. And last night I wanted to die."

Joanna exhaled, trying to understand. "What happened?"

"A hand reached for mine, and as I opened my eyes, I beheld a face I knew at once but had never seen before." Annat leaned across the table, ducking her head to whisper. "Do you believe such things are possible? That we could know the face of God? Because I looked into His eyes, Joanna. I looked into His eyes, and I knew."

Joanna shook her head, trying to take it all in. "Who was it? It was Jesus, yes?" A thrill went through her body. A worker of miracles walked among the people at last. "And then what?" she whispered, leaning forward again.

"He commanded the fever to leave, and it did." Annat clapped her hands together, and Joanna jumped, startled. "Just like that! A fever obeyed His command. I got up, washed, and served the men, including Jesus, a big dinner."

"How could He command a fever and the fever obey?"

"How could I ask for death and not know that what I needed was life?" Annat glanced toward the door, where the palace soldier stood. She kept her voice low. "Stranger things than my miracle happened last night, my daughter. This house became a whirlwind of miracles. Lepers were cured. Completely. Evil spirits thrown out. Diseases of every kind healed instantly."

"How?" Joanna asked, pulling back, a challenge in her voice.

"A word from Jesus. That's all. He commands the natural world. Wait. No," Annat shook her head, then swept her hands over her lap as if readjusting her robe. "I said that wrong. He doesn't just command the natural world. I'm telling you the truth. Jesus? He commands this world *and* the next."

Joanna sat in silence, letting the words sink in. Or trying to. Her mind seemed resistant to the idea.

"Any disease?" she asked. "Anything at all?"

Annat nodded.

"And the people who come to Him," Joanna asked, "what do they pay Him?"

Annat jerked back as if Joanna had slapped her.

"I did not mean to offend," Joanna said quickly. "I just assume that a man—"

"Who said He was a man?" Annat retorted. "Are you even listening to me, child? Miracles happened in this very room, in this house! Only hours ago, I saw, with my own eyes, the very nature of reality turned inside out! Anything is possible! I cannot explain how He does what He does, and I cannot even explain why He does what He does. But I can promise you this: He is not doing it for money."

Joanna nodded as if she understood, but she didn't. A power like that, so vast and unprecedented, to heal any disease or ailment, and Jesus collected no money? What did He want?

Was He amassing popular support? Joanna would sell her soul for a chance to give Chuza a child. And to think, she had access to the best doctors and medical care in the empire. The poor, who could not afford doctors or medicine, would gladly pledge themselves to war in exchange for healing.

She shuddered and drew her shawl closer around her shoulders. Herod and Herodias had not even begun to comprehend the power of their enemy.

Jesus would set the world on fire.

"Do you need a miracle too?" Annat asked. "How will you find Him?"

"You do not know where He is?" Joanna asked, her heart sinking.

"I rose at dawn to cook breakfast for the men, but Jesus was gone. Right away, I woke up Simon Peter and his friends. They left without their breakfast."

Joanna hung her head in her hands.

"He has a mother in Nazareth," Annat said.

Joanna lifted her face. Rising, she thanked Annat for the hospitality and summoned the guard.

How could the Messiah have a human mother? How could the Messiah come from Nazareth? Nothing worthwhile was there.

CHAPTER EIGHT

Summer, 30 CE
On the road to Nazareth

Much of the wheat had been harvested, the dull stalks lying crisscrossed, with only the dead brown root clumps remaining in the ground. Laborers, skin browned by the sun and sweat on their brow, gathered up the heads of grain to take to the threshing floor. The work made the air thick with chaff and dust.

In the far distance stood the Hills of Hattin, dark brown hulking shadows seen from here under the pale blue sky. The sole, lonely cloud that drifted slowly across the sky was a listless gray. The colors of this month were soft, washed, and muted, but the work was hard and the hours long. The thrill of the heavy harvest had changed into the reality of the work. A harvest was only a blessing if you had the strength to attend to it.

Children ran out from the fields, their bare brown feet stamping the earth in delight at the sight of a real, true, living palace guard.

Her guard was, she knew, an impressive sight. He rode on a camel that towered above her horse, and of course far above any adult or child on the ground. The camel wore armor, a blanket of tiny brass shields woven together and draped over its back. Its reins and tack were decorated with red tassels. She had thought it ironic that a sullen beast should be so elaborately displayed, but then, she hadn't known how sullen its rider was.

The guard's temperament was so mysteriously cold that it was almost a relief when the camel spat at her. At least she knew what made the camel mad. With the guard, she never had any indication of his thoughts.

Joanna loved the children's reactions as they passed through towns. And now she indulged herself again, laughing at their wide-eyed enthusiasm, though her guard remained stoic as he rode beside her.

She watched with delight as a little girl plucked a head of a white-flowered wild parsley and lifted it to her.

"Are you a queen?" the girl asked, her cheeks flecked with chaff from the harvest.

Joanna accepted the flowers and tucked them into the edge of her saddle blanket, just below the horse's neck.

Now she would have something pretty to look at while she rode. The guard certainly provided no pleasant distraction. He did not even deign to look down from his perch above her on the camel.

The flowers gave her an idea. Reaching across to the camel's bridle, she tugged on one of the tassels. The camel cast a sideways glance at her, and its eyes were lit with hate. It clearly was considering a bite.

Managing to quickly pull one free and then retreating to a safe distance, she handed the tassel to the girl, who cradled the strands of thread as if they were spun of gold.

"I'm not a queen," Joanna replied. "But I am your friend."

The girl's mouth fell open, and then she ran screaming for joy back into the fields.

The guard finally looked down at Joanna.

"It's forty miles to Nazareth," he said, his tone flat. "Are you planning on giving out gifts the whole way?"

She tossed her hair off her shoulder, ignoring him. He was a true guard of the palace, worried more about money than people.

"We'll stop at the Seven Springs," the guard said. "Water the animals. If you want to bathe, they have facilities. I know of lodgings there for us. Tomorrow we go to Migdal."

"Migdal?" She recoiled at the thought. She'd heard rumors of a tyrant of a woman who lived there, wealthy and lascivious. She was also crazy, possessed by many demons and prone to such indulgences of the flesh that men made sport with her in shameful, degrading ways. This woman, Mary Magdalene, was said to be fierce in every way.

Joanna really didn't want to deal with any more bullies. Besides, she'd always heard that Migdal stank of fish.

Sighing, she touched the white wildflower the girl had given her. They grew all along the road, and she made a mental note to offer it to her horse when they stopped and see if he liked it. She'd seen other animals eating them. The guard hardly gave the animals time to eat and drink along the road.

"I just realized something," Joanna said, trying to keep her tone civil. She'd been riding beside the guard for four hours today, and that was four hours too long. "This is going to be a long journey, and you are the only company I'm likely to have, but I do not even know your name."

"My name is Constans," he grunted, one side of his mouth turned down. "Though I do not think we should address each other as friends."

"Oh, I did not mean you!" Joanna exclaimed. "I meant my horse." She leaned down as if listening to her animal. "Really? That is a wonderful name! Quite distinguished. On your father's side, you say? Well, I am pleased to call you my friend and companion, Rufus."

Constans sat up, eyes straight ahead, not acknowledging her again. They rode in silence until the sound of water rushing over rocks reached them. Their animals perked up immediately, and their pace increased. Eager to get out of the sun, the animals trotted toward the sound of refreshing. The air changed, became cooler by degrees as the tree cover became thicker, and green leaves made a canopy. Passing through a clearing, they came to a small waterfall beside a rushing river.

Joanna didn't wait for assistance but lumbered down from her horse, stiff and sore from the ride. Why did blue water and green trees seem to call all God's creatures, seem to be so essentially good? She sat beside the brook and scooped the water by handfuls to her mouth.

She had never drunk water straight from a rushing brook. Her mother would have spat in the dirt to see her oldest daughter behaving like a shepherd.

"It's sweet! And cold!" she exclaimed, forgetting that Constans had no interest in her thoughts.

Constans shook his head and went to drink farther down, away from her. Perhaps he had done this dozens of times, but she hadn't. She didn't know water could be this cold, or taste like anything but ceramic pots.

Tilting her head back, she looked up at the blue sky. In the palace, she had been given every luxury imaginable. Or so she'd thought. That's what everyone in the palace believed. But had *they* ever drunk straight from a rushing brook?

What else in this world had she missed? Maybe her current plight wasn't all bad. Maybe there were treasures to be discovered in disappointments.

"Do we really have to go through Migdal?" Joanna wrinkled her nose. They were two miles away, but the smell was already overwhelming. The brine of fresh fish and tang of salted fish drying in the sun swamped the air. She had not known fish could have such varying degrees of stink. With any luck, they'd be out of the town before the tyrant-woman even knew they were there.

"It's the best road," Constans replied. Romans built wonderful roads. They taxed everyone within an inch of their lives, but they made travel a relatively easy burden.

The people of Migdal were the fish salters of the Roman Empire. If you ate a dried fish, it came from Migdal. Would the people smell of fish? With a shudder of horror, she wondered if she would smell of fish after spending the night there.

"Migdal must be easy to invade," she mused. "Invaders could sneak right up to them, and no one would be able to smell them. Even animals would be able to sneak into the city. But then, who would want to rule an empire of fish?"

Constans did not respond. He ignored her completely by now. It was freeing, in a way, to talk without any expectation of a response or rebuke.

As they approached the city, fish scales littered the path. Soon she spied the giant rack of crossed beams that had been erected for the work of drying fish. The sheer size of the rack was impressive. It was larger than most homes she had seen on the journey. Hanging from this rack were hundreds and hundreds of fish, drying in the sun. Their scales glittered, but the dull dead eyes made her blanch and turn away. One dead fish on her plate wasn't bad but to see hundreds at a time like this was nauseating.

Flies buzzed around the rack. Scales littered the ground, and she spied great hawks watching for the rodents that scampered about between the shrubs.

A woman sat at a market booth with alabaster jars. She nodded as Joanna and Constans passed, regarding them with a saleswoman's keen interest.

"Perfumers? Here?" Joanna asked.

"Migdal is famous for them," Constans replied. "Not just for the fish."

Joanna remembered suddenly a snippet of the story about the dreadful woman of the rumors, Mary Magdelene. She had made her money in perfume. Joanna wondered if the rumors were true, if she was really possessed of demons or if some enemy hated her too.

"She has gone traveling," Mary's sister said. The sister looked thin and worn, yet there was an unmistakable light in her eyes. Joanna judged her age to be no more than fifteen, yet the young woman looked as if she had seen dreadful things in her short life.

"Where has she gone? I was told she practically ran this city," Joanna replied, surprised. Mary Magdelene gone? Women didn't simply "go traveling." Such a thing was unheard of, even for a woman of her stature and wealth. Even for a woman possessed.

The young woman, watching her puzzled expression, burst out laughing. "Come inside." She gestured to the beautiful stone building not far from the well. Joanna had brought her horse there for a drink when she had chanced upon Mary Magdalene's little sister. She had introduced herself eagerly after seeing Joanna's expensive attire. Her name was Meira. No doubt Mary had trained her to treat wealthy travelers as potential customers.

Inside the home, Meira removed a stone crock from a shelf and dipped a ladle into the opening. She retrieved a honeycomb and placed it on a stone serving dish and set it before Joanna at a low table surrounded by cushions. Next, she retrieved fresh grapes and figs and a loaf of bread. Joanna raised her eyebrows. This was a great deal of food for one guest, and a stranger at that.

"I know!" Meira giggled, seeming to read Joanna's mind. "But if you had seen what I have seen, you would be celebrating too! I am just so grateful that I have someone to share my happiness with."

Constans was at the administration office outside the drying racks, sending a message back to the palace about the trip. Joanna could guess the message—the trip had been worthless so far. No sightings of Jesus. And yet, to hear what He had done for others, to drink fresh water and sleep under the stars, that was good medicine. Better than Herod's money could buy.

She decided to enjoy her unexpected good fortune. "Tell me, then. What are we celebrating?"

"My sister!" Meira dropped her cluster of grapes into her lap out of shock. "You haven't heard? Oh, of course not, you just arrived. But word hasn't spread? I thought everyone would have heard by now! She had a fearsome reputation!"

"Had?" Joanna asked. Meira spoke of Mary Magdelene in the past tense.

Meira turned red and blinked several times, flustered. "Yes, had. I mean to say, my sister is quite well." She burst out laughing. "That's it! Don't you see? The miracle! My sister is quite well!"

Meira reached across the table and grabbed Joanna's hands, pressing them to her cheek. "He did it. He did the impossible." Her eyes closed as she murmured the name over and over…. "Jesus."

"He's been here already?" Joanna asked, her stomach sinking.

"Yes," Meira replied. "Only two days ago. He was here with two rough-looking men. Fishermen, they said, but they didn't go near the water and do any fishing, not while they were here. But you should have seen what I saw!"

Joanna's shoulders sank. The farther she got from the palace, the further away her hope seemed. She had to get a miracle healing or get proof that Jesus was leading a rebellion. If she couldn't catch up to Him, neither one would happen. Maybe that was Chuza's plan all along. Maybe she would spend weeks, months even, chasing this strange figure, while Chuza relished his freedom.

A thought broke into her mind. What was God's plan? She caught herself and sat upright. Could God possibly have a plan in all these missed chances and lost opportunities? All she had managed so far was to hear stories of what He had done, of what He could do.

How could hearing of Him be part of God's plan?

She snapped her attention back to Meira. "Tell me everything."

Meira did. She described the quiet, unusual-looking man and His strange companions walking into town. She told of how many people rushed to Him, begging for healing.

"How did they know He could do it?" Joanna asked. "How did they know He would?" There was, after all, a difference.

Meira shrugged. "When you look into His eyes, you just know."

Joanna remembered those eyes. The young woman was right.

Meira's voice lowered. "He healed everything. Everything. Impossible things. Ailments that had existed from birth. Sickly children. Withered limbs. Sight restored to old milk-white eyes. Lepers healed. Paralytics made whole. I'm telling you the truth—it was as if nature reversed itself. As if the foundations of the world shook under His feet."

Joanna sat back, pondering Meira's words, her demeanor. Peter's mother-in-law had worn this same awe-filled expression. She had spoken of the healings with the same dazed and breathless voice. These women had witnessed something profoundly unnatural. Or profoundly natural. Which was it? Was Jesus setting things right, or upending the order of the universe?

"I don't know," Meira said quietly, as if reading her thoughts again. "I don't know what it all means. I just know who He is."

"Who is He?" Joanna asked softly.

"He is the Messiah."

The words hung in the air between them.

"And your sister?" Joanna asked at last. "What happened?"

"He called her name," Meira said, a smile coming to her lips.

"And?" Joanna leaned forward.

"That's it." Meira's smile widened. "He called her name. And at the sound of His voice calling to her, she was set free. I cannot describe it, other than something dark and shapeless lifted from her and dispersed through the air. And joy returned to her eyes." She dabbed at her own eyes with the corner of her sleeve. "You don't understand who my sister was. She was wealthy, that's true. But she was troubled. No one liked her. She didn't even like herself. She cut herself at night on the rocks. She drank to excess, she ate to excess too. It was like a battle raged inside her, and she punished herself with whatever she was gifted with…food, wealth, beauty, drink. It was awful to watch, to be helpless. But then… Jesus."

"Where is He now?" Joanna asked. "Did He say where He was going?"

"He didn't." She paused, a faraway look in her eyes before focusing on Joanna again. "He has family in Cana. Oh! Have you heard what He did at a wedding there?" Meira clapped her hands and began another story.

Constans's mood had only grown worse since leaving Migdal. A short two-day journey between the cities had now stretched out too long, and they would arrive in Nazareth on the third day. He muttered under his breath, trying to edge his camel past another family moving slowly.

The heat made Joanna grumpy, but she still had manners. She apologized to the family as she passed. She caught up to Constans on a break between groups.

"Where are they all coming from?" she asked. "The roads are crowded with families, not traders."

He huffed in exasperation, focusing on threading his way between the next group of travelers.

"More importantly…where are they all going?" she added.

"They are not going to their hometowns for a census," Constans replied. "No one has called for that. I've never seen anything like this. Look at them!" He wrinkled his nose, nodding in the direction of a family just ahead.

The mother carried a lame child in her arms. Their donkey was old and skinny, with ribs plainly visible even from this distance. They were obviously poor, and probably could not afford the trip. What were they doing?

Joanna decided to find out. Spurring her horse before Constans could scold her, she approached them. She immediately regretted it. They were not wealthy people, of course, but they were not even hygienic. Had they ever seen clean water, or perfume? Ducking her head down into her scarf, trying to hide her nose a bit from the smell, she drew her animal alongside the mother.

The woman looked at her with wary eyes, taking in the formal robes, then the woman searched Joanna's face and body as if looking for something. A flaw perhaps? Joanna had the distinct sense the woman was looking for a fault and was surprised not to find one. That made no sense. Why would a wealthy woman have an obvious flaw?

"Mother," Joanna asked, trying her most polite tone, "why are you and your family on the road? Where are you going?"

The woman looked at her, then down at her child, who slept in her arms. A tear escaped her eye and rolled down her cheek.

"To see Jesus," she whispered to Joanna. "He will heal my daughter."

"How do you know?" Joanna couldn't help but ask. All this trouble, this expense, to see a man who was rumored to have great power…but what if she was wrong? She didn't dare voice the full strength of her doubts. The woman looked too fragile.

"I don't know," the woman replied softly. "I believe. I think there is a difference." She looked at Joanna. "Are you seeking Him too?"

Joanna glanced back at Constans, who was busy trying to get his camel to sidestep a large amount of animal waste. Camels were not known for being easy to maneuver. There was a reason they were not preferred in battle conditions, after all.

"Yes," she replied. "I need a healing. My husband does not believe, though. And to be truthful…I don't think I do either. Will He hold that against me? Do I need to do something first? Pay for an offering? Or is there a fast I must complete?"

The woman shook her head. "I will do anything to see my daughter healed. What are you prepared to do? Perhaps you need to think about that on your journey."

Joanna reined her horse back and waited for Constans to catch up. She didn't have to wait long. He came charging up, his face red.

"You shouldn't have done that!" he yelled. "Do you know how many robbers are on the roads? And with your fine clothes they'll know you have money. You'll be easy prey for some criminal!"

Blinking rapidly to hold back the tears of shock and embarrassment, she stammered an apology.

"Your words are useless," he muttered, turning his animal to resume the journey.

After a while, her heart stopped hurting from his attack. She had never been far from him. The woman certainly hadn't looked dangerous. Why had he overreacted so violently?

"So," he asked, his eyes straight ahead, "why are they all on the road?"

"To see Jesus," she said. "Word about Him is spreading."

"You need to report back to Chuza that Jesus is amassing popular support."

She gritted her teeth to restrain a cross reply. He saw everything in such dark, ominous tones.

"And what kind of army do you think He is raising? One of blind beggars and cripples? No one cares for these people. They command no great army. And no great army would have them under their command. They do not fit in anywhere, Constans, certainly not in a master plan for a rebellion against Rome."

He rolled his eyes.

She gestured at the people around them.

"Look at them! Half of them can barely bring a cup to their lips without spilling the water. How on earth could these poor souls swing a sword or carry a shield?"

Constans turned his head and glared at her. Tapping one finger to his forehead, he spoke. "Think. Jesus's power is broader, greater, and far more menacing than you realize. If He can really heal, and really heal anything, then no one in the empire is safe. Don't you see? Everyone is afflicted at some point in their lives. Everyone knows sorrow." His voice wavered, and he cleared his throat before continuing. "If Jesus can heal, everyone will be in His debt. If you don't see the value in that, Chuza will."

Joanna leaned back, the impact of his words hitting. Chuza certainly understood debts, power, and pawns. Chuza would see Jesus the way Constans did, she was certain of that. Even if Jesus could heal her and grant her a child, Chuza would see Jesus as an enemy.

Why had he sent her to find Jesus? To get rid of her? Was she a fool to think Chuza still wanted a child from her?

She had to think of another's troubles, not her own. Her own troubles were so exhausting, and so stubborn. Nothing she ever did changed them.

What was the sorrow that Constans knew? What had made him such a miserable person? He detested her company, but then, it was clear he detested everyone. He hated life itself.

They stopped in Cana to feed and water the animals. The roads were becoming steeper, and narrower. More rocks were in the way, and occasionally the travelers had to wait while someone moved a large stone from the path to widen it.

Joanna sat on a stone bench near the well, listening to the travelers and locals mingling, swapping stories and information. Much of it was about Jesus. Much of it sounded too outlandish to be true.

Especially the bit about turning water into wine. That miracle had no place with the others, she thought. Healing the poor and sick? That was compassion. But providing wine at a wedding?

She spied the six giant stone jars he was purported to have used, still on display. Really, the size of the jars alone should have told people the story couldn't possibly be true...could it? Those jars held enough water to fill one of Herod's pools! What kind of wedding needed that much wine? No one in this region could possibly have had that many guests.

Chuza would have loved to see this, she thought. Not even Herod and his feast could go through that much wine in one evening. With a sudden pang of loneliness, she realized how much she missed Chuza. Or maybe she missed the man he used to be. She missed who they could have been, together.

With a deep sigh, she looked to the horizon as Constans brought the animals back. In the afternoon haze, the hills were dark waves, and she was at the center of their rolling story. She felt caught, trapped in a stormy sea, even here on dry land. Who could ever understand the pain of not becoming the woman she always thought she would be? The disappointment in Chuza's eyes when he looked at her, and the helplessness she felt? He could fix any problem, except hers. No wonder he could not bear to look at her anymore.

Crowds of people waited to look inside the jars. Debates broke out here and there about the symbolism of the miracle. Some merely waited in line for the thrill of touching one of the jars.

Please, she thought, *please let the rumors about this Jesus be true. At least some of them.*

A swarm of Pharisees marched into the crowd, waving them back, demanding the crowd part without touching them. *Pharisees,* she thought, with a sinking stomach. *Nothing is ever good enough for them, especially the common people.* She herself barely qualified for a passing glance.

"What is the meaning of this?" a Pharisee demanded. He seemed to be the leader. His head was swathed with a purple turban, and his outer robe was red. His girdle was adorned with jewels. His companions were only a little less ostentatious. The poor and common people stepped back.

Constans sighed. Joanna glanced up at him, but he motioned for her to keep quiet. Leaning down, he whispered. "Best to stay out of their way."

No one spoke to the Pharisees or answered the question. Mothers grabbed their children, pinning them to their sides. Fathers looked at the ground.

To touch a Pharisee, even by accident, was to incur their wrath. They took the ritual laws of cleanliness very seriously. They took all of Moses's laws very seriously. Pharisees wanted to remain—always—separate. Their very name came from an old word meaning "separate." They wanted to be separate from the Gentiles, from ritual uncleanness, from those who were not observant of the holy laws of Moses. It was very hard to be human around a Pharisee, so most people avoided them.

Also, they tended to cause accidents in the road and wherever else they went. They were self-righteous public safety hazards. When it was time for prayer, they stopped, even midstride, and bowed down. They didn't just say a brief prayer and get on with their business. No, they assumed that God preferred long prayers, so they stretched their prayers out if possible. It was said you could pass a Pharisee at his noon prayer, buy your meal, and pass him on your return while he was finishing the benediction. Yet none had ever performed a miracle. No one brought crippled children to the Pharisees.

One of the Pharisees circled around the stone jars, eyeing them with disdain. "These? These are the jars we heard tell of?"

A second Pharisee nodded. "Indeed. The stone jars for the ritual washing. And the story is that—"

"Stop!" the leader interrupted. "Do not repeat drivel. Gossip is a sin. Who has touched these vessels?" His angry gaze swept over the crowd. Few would meet it. "Stone jars protect the water within from becoming unclean, but if a crowd like you has touched them, looked inside, dipped your hands in to test the water…"

"If you have put your trust in this man Jesus instead of the teachings of Moses," the second Pharisee called out, "you must repent!"

Constans shook his head and whispered again to Joanna. "If you want to know what is hidden in the heart, watch how someone behaves when they don't get what they want."

"Reports of these miracles are nothing but lies!" the first Pharisee said. "Now I want to know if anyone put their hands inside these jars! These jars are part of our law, and Jesus treated them like a magician's trick!"

He snapped his fingers at his companions. They braced themselves against the stone jars, tipping them over roughly, shattering them one by one. Six stone jars fell and cracked open, staining the earth. The wine looked like spilled blood. The Pharisees' sandals stamped dust across the stain.

Joanna turned away.

She was anxious to get to Nazareth.

CHAPTER NINE

Summer, 30 CE
Capernaum

Constans was angry. "Chuza expected us back last week." Ignoring him, Joanna presented her husband's seal to the silk trader. Standing at his booth, the man's eyes lit with excitement.

"I need a place to stay for the evening, and information. We are looking for a man," Joanna said. "I will make sure you are well rewarded."

Hours later, Joanna helped alongside as the wives rushed from kitchen to dining table, then from kitchen to the crowds overflowing through the front door. After being introduced as an honored guest, Joanna found herself swept into wild preparations for a crowd of men from the synagogue.

Jesus was among them. And wherever Jesus went, crowds of common people followed, people without money for bread or the means to repay a host. Mira, the wife of the host, watched as her stores of grain and oil were depleted in a blink. And yet every time Joanna went back to a jar to refill a serving bowl, she found just enough.

She sweated through her robes, sweat trickling down her face, thankful for the distraction of work. No one seemed to notice or care that she was wealthy. No one noticed her hands trembling as she caught sight of Jesus.

A woman dressed in a beautiful linen robe with a lovely purple silk sash reached for the platter of bread Joanna held. Joanna smiled, happy to serve someone so much like herself here tonight. Jesus had been circulating through the crowd for an hour or so, talking to everyone, even women and children. Joanna had not seen any miracles take place, and yet the atmosphere was alive with hope.

At last Jesus settled in the center of the room. As each person reached for Him, He said only one thing, "Take courage, for your sins are forgiven."

Standing beside Joanna, Mira whispered in her ear, "I thought He was a healer."

"He is," Joanna whispered back. "He is healing what we cannot see." Her heart leaped. She had never expected a miracle like this, a miracle that took root deep in the heart.

As He spoke, she knew she had never heard teaching like this either. She had heard speakers who taught about God, such as John did. This man taught *for* God. She had never seen such authority paired with such humility. It was enchanting. The crowd soaked up every word. Even, she noticed, the religious leaders who had begun to trickle in.

The woman in the linen robe gazed at Jesus with such profound admiration and awe that Joanna was touched. She wanted to know this woman's story. After moving quietly across the room as Jesus spoke to each brokenhearted soul, Joanna discreetly touched her on the arm.

"What is your name?" Joanna asked.

"Mary," the woman replied, her eyes never leaving Jesus's face. "Mary Magdalene."

Joanna's mouth fell open. The woman possessed of many demons? Mary glanced up at her, then smiled and nodded.

"Yes. That Mary." Her eyes returned to Jesus.

Dust fell past Joanna's eyes, and she swept it away. "I did not mean to offend you."

Straw fell from the ceiling onto Mary's hair. She instinctively reached up to brush it away, just as a large thatch of straw came tumbling down. Joanna jumped out of the way just in time to avoid being hit on the head with the clump of mud and straw. The women, together with all the guests, looked up at the ceiling, where a large piece of the roof had been removed.

A mat was being lowered by a group of men, using what appeared to be ropes and sashes from their garments. As the mat lowered farther down, Joanna saw a young man lying on the mat, his legs withered and crippled. He had no muscle at all. She could clearly see the outline of every bone. She turned away, unable to look at his twisted, unnaturally thin legs.

Was turning away, pretending not to see, the only kindness she was capable of?

Jesus reached out and patted the young man. "Take heart, son. Your sins are forgiven."

At this, the religious leaders all over the house raised a collective, outraged gasp. They exchanged dark glances with one another. Joanna knew why. Such deformities were considered judgments from God for sin. This man had surely committed a terrible sin to have this deformity. Clearly, they thought Jesus had no right to dismiss it so easily.

Jesus, however, remained completely at peace. "Why are you thinking these things in your hearts?"

Every head swiveled toward them. The leaders grew red-faced, their eyes narrow slits of fury. They had never been made a public spectacle before, not for their own sin.

"Which is easier to say?" Jesus asked. "Your sins are forgiven? Or, take up your mat and walk?"

Everyone looked at the poor man lying on the mat with his useless legs. He'd likely never taken a step in his life. His legs weren't even strong enough to support his meager weight.

Jesus extended a hand to the young man, who reached back to Him. "But so that you may know that the Son of Man has authority on earth to forgive sins…" He looked into the eyes of the young man, who had begun to cry. "I tell you, get up, take your mat, and go home."

Joanna's breath caught in her throat. The young man blinked. Then sat up. He swung his legs off the mat, and the crowd exhaled in a huff of surprise. He looked up at Jesus, his eyes widening in indescribable shock. His legs had obeyed his will!

Jesus nodded as if in encouragement, as if to reassure the young man that he was not dreaming. The young man blew a short breath from between his lips like he was preparing for a burst of speed at the beginning of a race, then launched himself into a standing position.

A woman in the crowd was so startled she screamed and fainted. Several people rushed to attend to her. Several more had to catch the young man, who was tottering on his feet. He had no sense of balance. He listed from side to side, laughing hysterically, as they caught him and pushed him back aright.

Jesus laughed, and His eyes danced with merriment, watching the man explore what working legs could do. Only the Pharisees burned with anger.

The man bent down and grabbed his mat. "I'm going to run all the way home." He stopped and looked around the room, searching. "My mother's not here, is she? No. I can't wait to see the look on her face!" With a whoop, he shot out the door and into the night.

No one spoke for a while. They just watched the figure of a young man running. After a short distance he threw his mat to the side and lifted his arms, running as if in total victory.

Jesus continued His work late into the night. Joanna's eyelids grew heavy. She walked outside to refresh herself, hoping the night air would be cooler. The hottest month of the year approached, but breezes from the west provided a welcome relief.

Outside the door, she inhaled the fresh clean air, trying to process everything she had witnessed this evening. Her mind couldn't keep up with Jesus, with everything He was capable of. No, it wasn't just what He was capable of, she decided. What was so extraordinary about Jesus was what He was willing to do. He was willing to touch anyone, to heal anyone of anything. He broke every law of cleanliness and religious propriety.

And He did it in the name of God!

In the center of the courtyard, she spied women baking bread in the cool of the nighttime, preparing for breakfast. Breakfast? A quick glance to the east confirmed it—the sky had a tinge of pink. Dawn would rise in an hour or so. How fast this night had flown! She shook her head at the realization.

And then she had another: the smell of freshly baked bread was irresistible. How had she never known this? She had always had bread delivered to her at a table. She'd never been close to it while it baked. Heat was damaging to a woman's skin, just like harsh sunlight. This trip had truly opened her eyes to many things. She had much to tell Chuza…if he would listen.

Her stomach rumbled. She hadn't eaten in hours. Constans had disappeared, and she didn't have any money. Still, at least she could satisfy her curiosity, if not her appetite.

She edged closer to see how the women baked their bread. Their oven was made of stone and mud, about the height of her knees. She marveled that there were no leaping flames, but only glowing red embers inside. Loaves of bread were baking along the edges and walls. Each loaf about the size of a man's hand, golden brown on top, dark brown on the bottom edges.

"You are hungry?" A woman's voice startled her.

Turning, she saw Mary Magdalene standing next to her. The shock of being so close to her, this woman of many demons, left her speechless.

"I will buy you bread if you'd like," Mary offered, her eyes kind. She had a slight smile on her face, as if uncertain how Joanna would react.

"No." Joanna caught herself and remembered to be polite. "I was curious, that's all." Her stomach rumbled, and she felt her cheeks flush with embarrassment.

Mary glanced away, perhaps out of politeness. She reached into a purse attached to her girdle and offered a coin in exchange for a loaf. A woman was happy to make the exchange. Mary broke the steaming bread in two and took a bite.

"Delicious," she murmured.

Joanna's stomach roiled in hunger.

"It's really too bad you're not hungry," Mary said, taking another bite. "I'd hate to throw this half away."

"Oh, please do not do that!" Joanna blushed again, mad at herself for sounding so desperate. Biting her lip, she decided. "I am starving. Really. My guard has the money for our trip, so I cannot buy myself any bread until he returns."

Mary grinned and handed her the bread. Joanna took a bite then closed her eyes in ecstasy. It was incredible. Hunger and exhaustion made eating fresh bread under the stars truly a blissful experience. She had never known that hardship could also lead to incredible joy. She had never experienced such intense gratitude before.

She snuck a glance at Mary. The woman was exotic to her in many ways, even though Mary was a commoner. Mary was a businesswoman, wealthy from her earnings, independent, and she'd been healed by Jesus. She'd known darkness, but Jesus had delivered her.

"You want to ask," Mary said.

Joanna raised an eyebrow.

"You want to ask about the demons that were cast out. It's all right, everyone does," Mary continued. "Jesus heals many people. Those people can say that once they were crippled but now they walk. Or once they were mute and now they speak. Everyone knows a miracle occurred. But me? I can say that I was once tormented, and now I am free. No one can testify to my healing except for me. That is why I travel with Jesus and tell what He has done."

"Mary! Joanna!"

Joanna's heart caught in her chest. She knew that voice.

"Jesus!" Mary turned and embraced Jesus with abandon. He hugged her back. Immediately she bought bread and insisted He have something to eat. The women all fussed over Him, finding Him a place to sit, bringing Him drink and more bread. He waved them off politely and with many thanks.

"I need a word with Joanna, please," He said.

The women backed away, tending to chores in other parts of the courtyard. Joanna stood, feeling like a child with weak, trembling knees. She wasn't sure what to do with her hands. She clutched them, wringing her fingers back and forth, then held her arms stiffly at her sides.

"Good bread," He muttered, taking another bite.

"Do you know why I'm here?" she stammered.

He took another bite then looked up at her. He had incredibly piercing eyes that calmed and comforted her even as He intimidated her. What was this magnetic power He had?

"Of course," He replied. "It was hot inside. But the hottest month of the year is here. I need to do my work outside. Catch the breezes more."

"And the crowds," Joanna said. She couldn't believe she was making conversation with Jesus. "The roads were packed with travelers coming to see You. The roads are already packed with merchants bringing fresh fruit to market this time of year, plus the wheat harvest. I've never seen so many people traveling."

He nodded, watching her. His eyes narrowed a tiny bit, as if He was contemplating something about her. She cleared her throat.

"A lot of people are making money selling feed and bedding to the animals, or letting out extra rooms," she added nervously.

"Why?" He asked.

"Why are they coming?" she replied.

"No. I want you to tell me why you have come."

At last. This was her moment to ask for the miracle. Chuza would never believe a word of what she had seen. She needed to bring home the miracle, not just report one. Or trick Him into saying something that would get Him arrested. She could easily betray Him into the hands of Herod's court.

That idea seemed so silly now.

"My husband has money. I can pay for a miracle," she said. Her voice was weak. She did not have the heart to ask, not if it would mean putting this man at risk.

"I don't accept money for miracles," He said. He seemed even-tempered, neither offended nor perplexed.

"I can offer you safe passage too. My husband is the steward for Herod the Tetrarch. If you wish to travel to other countries, we can arrange that. Or, if you wish for an audience with Herod himself, that can be arranged."

"You still haven't answered My question."

She used the toe of her sandal to draw a shape in the dirt. Why had she come to find Him? For Chuza, and on his orders?

"I came to find You because I want to have a child. My husband loved me once, I think, but he does not love me anymore. He wants a son above anything else on earth. I cannot give him that. I want a miracle from You. I want You to open my womb."

His eyes filled with tears. He reached out and took hold of her right hand. "Take off the necklace from Herodias."

She'd forgotten she was wearing that! With her left hand, she removed it and threw it onto the ground. Jesus reached out to rest His hand upon the top of her head. A sudden relief swept through her body, like a cleansing breath. Her body did not hurt. Her stomach was no longer in knots. She could breathe deeply once more.

"Very good," He said. "And yes, you have been healed of what truly ails you. You are forgiven of your sins, daughter. Go in peace. And trust in God, in His plan."

She was aware of tears running down her cheeks. Her headache was gone. How long had it been there, in the background, a low ache? Since a year ago, spring? She had never felt so good, had never felt so much like herself until this moment. No wonder people came from far and wide to find this man.

"What can I offer You?" she asked, breathless.

"Your trust," He replied. "You need to return to the palace. Your husband is under much pressure."

How did He know that? Did He know Chuza? Joanna blushed. "But I—"

"Trust in Me," Jesus reminded her.

Joanna nodded. "When will I see You again?"

Jesus smiled. "I will meet you on the road."

"What—" Joanna began to ask, then caught herself. Jesus already knew, even if she didn't.

The next week

Traveling back to the palace in Tiberius

Joanna watched as her horse drank from a pool. It felt good to be done with riding for the day. Tomorrow she would be back in the area of Tiberius. Dread had begun to make her body feel heavy and cold despite the late-summer sun. There was still time to sail for Rome. Didn't Jesus understand that? Why had He sent her back when it was unsafe?

A group of men approached the well, pulling their bags loose. Joanna laughed out loud as Constans's face turned sour. Jesus had found her. Mary quickly wrapped Joanna in a hug. So many women traveled with Jesus and His disciples! Chuza would be shocked, but perhaps Herod would be relieved. A man planning for war does not summon troops of women.

After the animals had been watered and the disciples with Jesus had bought food for the evening, Joanna settled in with Mary near His feet to listen to Him speak. A fire crackled and hissed as the night sky stretched wide and blue above them all.

"Teach us to pray," a burly man said.

"That's Thomas," Mary whispered to Joanna. "He's always asking questions."

"When you pray," Jesus replied, "say, 'Our Father, hallowed be Your name! Your kingdom come. Give us each day our daily bread. Forgive us our sins, for we also forgive everyone who sins against us. And lead us not into temptation….'"

The whir of a moth passed her ear, and the sound of mourning doves punctuated His voice. It was such a simple prayer, she thought, so why did she feel as if the power of the heavens had been discharged into the words?

What mercy. On the eve of returning to face my worst fear, the Messiah teaches me how to speak to God. I do not have to wait to attend the temple, for a priest to offer prayers on my behalf. I can speak to God directly.

Looking at Jesus by the light of the campfire, she knew she already had.

The roads back to Tiberius were not congested. Joanna was anxious to bathe and refresh herself before presenting herself to Chuza. What news she had! What miracles she had seen!

Jesus was a real healer. And He *had* healed her. He never spoke of military action, not once. He never spoke about the government in Rome either. Herod would be relieved.

She entered the palace through the garden gate, and though she wished to stop and check the garden, she rushed through it. Guards at the outer door nodded in greeting, but she caught a strange look passing between them. *Never mind,* she thought, pressing on into the courtyard, careful to check for Chuza. She didn't want to see him until she had bathed.

She wanted to present her best self. She would be alluring, enticing, joyful. She would be her youthful, vibrant self again. Jesus had given her hope. She didn't just feel healthy and whole. She felt beautiful.

But first, she had to bathe. She still smelled like a horse.

Chuza was nowhere to be seen. Guards at the inner doors nodded in greeting, but again, a strange look passed between them. What was happening? She pressed through and took the stairs to the upper chambers on the far right, where she could bathe. Chuza's room was along this corridor, but he would not be in his room at this time of day. He would be working. She could get to the bath and call for Aresh to help her dress before he returned for the evening.

A guard at Chuza's door started as if frightened when he saw her. The door behind him swung open. Joanna ducked into an open room to her right. A soft, trilling laugh came from Chuza's room, and she leaned forward just a bit to see who was leaving.

Aresh. What was Aresh doing in Chuza's chamber?

"I found it, thank you!" Aresh said to the guard. "The scouts have seen Joanna approaching the gates. When she returns tonight, she would have noticed that her earring was missing. I will get this back to her room."

Joanna leaned back into the shadows as Aresh hurried past. Why was an earring from her collection in Chuza's room? On instinct, her hands went to her ears, checking to be sure neither earring was missing. They weren't. And when she left, she hadn't noticed that she was missing any earrings. In fact, she'd looked at her jewelry before deciding what to take. Everything had been there, accounted for.

The earring had gone missing while she was traveling. Someone had worn her earrings while she was gone. Someone had worn her earrings inside Chuza's bedchamber. Her body felt cold with grief. Forcing herself to take a step, then another, she walked past Chuza's room and to the bath.

Somehow, she knew water would not help.

CHAPTER TEN

Chuza did not send her to Rome, as she had feared he would. He sent her to the Black Fortress.

When she had arrived home to the palace in Tiberius, she discovered all the court preparing to leave for Machaerus, where John was imprisoned. Herod was throwing a birthday party for himself at the military outpost, although few nobles would be able to attend. Machaerus was simply too isolated to make travel practical.

The journey to Machearus seemed so much longer this time. The sun beat down on Joanna's head. She adjusted her shawl to create more shade over her face, but the day wore on and on. The sun refused to set. Maybe it was her unhappy heart, the bleak weariness that had returned. Chuza had been aloof when he saw her, not even commenting on her conspicuous absence during the best weeks for sailing to Rome. Had he forgotten his plan? It was irrational, but she wanted to remind him of it. She almost wished he still wanted to send her.

Why Machaerus? Did John know they were coming? Every hoofbeat was like a drumbeat and stirred the dust into a roiling carpet. Herod's traveling party was a slow dreadful storm snaking toward the imprisoned prophet.

As she rode with the caravan along the dusty roads, they passed through towns where fields of wheat had ripened. The abundant rains of Adar had made for a plentiful harvest. Perhaps, she thought, there is hope in that…a harsh storm might still bring life. She sniffled to hold back the tears.

Journeying through rich farmland, she lifted her head, listening to the workers in the fields singing, the sound of the scythes swinging, the call of the foremen to the laborers.

Did they find peace in the predictability of their lives? A grove of apricot trees on the hill to her left was flush with heavy golden fruit. Vines closer to the road were dark green, the grapes coming into season soon. So much life on either side of the dead, beaten road. So much life if she turned to her left or right, but her life was not her own. She could not turn.

Aresh rode to her right, having spoken no more than ten words all morning.

Joanna hadn't tried to say much to the girl. She was unwilling to question Aresh about what she'd seen when she got back to the palace, and Aresh had been uncharacteristically quiet since then.

Joanna's horse paused to steal a bite of grass, but she didn't scold him. The smell of the freshly cut wheat was surely tempting the poor fellow, and the scent of newly turned earth crushed underfoot made the air thick.

Aresh paused her donkey to watch the scene. Joanna smiled, thinking that the poor animal was probably grateful for a chance to steal some grass as well. The journey seemed long for everyone, even the beasts, surely. Jesus had unnerved the court. Women passed them carrying water pots to the edge of the fields and loaves of bread for the noon meal. Children who were too young to help with the harvest sat at the end of the rows, watching as older girls taught them to weave the green stalks into baskets. Occasionally a wild rabbit would bound out from the fields, disturbed by the laborers, and then the children would jump up, laughing, and give chase.

"What are you going to do?"

Joanna snapped back to the moment. "About what?"

"You need to conceive," Aresh replied. "And soon. No woman wants to go to Rome for Lupercalia."

"How did you—" Joanna stopped. If this was a peace offering, it was a poor one. "Aresh, you are a sweet girl. But again, I warn you, gossip is not acceptable."

Aresh's mouth fell open, as if she was offended. "Gossip? I never gossip! I was just looking out for you! The servants are talking, Joanna. I only repeated to you what they were saying. That's not gossip. That's loyalty."

Aresh was right, she did need loyal friends. But Aresh was wrong about the value of repeating gossip. "If I am not responsible for their words," Joanna said, "I do not want to carry the weight of them. Do you understand?"

Aresh spurred her donkey and left.

Joanna shook her head and urged her horse to continue.

Her husband was weary with her, Herodias was angry with her, and now her most intimate servant was gossiping about her. *Well,* she thought, *at least things can't get worse.*

A snake slithered out from the grass, crossing just in front of the horse. The poor beast, frightened, froze in midstride. Joanna fell forward with a cry. Several people in the caravan turned to see what the commotion was all about.

Including Chuza. The look of utter disappointment on his face was impossible to misread. He hated it when she called attention to herself in negative ways. She was, of course, nothing but a reflection of himself in the eyes of the court. And so of course she would command the court's attention in such an embarrassing way.

I'm wrong again, she thought. Things always seemed to find a way to get worse.

Summer, 30 CE
The Black Fortress

With two hours left until the party, the atmosphere in the palace was thick with tension. Joanna had exhausted every discreet resource she had—no one knew where John was being held. Maybe Chuza was wrong. Maybe John was not imprisoned in the dungeon here. But if he was, Joanna wanted to ask him about what Pilate had said. Was Jesus really just his cousin? That sounded suspicious. The Savior of the world wouldn't be someone's cousin. That seemed so…human, she supposed. If humans needed a savior, the savior couldn't be human.

Joanna had nothing left to do. She had no fancy clothes to wear and no one to dress her in them. Aresh had finished her hair an hour ago. To speed time along, Joanna decided to wander to the kitchens to watch the chefs prepare for the feast.

Passing down the corridor, she was startled by Salome's screams.

"I cannot! You ask too much of me this time!"

Herodias's voice was unmistakable with its mix of venom and shrill anger. "You will do everything, exactly as I wish. If you do not, I will see that you are married off into some distant empire that exports nothing but sand fleas!"

"I do not dance for men!" Salome's voice pleaded. "Dance is a sacred art, Mother. Even if you do not believe in such things, I do."

A tremendous crash of something metallic made Joanna lurch forward then brace herself against the wall. Her curiosity was irresistible—the weeks of rain and the indignity of this afternoon had weakened her. If someone else was having a worse afternoon than she was, she wanted to witness it. Especially if that someone was Herodias.

Joanna crept to the edge of the doorway to Salome's bedchamber and peeked in, careful to avoid being seen. A brass platter lay near the door, raisins scattered across the floor. Salome now wielded a matching goblet in her right hand, glaring at her mother as the cup dripped red, staining her robe and the carpet at her feet.

"Put that down, Salome! I command you!" Herodias shook her finger in her daughter's face.

Salome's expression was pinched and angry. "I do not want any part of this! I refuse to dance for Herod and his men!"

Herodias crossed her arms. "Do you know what happens to daughters who defy their mothers?"

Salome glared at her then shook her head.

"That's right. Because there are no stories about daughters who defy their mothers. Not in our empire. You are going to be married soon, Salome, and who do you think will make the match?"

"Herod! He holds the power!"

Herodias laughed. "He holds the title." She walked to the window and looked out at the sky, checking the weather. The rain had slowed to a steady roll.

"I can arrange a lifetime of misery for you."

Salome's grip on the goblet faltered, and the cup fell from her hand. "Mother, please."

Herodias's mouth curved in a wry smile. "One dance. That's all I am asking. It is his birthday, Salome, and you know how fond of you he truly is. He's been like a father to you since you were but a toddler. Do this for me, and I will arrange a marriage that exceeds your every expectation."

"I only have one request," Salome said.

Herodias's eyebrow arched as she listened, and she looked pleased to have won.

"Choose a husband who will take me far from you," Salome spat. "After tonight I never want to see your face again." A tear slipped from Salome's eye and down her cheek.

Joanna fled before she could be discovered.

A drumbeat announced the beginning of the party. The columns that flanked the courtyard echoed and amplified the drums that lined the inner courtyard. Joanna walked along the wall behind the columns, holding her fingers to her ears. Every strike of the drum reverberated in her chest. Where was John? Could he hear the drums too?

The outer courtyard overflowed with guests. These were the wealthy merchants, the dealers of fine linen and spices, the tax collectors. The truly important guests, however, were in the upper courtyard, near Herod's raised throne. Servants hustled along the back wall, dodging guests who wanted to explore the fortress courtyard before being called to pay homage to their ruler.

She made her way through them, identifying them by their clothes. Guests glittered with gold and silver and jewels of every color. Servants wore plain red robes and carried trays of food or wine. A few had abandoned their work and crowded at the edges of the balcony, or spied from the edge of the gardens, watching the spectacle of Herod's birthday party. Few sights equaled this, even in Rome. Herod indulged many people in many things, but he loved his birthday most of all. Wine and gold would flow tonight.

He sat on his throne in the center of the inner courtyard as throngs of well-wishers circulated around him. Herodias sat on his left, and a canopy stretched over their thrones in case of rain. The heavens cooperated this evening, though. The skies cleared, and the moon shone bright and full.

Chuza stood to Herod's right, accepting the gifts with what Joanna knew was a practiced smile.

Jugglers and dancers and magicians circulated at the outer edges of the crowd, weaving between inner and outer court-yards as the musicians played.

The palace was crammed with revelers, yet Joanna felt so alone.

She hated this time of year, what happened in the far distance, in the fields where the shepherds tended sheep. She wondered, if she strained, would she hear the sheep being led to slaughter? Glancing at the revelers, she felt a sudden chill down her spine. In the torchlight, their open-mouth smiles could easily be mistaken for grimaces. Celebrating here tonight with Herod, celebrating his reign, were they too being led to slaughter?

Where was John?

Herodias scanned the crowd, her face pinched with anger.

Herodias had applied extra cosmetics for the feast, and the edges of her kohl eyeliner were sharper and harsher than usual. As she aged, she lost more and more of her softness, and now used cosmetics to accentuate the hard angles of her face, making her more monstrous than human in the torchlight.

She called a servant forward and gestured to the crowd before dismissing the boy.

As the boy ran through the crowd, Joanna decided to follow him. Something had made Herodias angry.

She caught him on the back stairs leading up to the living chambers. She clutched his sleeve and stepped back when he turned so as not to alarm him.

"Why is Herodias angry?" she asked.

The boy looked side to side, although they were alone in the stairwell.

"You can tell me," she urged.

"Salome is crying. She does not want to dance at the party. Herodias said I am to go and remind her of the punishment for disobeying her."

Joanna's throat tightened. Salome was so young. "Which is?"

The boy leaned in. "Herodias is going to sell her to the slave traders. Them." He pointed to the main courtyard. Joanna followed his gesture and saw a group of harsh-looking men. One stood picking his teeth with his thumbnail, eyeing a servant woman as she circulated with a flask of wine. "Salome has to dance as if her life depended on it," the boy continued, "because it does. Herodias says that if Salome doesn't like taking orders from her mother, she might prefer to take orders from a slave master."

Joanna's hand flew to her heart. Herodias would make good on her threat. Salome had no idea what was at stake. Joanna pushed past the boy and rushed to Salome's chambers.

Salome sat alone at her dressing table. The girl was beautiful. Torches on the wall of the fortress cast darting shadows like serpent's tongues across the walls.

Salome looked up, startled. She visibly relaxed when she saw it was Joanna. "No."

The boy burst into the chambers seconds later, delivering the message. Joanna watched Salome's face crumple. "It is all right, Salome. Please do not despair."

"It is not right for a young woman to dance like this," she whimpered.

The boy looked from Joanna to Salome then fled. He seemed overwhelmed by the amount of emotion in the little room.

"I understand," Joanna said softly. "You have a choice. It is not a good choice, but it is one you must make. If you dance and please Herodias, you will be able to move on and forget this night ever happened. She will be so pleased, perhaps, that she might grant you greater freedom when we return to Tiberius."

Salome wiped her face. "It is only one dance," she murmured. "But even so…"

Joanna rested a hand on her shoulder. "Just one dance. Then we can all forget this night."

Salome reached up, resting a trembling hand on top of Joanna's. "Maybe I am being foolish to have such misgivings. You are right. One dance, and my dignity will be quickly restored by a good marriage. What harm could come from just one dance?"

Joanna returned to the party, taking several deep breaths to steady her nerves. Salome had come so close to a terrible punishment—her youthful rebellion might have cost her dearly if Joanna had not intervened.

Her braid had come loose. As she tucked it back into place, she realized she had broken into a nervous sweat. Across the courtyard, Chuza glanced at her and seemed puzzled seeing her in disarray. Aresh appeared at his side, handing him a goblet of wine. Joanna looked away, embarrassed. But for whom? Herself or him? She was so busy attending to someone else that she had neglected her husband.

The Jewish nobles of Galilee crowded around Herod. They lived far enough from Tiberius that to host him here in Machaerus was a rare delight. Everyone wanted to see him—or more correctly, everyone wanted Herod to see them. Everyone wanted something from Herod. Chuza was right—power must be the loneliest burden in the world.

Herod had already made one speech to them tonight, reminding them of his steadfast commitment to their community. Now he stood again, promising that he would continue to work with Rome to assure their prosperity. Joanna scanned their faces to see how much they believed.

Herod depended on their goodwill. He was caught between them and Rome, always.

Joanna felt the atmosphere in the room change. Salome had appeared, and the crowd parted as she walked toward Herod, bowing before his throne. When she turned, everyone saw the girl silhouetted in front of the full moon. It was as if the heavens had lit a stage for her. Her robes were but thinnest gauze, and with the moonlight behind her dazzlingly bright, the thin material of her robe was illuminated, outlining her body. Joanna looked away in shame, but she noticed that many men did not.

Chuza's eyes followed Salome with an avarice and hunger that shamed Joanna.

Herod and his men were no better. Salome's young body on display, used as entertainment, this was a shame upon the family that a Jew would call unthinkable. But Herod's true colors always came through, didn't they? And his colors were dark indeed.

The wine flowed from the wineskins, dripping from lips, down the front of robes, down the sides of goblets. Joanna shuddered, thinking how it looked like blood. In the torch-light, flames flickered in everyone's eyes. Joanna saw unre-strained desire on the men's faces.

Why had she ever convinced Salome to dance? What had she done?

Salome finished, and bowed. The crowd erupted into cheers. Herod leaped to his feet, applauding. Joanna laughed, a nervous relief that at last the girl was done. Whatever harm was done, at least it was over. Men had stared and yes, they had lusted, but at least it was done.

Joanna scanned the crowd for a servant, hoping to find something to eat. She was exhausted from the stress of the evening and famished. It was time to try and enjoy the party and be a good wife to Chuza.

Salome made her way through the crowd to stand before Herod and Herodias.

Joanna had certainly made a mistake by urging her to dance to avoid her mother's wrath. But it was just that, a mistake. And it was over. Chuza would be proud of her when he learned of how she intervened to get Salome to dance.

"Well done! What is your reward?" Herod's voice echoed across the courtyard. "Up to half of my kingdom!" His offer was meaningless, but then, he wanted more than anything to impress the Jewish nobles. He used the ancient tradition of kings, offering up to half their kingdom as a reward. No one dared remind Herod Antipas that he was no king, and his kingdom was just one-fourth of what it should have been. *One-half of one-fourth is not such a prize, Herod.*

Salome looked at her mother. Herodias beckoned with her hands, her eyes like chips of flint, glinting and hard. A slow, cruel smile spread across Herodias's face. It was as if she had anticipated exactly this.

Herodias had a plan.

Dread snaked around Joanna's ankles, working its way up, constricting her chest until she stopped breathing.

Salome climbed the short steps to her mother's throne and leaned toward Herodias. Her mother bent and whispered in her daughter's ear.

Salome jerked upright and would have stumbled from the platform had not Herodias's iron grip on her arm stopped her. Salome turned and found Joanna in the crowd.

Joanna tried to read the girl's expression, but it was impossible. The poor girl's eyes were wide and blank, and her mouth hung half open.

Chuza had noted the entire exchange, Joanna realized, his brow furrowed in alarm. Chuza knew Joanna was wrapped up in this.

Herodias glared at Salome until the girl seemed to return to life. Slowly, she turned to Herod.

"I want," she began, then cleared her throat. Herodias sat up straighter, glaring at her daughter as if in warning. "I want the head of John the Baptizer."

The Jewish nobles gasped.

Herodias sat forward in her chair, her eyes flashing in anger. The nobles quieted their voices to a low, hostile murmur. Chuza glared at Joanna.

"On a platter," Salome added. "I want the head of John the Baptizer brought to me on a platter."

Herodias sat back, her eyes sparkling. The torches' flames around her chair flickered and danced.

Herod rested his face in his hands, then lifted his head.

"As she has commanded," he said to the guards. He said nothing to the Jewish guests he had intended to impress. He had just condemned one of their prophets to death, and they would be witnesses. Herodias watched them all with a detached expression, as if she had already played this scene out a hundred times in her mind, and their reaction was nothing less than expected.

Joanna watched the guards turn and leave, moving toward the hallway that would lead to the dungeon. John was here. He had no doubt heard the party overhead, the drums and laughter and dancing. Had he heard the sudden silence when his head was claimed as a reward?

Joanna fled the party before the execution was completed. In the chambers about an hour later, she heard the nobles arguing as they left the party and the laughter of the fortress guards. Masculine voices recounted a hundred little horrors and unsavory details. The smell of iron was in the air. John was dead.

Joanna didn't even dare look out her window for fear the stars would tell more of the story. Instead, she sat on her bed and wept. She wept for the prophet, and for her people. And then, against her will, she wept for Herod and his wife. Despite the anger in her heart, the tears that began for John kept falling for them.

John was their only friend in the world.

John had dared to speak truth to Herod and Herodias. No one else would ever speak the truth to them like that again. Herodias had conspired to kill their only friend, and the last honest man in the court.

The truth would never again be a guest in Herod's palace.

Herodias now stood condemned to live a life alone.

CHAPTER ELEVEN

Every time Joanna heard music, she shivered, thinking of that awful night months ago. Her robes stank of alcohol all the time now too. Joanna slipped off the robe Aresh had set out and held a new one to her nose, but it also held the sharp tang of spilled wine. If she held her robes in a bright light, she often saw stains now where stains had never been. Since John's execution at the Black Fortress, Chuza had needed more and more wine before calling Joanna to his chambers. And Joanna, to her embarrassment, complied every time he called, no matter how many empty flasks littered the hallway outside his door. Chuza, perhaps, was desperate to forget what kind of ruler he had pledged his life to. She was desperate for a child. The threat of Lupercalia hung over Joanna's head. She would rather face Chuza in all his shame than the Roman priests in all of theirs. Thankfully, by the time the court returned from Machaerus after John's execution, it was too late to sail for Rome.

Lupercalia was being celebrated right now in those streets. She shuddered, thankful that the treacherous sea had been her salvation.

Seated at her dressing table now, Joanna had just a few minutes to prepare before attending to Chuza again for the evening. Her hand hovered over the bowl of rosewater. It sat on her dressing table with a jar of rich black kohl eyeliner, purest olive oil for her face, and a petal-tinted balm for her lips. Aresh would have known what to do to make her look fresh and new, but Aresh had been called to serve Salome earlier in the afternoon. Concentrating, Joanna picked up a narrow stylus and dipped it into the jar of kohl. If Aresh could do this, then so could she.

Moments later, she walked unescorted down the torchlit passage to Chuza's chambers.

Chuza did not look up as she entered. The servant at his table stepped aside with a polite nod, acknowledging her. She smiled, grateful to be seen. Even the tiniest act of humanity meant the world right now. She must remember that, she told herself. When people were broken, tiny acts of basic humanity were received as a great kindness.

"Has it been a good winter?" Chuza asked.

She glanced over his shoulder. He was updating the court purchase logs for the month. Two hundred flasks of wine, one hundred barley loaves, five hundred dried fish, plus more scribbles in the columns for fresh and dried produce and milk.

"Good?" Joanna stumbled over the word, and her hand went reflexively to her stomach. She had not yet conceived.

"I have called for you several times now," he added.

"You have," she agreed. She bowed her head, excusing herself, then left. Walking quickly and silently down the hall, she ignored the greetings of the servants as she approached Herodias's chambers. Inside was the sound of music and laughter. A guard held up his hand to stop her.

"I must announce you," he said.

"No," Joanna whispered. "I am not going in."

She peeked into the chamber to see how Herodias was amusing herself this evening.

Aresh was dancing in the center of the room while Herodias laughed and called encouragement. Salome stood next to Aresh, teaching her the steps. If it was improper for Aresh to dance with the daughter of the ruler, no one minded. Perhaps Herodias was grateful to have a companion for Salome.

Dark circles under Salome's eyes marred her beauty. Empty bowls of wine littered the floor, most of them around Salome's feet. Platters with plucked stalks of fresh grape clusters and leaves of fresh dates were stacked around the room. The fruit harvest was coming in, and this year was a good one.

"It is so good to see Salome enjoying herself again," Joanna whispered to the guard, hoping she did not sound as insincere as she felt. "It seems the unfortunate incident at Herod's party has not dimmed her spirits."

"We all knew what to expect." The guard shrugged. "He held the party at Machaerus, after all."

She cocked her head, confused. Taking his eyes away from the room of women, the guard explained Herod's strategy. "The Black Fortress is a desolate place. No one will ever know what Herod did out there."

No one will ever know. Sorrow filled her heart for all that had been lost under the seal of Herod.

The following evening

The bathhouse's white stone walls had been freshly plastered. The plaster was blindingly white. The columns in the bath had been freshly painted a deep blood red to match the square mosaic on the floor. None of the colors blended together—everywhere were sharp lines and edges, with no blurring or softening.

Aresh hummed softly, setting out jars of fragrant oils before Joanna's bath. She had carried a tray to the bathhouse loaded down with these jars, plus combs, kohl eyeliner, rouge, and jewelry. Joanna had looked forward to her bath all afternoon. She looked at the tray and noted that several sets of earrings were there. She sat waiting on a stone bench.

"I thought you might like to wear your jewelry after the bath," Aresh said. Aresh seemed happy, a lightness in her step that was unexplained. The girl's eyes lingered too long on the jewelry.

"You can pick out a pair. Something you think Chuza would like," Joanna replied, a creeping thought making her skin crawl.

Aresh's hand hovered over one set, just for a moment, and their eyes locked. Aresh's smile was an innocent flutter, but Joanna noted a tremor in her hand. Aresh passed over the earrings her hand hovered above in favor of another set.

Aresh set the earrings alongside the fresh tunic she had laid out and busied herself with final preparations. Had Joanna imagined the tension of that moment? Was she being unfair?

She rose and walked to a wall to test the work. She dragged a fingernail across the plaster. The plaster chipped immediately, revealing the plain stone wall beneath.

Such deception, she thought suddenly, looking around as if seeing this palace for the first time. It was all a lie. Everything here was a lie.

"The water is ready," Aresh said, motioning for Joanna to enter the bath.

She walked behind Aresh to the bath and stood between the mosaic columns that lined the pool's entry.

Joanna stepped into the water that was heated by pipes beneath the floor. The pipes held air heated by a furnace in another room. The water felt so good to her tired limbs. Her ceaseless thoughts had driven sleep from her chambers for weeks now. She needed this respite.

With every step, she felt the muscles in her body loosening. She sank lower into the bath and closed her eyes, wishing herself to be anywhere but in the palace.

After a long while, she opened her eyes. Her fingertips had wrinkled, and beads of sweat ran down her forehead. Her shoulders felt loose and heavy. She honestly didn't know if she had the strength to stand up.

Aresh sat on a stone bench in the corner, dozing. Joanna watched her, with her pretty chin tucked down to her chest.

Aresh sat up, rubbing her eyes. "Are you ready to get out?" She stood and grabbed a towel. "I have your favorite bath oil. I know Chuza likes the fragrance too."

Hearing her husband's name in Aresh's mouth brought back all her fears and suspicions. *I'm wrong, though,* she told herself. *I am imagining things.*

"How do you know which fragrance Chuza prefers?" she asked lightly, standing.

Aresh rushed forward with the towel, looking away out of decorum. "I told you, I pay attention to everyone. Oh! I asked the cook to make your favorite honey cake for dessert tonight at dinner."

Steam rose from the bath, swirling and dissipating between the women as they faced each other. Something was not right. Joanna felt that same catch in her throat as when a clay pitcher rested too close to the edge of a table or when a goblet tipped and wine brimmed to the edge.

She reached out and rested a hand on Aresh's arm. "Aresh, do you want to tell me something?"

Aresh recoiled as if Joanna had burned her. "I have done nothing wrong."

"Then why are you so upset?" Joanna heard the uptick in her own voice, the shrill note at the end. They were both upset. She felt as if she was teetering on the brink of a steep hill, about to fall headlong into darkness.

"Everyone knows you cannot conceive," Aresh said, tears in her eyes. "Herodias swore to me that it is a common practice to give a servant to the husband. She says it would solve your problems."

"What?"

"And Chuza is miserable. Look at him, Joanna! He rarely calls you to his chambers anymore. When he does, you upset him. I am just a servant, but at least that gives me one advantage. I know how to make other people happy. You were born into wealth, so you expect Chuza to make you happy. That is why you are going to lose him."

"What have you done?" Joanna's blood ran cold.

"Nothing. Except listen to authority greater than yours." Aresh tossed her hair, wrapping her arms around herself. "Remember your kindness to me in the garden? I have not forgotten that. I could help you have a child for him. Everyone wants that. It is the simplest solution."

Joanna stood speechless.

"You made Chuza seem like a cold man," Aresh said softly. "But he's been very kind to me, Joanna. I don't think you know him at all."

Joanna sucked in air, feeling the words like a punch to the stomach. Her pride rose like a roaring lion. "Do you seek to supplant me? Do you really think a servant could take my place as a wife?"

Aresh's mouth fell open. "I am trying to protect you. And now I wonder why I bothered."

Joanna dressed herself now, not waiting for help.

"If you are angry with me," Aresh said, "you are angry with the wrong person."

"I am angry at Chuza, at Herodias, and at myself. And yes, Aresh—I am angry at you."

The honey cake stuck in her throat. Sitting beside Chuza at dinner, she tried to recapture the charm she once had. What had drawn him to her long ago? She tried to remember, but too many disappointments now obscured the love they once shared. Aresh had attempted all evening to catch her eye and smile with soft eyes. The little gnat of a girl was probably determined to annoy Joanna with her youth and beauty. She probably did want to help Joanna, which made Joanna feel all the worse.

All evening, the girdle around her waist had seemed to grow tighter, and not because she was eating. No, she had been unable to eat more than a few bites.

Something was in the palace air. Worse, everyone seemed to know what it was except for her. She passed Chuza a plate of fresh apple slices drizzled with honey and allspice. He accepted it without looking at her.

"So," he said quietly, "tell me. Will I have a child?"

She dropped the goblet of wine she held, shocked by his direct, abrupt question. This was his first comment to her all evening.

Servants rushed forward to clean the mess, and her cheeks burned as Herodias and Aresh watched her. Once again, she had embarrassed herself in front of the palace court. In her mind, she had been planning to ride back to the palace in triumph all those months ago. She had procured a miracle from Jesus, and once she returned here, all would be well. How was it possible, then, that once she returned here, all was worse than ever?

Was this how miracles worked? She wanted to run back to Jesus and ask about that. A seed of anger was planted in her heart. Nothing about this had unfolded according to her expectation.

"I just need a little more time," she murmured softly, trying to remember what she had sounded like in the days when she had been young and innocent. She probably sounded like a fool now, she thought.

Herodias clanked a spoon against her goblet. Everyone turned their attention to the ruler.

"Joanna has interesting news for the court," Herodias said. Salome sat next to Herodias and clapped her hands with a detached expression. The poor girl's eyes were lifeless.

"You have seen Jesus," Herodias said, sweeping an arm out as if to prepare for a great story. "You have talked to Him face to face. You have even—so I have been told—asked Him for a miracle."

Whispers rose from the court. Everyone looked at Joanna, their eyes raking her face and body, trying to guess if she was pregnant. Everyone knew she was barren. Joanna wanted to be swallowed up and disappear, the shame of being scrutinized for weakness and flaw being overpowering. She reached for Chuza's hand, but it was not there.

She stood on weak knees and took a deep breath. No one spoke. No one moved, not even to lift a spoon or goblet to their mouth. Everyone was rapt with attention at the mention of the name Jesus.

"Who is this Jesus?" Joanna began, clearing her throat quietly. "Some say He is from Bethlehem. Some say He is from Nazareth." She ignored the snickers and continued. "Some say He is the Messiah, the long-awaited Savior of the Jews. I cannot say any of those things. I can only say that He is…"

The court was held captive as she searched for the next words.

"I can only say that He is my friend. I brought Him my troubles. He listened." A smile crept across her face. "I tried to offer Him money." She glanced at Herodias and Herod, to be sure they understood her point. "He does not want money. He is not interested in wealth or power."

"What does He want?" Herod asked, leaning forward. "Most of the Jewish teachers dislike him. He cannot hope to become a rabbi of much influence."

"He has not spoken of any plan," Joanna said. "He just loves people."

Herodias threw her spoon on the table, her face wrinkled in disgust.

"He wants to heal us," Joanna quickly added.

"So, did He heal you?" Herodias snapped. Her eyes were the eyes of a viper, cold slits that watched its prey. Her eyes rested on Joanna's neck, with its missing necklace. "Do you trust this Jesus to give you a child? I offered you all the resources of this court. Have you made your choice, then? Whom do you trust with your fate?"

Herod turned to look at his wife, scowling. Herodias had overstepped her authority, threatening the wife of his steward in public like this. Joanna felt her face burning in humiliation. Her barrenness had been turned into political sport. Herodias used her barrenness to force a choice between Rome and her Jewish roots.

Chuza leaned toward Herod. The two men conferred as Chuza motioned to a servant to pour more wine. Joanna knew he would be drunk tonight.

"What is your choice?" Herodias prompted.

Everyone, even musicians with their lyres and harps, sat breathless and still, awaiting her reply. Her troubles did not matter to them. But Jesus's power did. If He was real, if He could heal, then there was hope for them too.

Herodias leaned forward, eyes blazing.

"I have made my choice," Joanna said, her voice threatening to crack. She forced herself to stand taller. "Because I have no choice. Because no healer, no charm or spell here or in Rome can help me. Jesus was—is—my only hope."

Herodias's mouth opened in outrage. Herod put a hand on her arm and cocked his head, listening. He had always been fascinated by the teachings of John. He clearly wanted to hear more about John's cousin. Herodias had silenced John forever. Joanna had to choose her next words with great care.

"I am loyal to this court and faithful to my husband," Joanna said, raising her palms in supplication. "I obey Roman law."

Herodias took a sip of wine and then motioned for a server to refill her goblet. Chuza watched Joanna, rubbing his chin with one hand, making Joanna remember him as he once was. In the days of their early marriage, when he was thoughtful and kind toward her.

A noticeable change began in the room, as servers shifted their weight from side to side, and noblemen cast quick glances at Herod and Herodias to see how they would react. "I have listened to the healers and had the attention of many wonderful physicians. I have done everything that medicine and logic would require."

Herodias grabbed a knife from the table, careful to catch Joanna's eye. Slowly, deliberately, she sawed through the bread on her plate. Crumbs fell from the jagged edges and tumbled to the floor.

"Only Jesus deals in miracles," Joanna went on. "So, yes. I asked Him to do what no one else could do. I asked for the impossible." She raised her chin and met the gaze of everyone who stared at her. Everyone here had secret heartaches. Everyone here needed miracles.

Herodias leaned toward Herod, whispering in his ear.

"This dinner has concluded," Herod said, standing. Everyone had to immediately stand and leave their food and drink. Herodias and Herod swept through the crowd back to the royal hall. Neither looked at Joanna.

"You've misunderstood her intentions," Aresh whispered crossly, appearing at her side. "She thought you brought good news of this man."

"I did!" Joanna replied, stung by her rebuke, unwilling to make peace with her.

"A miracle worker would be more powerful than Herod. Do you not see?" Aresh snapped. "You are so focused on what you do not have that you ruin the good you have left! Let me help you, Joanna!"

Chuza rested his hand on Aresh's arm to quiet her. Joanna was startled. He had moved so quickly to the young woman's side. The gesture was one of improper familiarity.

Chuza quickly dropped his arm, and Aresh's face turned bright pink. Aresh looked at the floor, but whether it was out of shame or embarrassment that they were caught, Joanna could not tell.

"I cannot call you to my chambers this evening," Chuza said abruptly to Joanna. "The mess you made at dinner means that Herod will have no peace tonight. He will want to review his books."

Herod needed an official excuse to avoid the company of Herodias. And it meant of course that Chuza would have to work alongside the ruler, reviewing all the accounts.

Chuza departed before Joanna could reply. Her attention turned to Aresh. Aresh had seemed like an innocent victim when she had first met her in the palace garden. Joanna wasn't sure whether Aresh was still so innocent. This palace turned people into strange shadows of who they once had been.

"My heart was laid bare before the whole court tonight," Joanna said. "What about you?" She stared at Aresh. "What is really in your heart? What is the future you envision for yourself? You cannot want to have a child for another man's wife. Surely you want to be a wife, Aresh. Surely you would want to have a family of your own."

"You do not understand how different we are. You speak of baring your heart?" Aresh looked up, a sorrowful expression on her face. "That is one more luxury a servant like me cannot afford. We spend our entire lives getting our masters what they want. We cannot afford dreams and desires for ourselves."

Aresh was too young to be bitter, but the strident note in her voice said otherwise. Joanna knew she had dreams.

"Aresh, please forgive me." Joanna softened her tone. "You must be lonely, and I did not see it. If you want a husband, I will find one for you. You do not have to follow orders from Herodias. This is her court, but I can always send you away."

Aresh stiffened. "You want to get rid of me? This is the only home I have! You worry Chuza prefers me, don't you?"

"No! I am trying to make you happy," Joanna replied. "I am trying to be a friend." Joanna had never had a friend in the palace. The statement sounded hollow but only because it was new.

"You and me? Friends?" The disbelief in Aresh's voice said it all. Aresh turned and left.

Joanna started to follow, but then stopped. Every time she reached out to Aresh to untangle the knot that was their relationship, a new twist appeared. *Perhaps it is better not to try.*

Early spring, 31 CE
The palace of Tiberius

The rain was a dark, gloomy presence outside Joanna's chamber window. Thunder growled in the distance. The latter rains had arrived, bringing long gray afternoons. Her only companions were boredom and unrest. Chuza had called for her twice. On one occasion, he had already passed out from drink when she arrived.

Joanna sat at her dressing table, frustrated. Removing the polished ebony hair pin, she let her dry curls fall back down again. Aresh now served Salome. *No doubt it made infidelity so much easier.* But without Aresh, Joanna struggled to style her hair in a pleasant way or get the lines of kohl straight on her eyes. She hated feeling embarrassed every time she saw Chuza with Aresh, knowing that she did not look her best. How unfair that Aresh took that from her too.

"Do you need help with that?"

Joanna whirled around. Aresh stood in her doorway. Joanna stiffened in her chair, unable to decide what to say. Too many words rushed to the tip of her tongue at once.

Aresh walked across the bedchamber and picked up a comb from the table in front of Joanna. Standing behind her, Aresh began to gently comb out Joanna's hair. She hit a snag and stopped, checking in the bronze mirror to see if she had caused Joanna any pain.

Joanna refused to show any reaction.

Aresh sighed and resumed her work. She applied oil to Joanna's tresses next, working it through them carefully, thoroughly, then combing each section with long, delicate strokes. Joanna's hair was now smooth and shining.

Aresh worked the satin strands into a braid and then wound the braid into a crown at the back of Joanna's head and secured it with the ebony pin Joanna had given up on.

"Thank you," Joanna said, her throat constricting on the words. "You did not have to do that."

"You needed my help. And I don't think it's fair that you don't have a maidservant anymore."

Joanna turned and looked up at her. "Why did you come to see me?" Knowing Aresh, she was in trouble.

Aresh would not meet her gaze. "I need your perfume."

"Excuse me?"

"Chuza said there's a perfume you wear that he loves and that I should come here and take it. We are leaving for Jerusalem."

"Jerusalem?" Joanna sat up, intrigued. She had assumed Herod would avoid Jerusalem after he'd murdered John.

"Passover." Aresh sighed, as if the thought bored her.

"Why has no one come to prepare me for travel?" Joanna asked.

"I thought you knew," Aresh replied, taking a step back. "You are not going."

Joanna knew a strong woman would fight. But what was she fighting for? A man who didn't want her. There could be no victory in that battle.

Aresh stood, chewing her lower lip, sneaking nervous glances at Joanna. Something Jesus said echoed in Joanna's mind. "You must love even your enemies." Mary had recited those words to her too, urged her to keep them locked in her heart. Now the words floated to the surface at just this moment.

Joanna reached across the dressing table to an alabaster jar, her arm tingling with a strange pain. She handed it to Aresh.

"Thank you again for helping me today."

Aresh walked out of the chamber, carrying the jar of perfume Chuza had bought Joanna to celebrate their wedding.

Joanna rested her arm in her lap, the pain of sacrifice still stinging.

She watched the younger woman walk out the door bearing away Joanna's broken dreams and lost hopes.

CHAPTER TWELVE

Early in the morning, Joanna awakened to the strange quiet. The court had left for Jerusalem to attend the celebration of Passover. Even if Chuza had arranged this, it had probably been Herodias's idea.

Finches flitted past her window to the gardens below. Wrapping a delicate fringed shawl around her shoulders, she walked to the window to listen to their trills and calls.

Below the palace, on the side of the hill, workers moved between the rows of grapevines. Smoke rose from the vineyard with the comforting scent of wood fire. Searching, she saw a small fire in a stone pit at the edge of the vineyard.

Resting her head against the window, she let a tear slip down her cheek.

"How could God let this happen?" she asked the finches, who sang back to her. "How can a woman stand before Jesus and witness His power, and yet nothing in her life changes?" Doing the right thing hurt, and there was no end in sight.

A beam of sun hit her face, and she closed her eyes, leaning into its warmth. The day would be cool, so the warmth was welcome. She had hoped to be with child by this season and to enjoy the relief from the sun of summer past. She had thought a new season was coming in every sense. But she had been wrong. Now she felt the absence of warmth everywhere she went.

She decided to walk down to the vineyard and watch the vineyard dressers at their work. After a short walk, she was among them. They sang as they tended the vines, and she found a flat spot under a tree to watch. A little boy brought her a dried fish wrapped in a leaf from his breakfast. She thanked him and carefully peeled away the fragile leaf, trying not to lose any fish in the process. He giggled as he watched her. She had servants who usually did this for her, though, so she could not help being clumsy.

At the edge of the vineyard, a haggard old woman walking behind an ox plowed under a section of dead field peas. Peas and even hyssop were often planted at the edges of vineyards. A mixture of crops yielded a better harvest, someone had told her.

Dead stalks and dried pods fell and were crushed under the ox's heavy hooves. The sharp blade of the plow cut into the earth in a long, deep gash as the ox pushed on, ripping up the roots of the field peas.

Joanna shifted on the ground, feeling her sadness like a weight in her empty womb.

A man walked past with a curved pruning hook. He was not much older than she was and whistled a happy song as he walked past. She leaped to her feet, wanting a distraction.

"Can I watch?" she asked.

"Of course," he answered with a grin. "Never had an audience from the palace before." His skin was taut and red, especially over his nose and brow. His cheeks looked tough and leathery. He had lived in the sun; his face was a testament to its harsh treatment.

The field hand walked to a vine and ran his hands along the thick brown center of the vine, inspecting the shoots that ran off from it. Every so often, he'd peer closely at one. Finally, he stood aright and placed his pruning hook at the base of a shoot. The knife's edge glinted in the sun. *It all seems so harsh.*

He must have sensed her anxiety, because he hesitated.

"Look around," he said, gesturing to the vineyard. "The green leaves are gone. We are careful to prune only at a specific time. Right now, we can clearly see the outline of the vine. We want to see the whole vine, as it is and as it could be, before we even begin."

She bit her lip before replying. "I do not understand how hurting a vine helps it."

His face grew serious. "I would never hurt it." He pointed with the tip of his knife. "Can you see the spurs and canes growing off the main vine?"

She leaned closer then nodded.

"The vine will feed every cane. But not every cane will produce fruit. My job is to know which cane will produce fruit and which will use up resources but never produce fruit. Those dormant canes lessen the quality of the whole harvest. No one wants that."

He studied two canes that were side by side. "Do you see this one?" he asked, pointing. "This one can stay. It will produce fruit next year. But this one?" He placed his knife at the base of the other. With a flick of a wrist, he removed it.

The little boy who had shared his fish ran forward, collected the dead cane, and ran toward a stone pit. Workers took the cane from the boy and tossed it into the fire burning inside the pit. A boy scooped ashes from the outside pile and carried them to another garden, spreading them at the base of the plants.

"It's a process I use even with flowers." The field hand continued speaking as he worked. "Every plant needs pruning."

He rested the knife at the base of the good cane, the one he had just said would remain. He slid the knife up a bit, then cleanly sliced through the good shoot.

"Why did you cut that one?" she asked, aware that her throat was tightening in sorrow. She felt like she'd been pruned these last few months, but no blessing had come forth. Every little injury had cut deep, the blade as sharp as this man's pruning hook. Yet where was the reward?

"I promise, it will produce even more fruit." He smiled. "I didn't cut it entirely off. Just cut if off near the buds."

She turned back for the palace. All she could think about was that she had sought out Jesus and asked Him for a miracle. She had seen nothing but trouble since then. It wasn't fair. People came to Him for miracles, and He instantly solved their worst problems. Why did she still feel a dozen tiny nicks and stings every day?

"Come back when the harvest comes in!" the field hand yelled after her. "You'll see! This cane will be heavy with fruit!"

As she walked back up the path, Joanna paused to watch a finch fly past and alight on a branch, singing. A new thought came to her in its music, a thought that was not of her own mind. It was just a whisper that the wind carried: without pruning, the gardens she loved would be a wilderness, not a refuge.

Once, she told herself that to walk in a garden was to know peace. Maybe she could endure the pain of the palace a little longer. There could still be good fruit from this barren season.

Early summer, 31 CE
The palace of Tiberius

A month had passed since the court had returned from Jerusalem. Already the moon had completed half of its monthly dance of veils, and yet only once before tonight had Chuza called for her to come to his chambers. Aresh must be utterly enchanting, she thought gloomily.

Would Chuza demand to know again if she was with child? He had been gone over a month, plus the time since he returned. He would insist there had been time for the signs to make themselves known. Her hand went to her abdomen. No signs of life were there. She still had hope…a tiny sliver of hope. Jesus's miracle could still come to pass. She had told others about Him, she had done her best to trust and to be a good wife…surely the miracle would happen soon.

Her steps quickened on the way to Chuza's chambers, the echo of her sandals against the stone floors rapid and faint like a bird's heart when it was caught in thorn branches. The torches gave the white walls an orange glow.

A guard announced her arrival, and as he swung the door open to Chuza's chamber, she raised one hand to shield her eyes from the glitter of gold. At a glimpse of his face, though, she wanted to rush forward and hug him.

Coins were piled upon his bed, so deep his straw mattress sank in the middle. Chuza sat at his desk, empty wineskins at his feet, another upright on the desk beside him. Surely he had not drunk all that wine by himself. That would not be like the man she knew. Or the man she once knew. He had always been a good and careful steward.

He stood and turned as she entered. "You look well," he said.

She kept her arms pinned at her side, like broken wings.

"You are celebrating?" she ventured, careful to keep her tone neutral.

He stepped toward the bed, and she noted how his gait faltered ever so slightly. He had drunk the wine alone. Constans's words came back to her suddenly—*"Watch how someone behaves when they don't get what they want."* Chuza hadn't gotten the son he wanted, and he was disintegrating into drink and infidelity.

"Not exactly," he said, sitting down on the bed. He patted the bed covering. Hesitantly, she walked over and sat beside him. She was overwhelmed with longing for him, and for the man she had once known. His eyes were the same, although now they were lined with worry and shadows. She reached out and rested her hand on top of his. He drew a deep, shuddering breath, closing his eyes.

In the night, outside beyond his window, crickets sang one note over and over, and the wind gently rustled the leaves of the olive trees.

"Why are you unhappy?" she asked.

Opening his eyes, he leaned over and kissed her softly on the lips, then withdrew. A tear ran down his face as he traced the curve of her cheek with one finger. "Forgive me. I have been a poor husband to you."

She tried to be patient with him. He had been drinking, perhaps for hours. But she wanted to tell him everything, to yell at him for everything else she couldn't say, and then storm from this chamber and never speak to him again. And yet… after all he had put her through, all he had demanded, he was still her husband. She was bound by her vow and oath.

How could one person make her feel all possible human emotions in one breath?

Chuza shook his head and blinked several times. He gestured to the gold on the bed with them. "This gold? A gift from a synagogue official in Capernaum. A man of great learning and influence."

Joanna leaned back to study the gold. It was truly an extraordinary amount. She picked up a coin. The coin bore no image of Herod. Herod Antipas refused to have his coins imprinted with his image as a way of appeasing the Jews, who did not like this form of idolatry. How could Herod follow the Jewish law and miss its heart?

"What does he want?" she asked.

Chuza leaned forward again and kissed her forehead. She was dizzy from the attention and affection.

"Healing," he replied. "His daughter is sick. No one has been able to cure her. But I can send for the greatest physician in Rome, if the mood strikes me."

"And for this amount of gold," Joanna replied, "I am guessing that the mood struck you, indeed."

"A messenger has already been dispatched. The weather is excellent for sailing."

Joanna flinched without meaning to. Furrowing his brow, Chuza looked at her, puzzled. "It is all right. I have arranged for a fast ship. The physician will be here in a month's time."

Joanna exhaled, grateful Chuza was too inebriated to understand her fright. She wanted him to forget Rome, forget sailing, and most of all, forget the idea of ever sending her to Lupercalia. She would be in danger of that again until the seasons changed this year, until the first cool winds of winter began to blow.

Chuza walked to the desk to pour himself another cup of wine.

"Will the daughter live that long?" she asked.

"She has lived thus far." Downing the wine, then running the back of his hand along his mouth, Chuza pointed at her with his cup. "There is a lot of money in healing. That is what I wanted you to see." He chuckled, as if sharing a joke with her. "I do not know why I bothered. I know you are not impressed with money. Unlike—" He caught himself and cleared his throat.

Joanna looked at the gold. Judging by the amount—enough to bury her hands in—the father was desperate. Whatever the daughter had, she was suffering.

Chuza's expression softened. "I did not mean to pit you against Herodias and Herod. I only sent you out to seek Jesus for selfish reasons. I wanted to gain a son or gain an edge to keep advancing my own name here in the court. And it seems now I've gained neither. You angered Herodias, and I can see that you are still barren."

She closed her eyes, not wanting to see that word on his lips.

"You might still have a son," she said, careful to keep her voice soft. "I asked Jesus to open my womb."

Chuza's expression became still, his eyes focused. "You believe He can really work miracles?"

"I do. I've seen them. Unimaginable miracles."

"Good. Why do we have to assume this Jesus is an enemy of the court? If He can work miracles, He could be our greatest ally." Chuza poured himself another cup of wine and downed it in a blink. His hand shook as he tried to set the wineskin back on the desk. It missed the edge and fell to the floor. Not that it mattered; it was empty by now. "Jesus could make Herod the king. I want Herod to see that."

Joanna stood, arms extended. Chuza walked to her and embraced her, nuzzled her neck, whispering her name.

"You could bring Jesus to us, Joanna."

"I have a question," she whispered.

"Mmmm?"

"The daughter who is ill, what is her father's name?"

"Jairus. His name is Jairus."

Joanna took a step back, careful to lead him gently so he would not trip over his robe or hers. He kept repeating her name and murmuring his apologies for his harsh treatment. Chuza was in her arms again.

What if this was her miracle: A chance to start over with Chuza? A chance to be a wife again, and if it pleased God, a mother? Tomorrow she could wake up in his chambers and, after that, deal with Aresh once and for all. This Jairus, with all his gold, had given her the chance she needed to take back what was rightfully hers.

And yet somewhere in the night a woman was holding her suffering daughter, praying for a miracle of her own. A miracle that would never come from Rome.

"You really want me to go and find Jesus?" Joanna whispered.

Chuza nodded, his head flopping up and down. "Leave tomorrow. Take the guard Constans. I trust him. Take a purse full of gold! As much as you please!"

She led Chuza to the bed and helped him lower himself safely down amid all the gold coins. He grabbed her hand. "Stay with me tonight." She leaned down and kissed him on the forehead.

His eyes closed, and he snored as she stood up, wrapping her shawl around her shoulders. She had to find that mother. She had to tell her of Jesus. Jesus was in the area—He never traveled too far from Galilee. He could be at the daughter's side before Chuza's messenger made it to Rome.

If that daughter had any hope of living, it was Jesus.

Pausing at the doorway, Joanna looked back at Chuza asleep on his bed, gold coins around him glinting in the torchlight. She had made her choice. But then, so had he.

Summer, 31 CE
Traveling through Galilee

By now, it wasn't hard to find Jesus. Joanna knew to follow the crowds. On the roads, families streamed in one direction. These people carried the ill and infirm on their backs or the backs of animals. Coming the other way were those returning with outrageous stories, faces radiant, words coming so fast that the people were nearly incoherent with praise and thanksgiving. Jesus healed a leper. Jesus gave a blind man sight. Yes, a man born blind, now he saw! And the lame walked. Jesus stretched out His hand and the lame got up and walked! And even more unbelievably, one man claimed that Jesus had raised a boy from the dead. All because Jesus had compassion on the boy's mother, who was a widow. Jesus had called the boy back from the shadowlands, and his spirit had returned to his body. He had been dead, then he sat up and talked as men carried him to his grave.

Smiling politely as a mother passed on her left carrying a sleeping infant with bloom-fresh cheeks, Joanna seethed inwardly. Really, if Jesus was doing that for strangers, what had gone wrong for her? She could have been useful to Him. Chuza would have been a powerful ally in the court. She hadn't asked for power or wealth, she had only asked to honor her husband. What was wrong with that? Why did Jesus grant miracles to other women, yet deny her the one small, honorable thing she requested?

Why did He speak in parables and go away to pray when the crowds grew too large? Leaders wanted more followers, not fewer.

Heat made the horizon shimmer.

"I do not like riding a donkey," Constans remarked yet again.

"And I do not want to draw attention," Joanna replied.

Constans kept pace with her, though, shielding her when frustrated traders pushed through groups of slow travelers.

Joanna ignored Constans as best she could, preferring to think about her own, very real problem. The only plain fact was that Jesus had denied her the one thing she wanted more than anything in the world. How many other women had He disappointed? Life wasn't fair, but was Jesus? That mystery was driving her mad.

Hours later, they found Him.

Or, she heard Him. The crowd was pressed so thickly around Him that she couldn't see over their heads or around their bodies. She'd never seen so many poor people! Robes torn, mended and patched, and some of the patches had patches. Their faces were lined from hard years of labor in the sun, and dirt from the roads had settled into the lines. They didn't bathe daily like she did, if they bathed at all. She lifted her robe to her face, not for disguise but for disgust. The smell was overpowering. Some had sores that had not healed, and they were all pressed against each other, pushing and shoving, trying to get His attention for a healing.

Women's voices rose shrill and urgent. Children screeched for attention, their little bodies darting like fish between adults.

Constans held out a hand to stop her from riding farther. Her donkey was pushed roughly aside by a man trying to get his son to Jesus. The animal swung its head, trying to bite the man. Joanna grabbed its neck for balance but didn't scold it. She couldn't blame the poor thing.

"Are you all right?" A woman's voice at her right side made her turn.

"Mary!"

Mary Magdalene had found her and was standing beside her, watching the crowd too.

"He may need to get into a boat and teach from the water," Mary said. "Sometimes it's the only way to keep Him safe and the crowd under control."

"How long have you been—" Constans barely concealed the shock in his voice.

Mary laughed, her head leaning in close to Joanna's, as if they were sisters, sharing a story late at night. "Yes, you can say it, Constans. I've been traveling with Him and the disciples. The old ways are changing."

"What do you do?"

She stepped to one side, making room for a woman leading an elderly man through the crowd, the man's eyes clouded with cataracts.

"I speak to women," Mary said, raising her voice to be heard. "It's helpful for Him. Many desperate people come to Him, every day. But some forms of desperation keep people stuck where they are."

Joanna nodded, understanding exactly what Mary meant. She scanned the edge of the crowd, looking for a place to talk. Dismounting, she grabbed the reins and then began to weave through the crowd. Mary and Constans followed her.

"Since it is easier for a woman to speak to another woman," Mary said, "and our laws make everything complicated, I look for the women who are in pain. I go to them. I tell them about Jesus. When they're ready, they come to hear Him teach."

So much emotion rose from her heart all at once that Joanna swallowed as if she could keep it back.

"There was no miracle for me, Mary," Joanna confessed, and tears spilled from her face. Constans looked at the horizon and then turned away.

Mary grabbed her by the arm, leading her to the edge of the crowd. There, Mary took her into her arms, and Joanna wept.

"I needed to conceive," Joanna confessed. "I wanted to conceive. Somehow it all went terribly wrong. I have lost my husband's affections. I have lost my standing in the court. All I have left is hope, and for reasons I do not understand, that hope is in Jesus. He is all I have left."

Mary pulled away and looked Joanna in the eyes. "If all you have left is hope, and that hope is Jesus, then I promise you this: you already have everything you need."

Constans sat on his donkey not far off, looking unnaturally solemn. Mary crooked a finger toward him. "You! Come and assist us. We want to hear Jesus."

Constans dismounted and walked his animal over. He helped them navigate the crowds until they found a smooth, low rock to sit on. Wind blowing in from the Sea of Galilee cooled the afternoon sun as palm trees overhead gently rustled and swished. The murmurs of the crowd were a steady pulse, and Joanna felt swept into a swelling crowd of people, all of them eager for hope and healing. Birds soared overhead in the brilliant blue sky, circling in wide, lazy patterns on the currents. Joanna began to feel better almost at once. Glancing at Constans, she noted that his dark glare had softened slightly. Everyone was here for Jesus, and the air was expectant.

After making His way through the crowd, He stood at the top of a slope so more could see Him. Somehow, His eyes sought out Joanna's in the crowd. He knew she was there.

"What is the kingdom of God like, and to what shall I compare it? The kingdom of heaven is like a mustard seed, which a man took and sowed in his garden."

Joanna noted the confused smirks of the rough-looking people, those who lived from the land. Surely a mustard seed was more deserving of respect than what they displayed!

"When it is sown upon the soil," Jesus continued, "it is smaller than all the other seeds."

The people nodded in agreement. *Does everyone know what a mustard seed looks like?* Joanna had never seen one, and certainly never planted one.

"But when it is full grown?" Jesus asked. "It is larger than all the garden plants, and forms large branches, and becomes a tree, so that the birds of the air can come and nest in its branches."

Joanna did not understand, so she watched the people around her. Most seemed pensive or talked quietly one to another. Why did Jesus compare a mighty kingdom to a seed, which has to be buried in the earth?

"Mary," she whispered.

"Do not ask me," Mary whispered back. "Ask Him. He will explain if you wait. Stay with us tonight."

"I cannot. I must find a man named Jairus. His daughter is ill. Chuza is sending for a physician from Rome, but I want Jairus to bring the girl to Jesus."

"How can I help?"

"Do you know where Jesus is going?"

Mary's face lost its color. "Yes, but do not look for us there. He goes to Decapolis tomorrow."

Joanna arched an eyebrow. "What is in Decapolis?"

Mary grabbed her hand, squeezing it as if frightened. "Not what. Who."

CHAPTER THIRTEEN

Jesus finished teaching and got in a boat to cross the Sea of Galilee. It was a calm, peaceful night, but Joanna felt fear nipping at the edges of the evening. Mary's dread of Decapolis unsettled her.

As the crowd began to disperse, Joanna found Constans. "I am staying with Mary to follow Jesus. I think she needs me somehow. You ride ahead to find Jairus and tell him not to wait for the physician from Rome. Tell him to find Jesus."

"No." Constans folded his arms.

"You must go," Joanna urged. "Besides, you can take a horse now. You will make fast time."

"You are my charge," he replied, his tone resolute. "I will not leave you."

Joanna narrowed her eyes and moved so that her toes were touching his as she stood facing him.

"You would let a little girl die?"

He hesitated with a quick glance down. "The daughter is very ill?"

His posture softened, and Joanna knew she had won. She breathed a sigh of relief, knowing that the girl had a chance now. But what of Decapolis? What waited for them?

A grouping of cities east of the Sea of Galilee, the region was notable for the blend of religion. Zeus, the Greek god, was the main god that people honored, followed by the Phoenician gods and Arabian gods, and an assortment of demons that were said to hold sway over illness and bad fortune.

Demons. *Oh, Mary.*

Mary trembled as the women arrived in Decapolis in the eerie half light of dawn, when dreams seemed too real and the imagination played tricks. A group of pigs lounged near an outcropping of rocks, resting in the early hour. Fat from eating the waste of sacrifices, no doubt. With gods and demons, there was always waste. Their herdsmen regarded the women with suspicion. If only she had not sent Constans away! Had he reached Jairus by now? Would the ruler consent to ask Jesus for help, or risk waiting for Rome?

A jackal cried as the sun rose in the distance like a yolk slowly spreading against the empty sky.

Together the women huddled without speaking at the edge of the Sea of Galilee, waiting for Jesus and the men. When the boat thumped against the shore, the men poured over the sides, talking rapidly of a strange and powerful storm that had swept over the sea without warning. Jesus stepped onto the shore. As the disciples spoke, a fog crept up from the cemetery behind them, snaking underfoot, muffling their words, chilling the air. Mary wrapped her arms around herself, and Joanna placed a hand on her arm in comfort.

Joanna wondered where the crowds had gone. No one had wanted to follow Jesus here, not even Mary.

Another jackal answered the first, a piercing cry that brought goose bumps along Joanna's arms. Chuffing sounds alarmed her. Whipping her head side to side, she caught a thick low shape slinking between the pillars in a crypt.

"What is that?" she whispered. The skin on Mary's arm was ice.

"Bear," Mary said. "Or lion. I do not know."

Two men emerged screaming from behind a broken tombstone, chains trailing from their arms and legs. Cuts, bruises, and black-crusted sores covered their bodies like thatched roofs. Their eyes burned with an inhuman glow. The disciples yelled in panic, some rushing back to the boat.

"The demoniacs of the Gadarenes," Mary said. "Captives, like I once was." There was no life in her voice. "No one can cross through this region because of them. They are far too dangerous."

Mary and Joanna fell back, following the disciples. Only Jesus continued walking forward, His stride undisturbed.

"Come out of the men." Jesus's voice rang clear in the chaos.

The first man burst into a run toward Jesus, causing Joanna to cry out in fear. She noticed Peter reach for the dagger at his side.

The man fell at Jesus's feet with an unearthly wail, sending birds to flight from nearby rocks.

"What business do we have with each other, Jesus, Son of the Most High God?"

Joanna struggled for breath, unable to believe what she was seeing.

"Have you come here to torment us before the time?" the voice screamed. "I beg You by God, do not torment me!"

The second man's mouth was moving, but no sound came forth, only flies.

The voice of the first man was not of this earth.

"What is your name?" Jesus asked the first man.

"My name is Legion, for we are many." The man's head swiveled, and he found Mary in the crowd. Both men looked at her, and their eyes lit with dark recognition.

Joanna's head swam as she clung to Mary.

What happened next was a blur. Jesus commanded the unseen evil to enter the pigs. The animals screamed in terror and tore as fast as they could into the sea, drowning themselves. Joanna watched as their heads disappeared, one by one, into the surf. After a moment, the only sound was the waves gently breaking upon the shore. Joanna turned to look at the demoniacs, but they were gone. In their place, two men stood. Shaking her head to clear her vision, Joanna looked again. Their skin was entirely clean, glistening in the morning sun. John was wrapping them in linen for modesty, but no other disciple dared approach yet. When the first man spoke to Jesus, Joanna could not hear the exact words of thanksgiving, but she knew this: she had never heard his voice before.

How long had it been since even he had heard it?

Oh, Jesus, the things You restore to us!

Mary pointed to the water. In the spray breaking over the rocks, a rainbow shimmered. Joanna watched the droplets of water play in the rainbow's crescent. The sun had risen strong and clear over the Sea of Galilee.

Two days later
Summer, 31 CE

The sea remained calm. Peter arranged for several small fishing vessels to take them all back to Capernaum. The shock of the exorcisms in the Gadarenes had left them weak. Joanna's legs had trembled for the remainder of that entire afternoon.

Approaching the shore, Joanna was relieved to see Constans among the waiting crowd spilling down from the trade road. He was not a warm man, but he was dependable. He kept his word, and his word had been given to watch over her and keep her safe. Larks sang and flitted overhead as the boats drew closer to shore.

Pushing his way through the crowd, Constans cleared a path to Jesus as He stepped from the boat. A group of Pharisees stood on shore. One man in the center did not wear the traditional robe and turban. That man had red eyes and a strained face. His shoulders stooped as he fell.

Jairus! Constans nodded as Joanna's eyebrows lifted in surprise. He had found Jairus!

Jairus fell at Jesus's feet as Jesus emerged from the waves. Water lapped at the man's knees, dark stains rising across his costly tunic, the corner tassels coated in mud. Joanna climbed from her boat and got closer, shocked at the spectacle. A synagogue ruler oversaw every aspect of Jewish life and faith. Jairus decided who studied at the synagogue and who was excluded.

"Please come," Jairus said. "My daughter is dying. Place your hands on her to heal her. Then she will live."

Jairus held all the power in his community and now here he was, begging, on his knees. And to a man who had angered so many Pharisees!

Everyone froze, seeing the man who had control of their lives giving control over his daughter's life to Jesus.

Jesus extended a hand and lifted Jairus to his feet. Together, the men turned for the road, the crowd pressing in from all sides. Jairus's companions, the Pharisees, frowned as they fell behind and were jostled by the people.

Joanna and Mary picked up the edges of their robes and hurried into the crowd, eager to see what Jesus and the other Pharisees would do. The ruler of a synagogue had yielded his spiritual authority to Jesus. No matter what happened to the girl, her father would never reclaim his position in the community. His family would be thrown out of the synagogue.

"Tameh! Tameh!" a Pharisee screamed, pointing at a shrouded woman near him. "That woman is *zavah*! She is unclean."

Mary grasped Joanna's arm, nudging her to look in the direction of the uproar. A man balancing on a crutch hovered near the shrouded woman.

"Tameh! Tameh!" the Pharisee called again. The man lifted his crutch and swung it wildly, causing the Pharisee and all who stood with him to stumble and fall away. The woman charged forward, head down, muttering something to herself repeatedly. She did not stop until she reached Jesus. Falling at His feet with outstretched arms, she grazed her fingertips over the edge of His robe, and she said no more. The crowd surged forward, moving past and around her, covering her from sight.

Joanna and Mary exchanged looks of concern. Jesus stopped. Jairus looked back at Him, his brow wrinkled in alarm. Constans moved toward Joanna, maneuvering her and Mary closer to the outside front edge. "We've got to get away from the center."

"Who touched Me?" Jesus called.

The people around Him shook their heads and held up their hands.

"Someone touched Me," Jesus insisted. "For I recognized power going out from Me."

The disciples whirled around in confusion. "You see all the people," Thomas replied. "They are crowding against You. How can you ask which one touched You?"

Jesus seemed to ignore the disciples, looking intently at the faces around Him, searching.

A woman stood, and as she did, her shroud fell away. A knot of tension gripped Joanna's stomach.

"It was I," the woman said, kneeling at Jesus's feet. "I am the one who touched You, my Lord. I have been zavah for twelve years."

The shouts of "Unclean!" rippled through the crowd. Joanna strained to hear the woman's story as she spoke to Jesus. The woman said she had bled for many years and was now destitute from paying for healings that never healed.

"The very moment I touched the fringe of Your garment, I was healed," the woman said.

"Daughter, your faith has made you well," Jesus replied. "Go in peace."

Before Joanna could loosen her grip on Mary's arm, before she could open her mouth to exclaim in wonder and joy, a messenger on horseback crested the hill. He rode straight for Jairus, dismounting in a leap.

With a deep and ragged breath, the rider lowered his head.

"Your daughter has died."

Jairus fell to his knees. A Pharisee rushed to his friend's side as the messenger went on. "Why bother Jesus anymore?"

The intent was plain. Why risk everything for someone who can give nothing now?

Jairus looked between his friends and Jesus, his head turning back and forth, the weight of each world pulling him back again. Did Jairus realize that tears streamed down his cheeks?

Joanna's heart broke for him. The end of life was the end of hope. That unclean woman had interrupted their journey and stolen his only chance. Joanna knew what that was like, to have another steal your only hope. What would Jairus do now? If he walked away, he could still return to the synagogue. Maybe not as the ruler, but he could still salvage something from his old life.

Then Jesus spoke.

"Don't be afraid. Just believe."

Joanna's eyes watered as she squinted to be sure. What man stood in the doorway of Jairus's house?

When Chuza recognized Joanna, a cold flinch turned him to one side, like she had slapped him. As she approached, he did not acknowledge her or speak her name. The air between them was thick with unspoken accusation, so thick that he made wide arcs to avoid her. She had not brought Jesus to Chuza. No, it was clear now that she had used Chuza's gold to bring Jesus to Jairus. Chuza would not profit from Jesus's miracles. And worse, the daughter was dead. Jesus had come too late. She had failed Chuza and Jairus.

Chuza thought she had chosen sides, but he did not understand Jesus. To choose Jesus was to choose life. She had thought she was doing the right thing.

Jairus stopped in the road in front of the home, staring with blank eyes at the doorway a daughter had once run out of, calling for her *abba*. Slowly, his knees buckled, and he fell to the ground. Jesus lifted him to his feet, but Chuza rushed forward and separated them.

"I arranged for the finest physician in the empire," Chuza said. "He would have been here before the new moon. But I'm afraid there was nothing anyone could have done." Chuza's voice rested heavily on the word *anyone*.

Mourners streamed out of the house. Their cries pierced Joanna's heart. The disciples walked into the crowd, offering words of comfort and assistance for the older women who could not bear up under the grief.

A woman fell to her knees beside Jairus. "My precious daughter," she sobbed. "She was only twelve years old. Twelve!"

"Why all this confusion and sobbing?" Jesus asked, speaking softly to her like a father comforting his daughter in a storm. He took her by the arms and lifted her to her feet. "The child is not dead. She is only sleeping."

The mourners laughed, but it was a bitter laugh, short and hard at the edges. Jesus released the mother to John's care. Another disciple brought her a drink of water and fanned her for fresh air until her shuddering breath became steady.

Jesus took her by the hand and motioned for Jairus to follow, leading them inside the house. A mourner followed, but Jesus stopped and denied the woman entrance. Only the parents and Jesus's disciples could enter the home. Joanna felt sorry for them—she would not want to see a little girl dead.

Chuza snapped at Constans, demanding a report of his time on the journey with Joanna.

Mary walked toward the house, then held out her hand for Joanna to follow.

Joanna, with a last look back, followed the disciples into the house.

Dust motes swirled in the light that stole in from the thatched roof. Jairus's daughter lay on her bed, unnaturally still. Her skin had the dull rime of a body dead for hours, but her face held the beauty of a child. Her black hair had been neatly combed on either side of her head, and her hands had been folded on top of the sheet. There was no rise and fall under the sheet from her breath. The child was dead.

Jairus wailed, a cry so loud Joanna wondered that his chest did not cleave open from grief.

Jesus took the little girl by the hand, with a tenderness that embarrassed Joanna. To touch the dead made a man unclean. How many times today would Jesus break with Jewish law and tradition?

"Little girl, I say to you, get up!" Jesus's voice disturbed the quiet of the room. Dust motes exploded upward toward the light as a great wind swept through the home.

The little girl sat up. *"Imma?"* She blinked. The mother became as still as stone.

Then the girl's sleepy eyes landed on Jairus. "Abba! You've come home! What have you brought me?"

Joanna looked at the faces around her. Each was pale and glassy-eyed. She imagined her own was too. She had no words to express her shock.

"Who are all these people?" the girl asked. Jairus fell forward, wrapping his little girl in a hug.

"Give her something to eat," Jesus said to the mother, resting a hand on her shoulder. "But do not tell anyone what has happened." The mother kissed Jesus on the cheek with a resounding wet smack and fell into the hug with Jairus and her little girl.

Joanna wanted to know how the girl heard a voice calling her back. Where had she been?

Walking outside, she faced Chuza.

"What is happening in there?" he demanded. "We all heard screams. Is the little girl alive? Was this all a trick?"

Joanna started to tell him but remembered Jesus' warning. She fell silent.

"I did not tell you to join Jesus. I told you to bring Him to us," Chuza said, his voice tight and dry. "Now look what you have done. If Jairus tells people I could not help him, but Jesus did, my power is over. Herod's power is over. People will not come to me anymore, people will no longer seek Herod's help. They will look to Jesus."

She remained silent.

"Did you mean to start a rebellion against Rome?" he asked. "Is that your revenge?"

"Why would I seek revenge?" she asked, the hair on her arms prickling.

Chuza walked to her, and he reached for the hem of her outer robe. She did not move. Her confusion made movement impossible. With both hands grabbing the hem, he tore a corner off and threw it in the dust at her feet.

"You are not my wife," he declared. "And I am not your husband."

Stars swam at the edge of her vision. He had just recited the vow of divorce, of dissolving the bonds of marriage.

"I will return your dowry plus give you a large sum of gold. I will send it with a messenger with the written vow," he continued. "From this day on, I want no part of you. I want no part of Jesus."

Joanna's head swam. "I will need to collect my things."

"Buy new ones. I will send enough money. Do not come back to the palace. Herod will send you to the Black Fortress for this."

He turned to leave. It had been so fast. He knew exactly what his offer would be before he ever knew her crime. Joanna realized he had made up his mind about her long ago.

"How is Aresh?" she called out.

"Pregnant." He did not look back. "And by next week she will be my wife."

CHAPTER FOURTEEN

Six months later
Early spring, 32 CE
Sea of Galilee

Joanna watched the waves lap at the shore of the Sea of Galilee. Dawn would break soon.

She shivered, wrapping her shawl around her shoulders, eager for the sun's warmth. Without servants who rose before dawn and lit fires in her bedchambers, she was cold most mornings. Summer would arrive in two more months. But the mornings were still cold, the way only a woman alone in the world could feel. True to his word, Chuza married Aresh the week after he dissolved the marriage to Joanna.

Perhaps if she had stayed with Jesus and the disciples, the sun would feel warmer. After Chuza erased their marriage, Mary urged her to travel with her, with Jesus and the disciples. She did, at first. Jesus returned to His hometown, Nazareth. There, His own people treated Him with such disrespect that Joanna's faith was shaken. They had known Him best, years ago. They could not believe He was the Messiah. Was she a fool because she could? Their disrespect stole whatever confidence she had left in her decisions, even her decision to trust Jesus.

After Nazareth, Jesus broke the disciples into pairs to send them out to preach and heal in His name. Joanna fled in the night. She did not think she could withstand the pain of so many goodbyes the next morning.

Life was exhausting now. Doing everything for herself took so much time! Washing her face, hands, and feet required a trip to the well first. That took twenty minutes each way. Eating required a trip to the market, which was a fifteen-minute walk to the main streets, then time to shop and select, then the hopeless tangle of negotiating. She was terrible at that. Embarrassingly, she had not yet mastered how to measure the worth of each coin in the empire compared to an hour of a man's labor. She had never offered a coin to one of her maids in exchange for a day's labor. It was hard to know how much time was worth, compared to a linen shawl, or an egg.

Thankfully, though, Chuza had been generous when he divorced her—if that was what he had done. The law he had used was more like an erasure of the marriage. In the eyes of the law, it was as if she no longer existed. The marriage had been just a dream. Chuza had paid her well to leave him. She had freedom, and she had wealth. The irony was that she wanted neither.

She returned to counting her sorrows. Most days, so far, she was too exhausted to prepare her food. At first, she had bought roasted grain, because that was what the women of the village did. They made their own bread.

Now she just bought bread. Her first night alone, she had spent a whole evening staring at the grain, wondering what to do with it, not knowing how the women transformed the hard-shelled grain into a fluffy loaf of bread.

A cat stalked near the water's edge. Joanna watched as it delicately turned over a rock with its paw, looking for something. Seconds later, it lashed out with its claws, snagging a sparkling silver minnow, and trotted away with its prize. Joanna smiled as its pranced past, its tail held high.

She turned back to stare at the hills in the east, dark hulking shapes that hid the sun's path.

"He's there right now, you know." A man spoke from behind her. Her hand flew to her chest, and she whirled around to see Constans. He stood a respectful distance away.

"What are you doing here?" Her tone was colder than she intended, but then, she hadn't seen him in ages. She had fallen so far since then. And he had always delighted in making life difficult for her, hadn't he? "And why are you not in uniform?"

"I left the palace guard," he replied, his eyes trained on the hills. The darkness began to lift in small degrees. She could make out the lines of his face now, and the familiar brown of his eyes.

She turned back to watch for the sun's ascent. "I did not know that." She offered no details about her own situation. She could not bear disdain, and she did not want pity.

"Jesus often goes into the mountains to pray before dawn," Constans said. "The crowds overwhelm Him at times, I think. Everyone demands something of Him."

The edges of the hills glowed orange and yellow. Joanna's breath quickened. Dawn had come. Why did she love this ritual, waiting for the sun every morning? Was it the splendor of dawn or the promise of a new day?

The sun showed itself, a crown of gold edging over the top of the mountain.

"I've listened to Him many times now," he said. Why was he talking to her as if he was her friend? Why did he want to talk about Jesus? "He offers eternal life to anyone who believes. He heals anyone who asks. Some people do not have the courage to ask, so they just reach out their hands and touch His robes. They are healed. It is like nothing the world has ever seen." He cleared his throat. "I too touched His robe, Joanna."

Joanna closed her eyes, the realization softening her heart against this man who was once the thorn in her side.

"And what happened?" she asked softly.

"You've heard the stories of how He restores withered limbs?" Constans replied.

Joanna nodded.

"He did that for my soul. My soul was withered with rage. I was angry at myself mostly. I sound like a madman, I know." Constans's cheeks turned deep red. "Years ago, I was alone with my sister and mother while my father was on a journey. I was thirteen. My father entrusted their care to me. While he was gone, a group of mercenaries raided our village."

Joanna swallowed. "Did they kill your mother and sister?"

Constans looked at the ground. "No. Not right away." In the silence, she heard the story he could not share. Blanching, she looked away.

"I never forgave myself," he went on. "I could not. Some acts of forgiveness are beyond us. The debt is too great." He kicked a pebble at his feet. "Jesus healed me of the rage I felt toward myself. A strange miracle, perhaps."

The sun rose higher, until an orb of orange flame rested over the mountain, and yellow light pierced through the clouds. It looked as if the mountain had burst into flame, and the flames reached into the heavens.

And Jesus was there, praying, she thought. Maybe she witnessed more than a sunrise.

"We live in extraordinary times," Constans said softly.

"Who do you say He is?" she whispered to Constans, sincere now. Jesus was no simple mortal. He was something entirely new. He was—

"He is the Son of God." Constans finished her thought for her. "I know the palace would kill me for professing that. That's why I left. I follow Jesus now. I am not one of the twelve, nor do I have any great responsibility or authority."

He took a few steps to stand closer to her. "I am a man who has learned to value forgiveness. Please forgive me, Joanna, wife of Chuza, for the times when I was harsh."

She could not tear her eyes away from the sunrise. "I am no longer Chuza's wife. I was thrown from the palace." She looked at him with a sideways glance, a gentle, wry smile. "At least you left by your own free will. You left with dignity." She watched as the sunrise continued to burn a hole in the heavens. "I am disgraced. Chuza has married a servant in my place."

"Then Chuza is disgraced, not you." Constans's voice was steady and strong. Joanna found comfort in it.

The clouds dispersed as the sun rose higher and claimed the sky. The horizon was shot with light from side to side. Joanna and Constans blinked in the overwhelming rush of gold rays.

Joanna caught sight of his clothes. In the new morning light, she saw that he was dressed plainly, with a rough linen robe of unsteady red dye. He had probably bought it second-hand. A shawl draped over his shoulder had been patched several times, by someone with poor eyesight. The stitches were large and uneven. His pride had once been his only earthly possession. But now, he worshipped at the feet of flaming mountains and watched miracles seed the earth.

"You gave up everything you once knew to follow Jesus," she said.

Constans looked at his robe then back at her and smirked. He did not mock her, but seemed to mock himself, or the man he had been. He was entirely different now, she realized.

"All my life, I have followed orders," he said. "When I lost my family, I was sold into slavery. I earned my freedom, but life as a soldier was the only trade I could take up. I've been a soldier since I was nineteen."

"So you left because you wanted freedom," she said.

"No!" He raised an eyebrow. "You and I went in search of Jesus, and I listened to His teachings."

Her mouth dropped open a little before she caught herself and closed it. "You understood those stories?" She hadn't understood any of His parables.

"No! I mean, yes!" Constans's face grew red again. "Let me speak. Please."

Joanna pressed her lips together, restraining a sudden and overwhelming urge to giggle. He was flustered. And with his cheeks bright red, he looked like a young boy.

"All my life I have followed orders," he began again.

She nodded, determined to remain silent this time.

"I took pride in doing my work well. I was an excellent soldier. But then I met Jesus, and He asked me a question that haunted my every waking moment. *What good would it do you, Constans, to be the best soldier in the world, if you lose your very soul?* I didn't know what He meant. I didn't even know if I believed that I had a soul."

He took a few steps away, then turned and looked at her. "I realized what He was saying to me was this—at the end of my life, I want to be proud that my commanders could entrust me with anything. But the bigger question was the one I had never asked: Would I be proud of the commanders I had chosen to follow?"

Joanna moved to a nearby rock and perched herself on the edge, listening. This was more than Constans had ever spoken to her, and every word came from the depths of his heart.

"My name will never be remembered, Joanna. Many of us who follow Jesus will be forgotten in the ages to come. And yet we follow. Why? Not for fame. Or riches. He is worthy to be followed. And that is what will make all the difference."

The sun was high above the hills. Fishing boats appeared on the horizon, bringing back their catches from the night's work.

Women trudged toward the shore, ready with breakfast for the fishermen, eager to collect their catch and take it to market.

"I'm sorry for your heartache," Constans said. "I will always owe you a debt, because you introduced me to Jesus."

Joanna waved his words away. "We were both following orders, that is all."

"True. And yet, aren't we the lucky ones?"

Joanna snorted, an ugly little noise that embarrassed her. She blushed and looked away.

Constans reached over then caught himself, perhaps still aware of the difference in status that once stood between them. "All I meant was that everyone follows orders. Our present circumstances force us to remember whose authority matters. If you think about it, we were given a gift. As I said, we live in extraordinary times."

Their eyes met, and Joanna's heart lifted to see not a servant, but a friend.

With that, he was gone, and another day in her uncomfortable new life began.

One month later
Spring, 32 CE

Joanna selected a perfect fish for her lunch. The merchant's wife had roasted it with olive oil and leeks and wrapped it in a thick, broad leaf for travel.

"For a fair price, I will give you bread too, sister," the woman crooned, her eyes crinkling with interest as she watched Joanna.

Joanna didn't want to admit it, but she wasn't certain what a fair price was to offer the woman. Not for a full meal like this, presented so beautifully. Rummaging through her coin purse, she picked through several coins from the money Chuza had given her. She hesitated, sorrow sweeping over her.

"Perhaps wealthy women think they are too good for our food," the woman said, growing impatient, dismissing Joanna with a wave of her hand.

Flustered, Joanna grabbed two coins and thrust them at the woman. "Forgive me. I was thinking of a sad memory."

The woman snatched the coins from her. Joanna took the fish and turned to leave.

"You know you just paid a week's wages for one fish?" Mary Magdalene stood, hands on hips, shaking her head.

Joanna, shocked to see her, and embarrassed, shrugged meekly. "She gave me the bread for free."

Mary burst into laughter. "Free? I think we need to talk about what that word means." She looped her arm through Joanna's. "Now, Constans tells me you've been staying near the water. Why don't we go there and talk?"

Joanna navigated through the market crowds, carrying her meal in one hand, Mary Magdelene hooked on to the other arm.

"You see this?" Mary asked.

"No." Joanna didn't see anything unusual. It was a market day. Stalls were set up with linen canopies to provide protection from the afternoon sun. There were merchants of fish, fruits, vegetables, linens, jewelry…and a few religious leaders, wandering about, casting sour glances at young boys who were not at the synagogue studying.

"Exactly. This is what I've come to talk to you about," Mary continued. "No one pays us any attention. We are just two women walking through the market together."

Why did Mary care that no one paid them any attention?

As if to prove a point, Mary stopped and considered a sash of pale-yellow linen, then set it back on the merchant's table and continued the walk. "Notice that the religious men don't bother looking twice at us. The very thing that makes us so weak in our culture makes us powerful in the kingdom."

"What kingdom?" Joanna was confused. "Jesus refused offers of money and power."

"That's why I've come to talk to you." Mary squeezed her arm. "You no longer have a husband, but you do have a family. Jesus is creating a new world. Now, hurry, before your meal gets soggy."

"Two more hours, and we should find the group," Mary said. She rode just ahead. They had bought donkeys and ridden north to join Jesus and the disciples.

Joanna had arrived with Mary on the outskirts of Tyre just a week after Mary had found her in the market. Along the way, Mary had shared more of Jesus's teachings and more of the miracles He had performed.

Joanna knew miracles were happening. She had already made peace with the strange, supernatural occurrences that were taking place. Heaven had opened up, and anything was possible…for other people. Jesus's teachings were striking and new. The more Mary explained His words to her, the more her own desire grew to be near Him again and learn.

And yet she had to know. Why had her miracle not worked? Why had He failed her?

She reined her donkey in to let another traveler on the road pass by. Sudden fear clenched her heart.

"What am I going to say to Him?"

By now, Mary knew everything that was on Joanna's heart and in her mind. Joanna had never had a friend since she married. She liked the experience of unburdening herself of her fears, except that Mary sometimes had advice that seemed wrong and unpleasant. Joanna wasn't sure if she was obligated to follow advice from a friend.

"Everyone always worries about what to say to Him!" Mary exclaimed. She sounded aggravated. "A few of them should worry more about what He might have to say to them!"

This was another new thing for Joanna. Friends could aggravate each other in a thousand small ways without consequences. That was somehow expected as the price of the friendship.

"Joanna," Mary said, turning on her perch to look at her just for a moment, "stop focusing on what you're going to say to Him!" Mary turned back around and raised her voice to be heard. "I promise, whatever He's got to say to you is so much more important. Stop worrying. Stop planning. All you must do is kneel before Him. Everything else will fall into place, I promise."

Mary had run a successful perfume business. She was used to being in charge. But she was so bossy. Joanna rolled her eyes.

"And don't roll your eyes," Mary called, though she didn't turn around.

Joanna burst out laughing.

CHAPTER FIFTEEN

As a woman named Martha washed her feet, Joanna sat on a bench by the door, secretly grateful to be back in a familiar routine. After a long journey, having a servant greet her at the door with a jar of water and stack of linens was a joy.

"When will we meet the other women, the ones who travel with Jesus?" Joanna asked Mary. Mary had just returned from the kitchen, where no doubt she'd already given orders about the evening meal. Joanna wondered why Mary hadn't lingered awhile longer at her own foot bath. It was so relaxing. This woman did it so well.

The woman washing her feet looked up, confused. Joanna saw another woman following behind Mary. The two women exchanged glances as if Joanna's words had offended them.

"Joanna," Mary said softly. "These are the women."

Joanna looked down at the woman washing her dirty feet, the mud from her toes now running through the woman's fingers. "I thought she was…you were…"

"I am not a slave, nor a servant." The woman rinsed her hands in a basin of clean water, dried them with a linen wrap, then stood. "Welcome to my home. I am Martha. I live with my sister Mary and my brother Lazarus." She pointed across the room. "And this is Seraph. She serves with us."

Joanna wanted to run away and never return. She'd just offended the host in front of the other women. Besides hating her for appearing rich, maybe now they could hate her for being rude. Joanna felt tears building.

A knock at the door broke the tension. The other women turned away to speak among themselves. Seraph excused herself and returned a moment later, frowning.

"A man outside wants to know when we plan on feeding Rufus the Second? He says the donkey has a taste for meadow flowers and white parsley."

Joanna sat up, thinking the name seemed familiar. But who would name a donkey?

Oh! She would. She had named a horse Rufus once, in fact.

"Constans!"

He came through the door just then, followed by men, then Jesus.

"You name your animals?" Matthew asked, looking in confusion between her and Constans. "A donkey is called Rufus?"

"I was lucky. She wanted to call me something far worse." Constans clapped him on the back, laughing.

The women immediately busied themselves setting out food, bowls of water, and linens for ceremonial hand washing and feet washing.

Joy bubbled up in her heart at the sight of her friends and the flurry of activity. She wanted to speak with Jesus, but a sudden shyness stopped her.

She watched the way Jesus hugged Mary in greeting. Far from being scandalous, as some might suggest, when Jesus hugged her it was as if Mary was transformed into an innocent child, and His arms were her haven.

Joanna gripped the bench. She wanted to jump up and run to Him too. These were all the feelings she should have had as a child but didn't. She had been raised to think real life would begin when she met the man who became her husband. When she pleased him and earned everything she had been given. But then she had failed and fallen. Her real life was now something very different than what she had imagined it would be.

Her heart softened in Jesus's presence, though, a tenderness that eased into that empty hollow place in her soul. He knew. She could see it in His eyes. She jumped up and ran to Him. He opened His arms and embraced her.

"Peace, be still, child," He whispered.

And she was.

Summer, 32 CE

She was glad to be so far from the palace, starting a new life in a new place. Each sunrise was a bright affirmation. Far from home but completely at ease, Joanna felt she had finally returned to the girl she had meant to become long ago, before she was told whom she had to please.

After staying with Martha and Mary for a few nights, the group moved on, heading north. One evening, about two weeks later, she was one of the last followers awake. Most had gone outside to sleep under the stars. She, Mary, and the other women were up late preparing bread for the next day's breakfast. It would rise through the night, then they would get up before dawn to bake it.

Her arms ached as she kneaded the dough. But she was getting stronger. Every day, she grew stronger.

Much work had been completed here in the northern region of Tyre and Sidon. From the other women, Joanna learned of miracles and ministry that had happened in towns all over the region. Unlikely places too, but none more unlikely than this. Tyre and Sidon was the ancient territory of Jezebel. In the minds of many Jews, the land was stained by the memory of Jezebel and Ahab. Their daughter had continued their brutal legacy among the Jews.

Jezebel's daughter, Athaliah, had ruled in Judah and nearly destroyed the bloodline of King David. Why did Jesus care about the homeland of His people's enemies? Maybe because Jesus didn't have any enemies. Although the religious leaders hated Him, He welcomed anyone to break bread with Him. Why didn't He have clear rules about who could share His table, hear His teachings, ask for His healing?

She glanced over. He was eating in silence. So many people had been healed today. His shoulders slumped as He leaned forward over the low kitchen table.

Joanna still wanted answers from Him about her own failed miracle. She was no longer desperate for them, though. Answers were useless now. Chuza had a new wife. Joanna had no need to hold on to hope.

But the truth was, a hollow ache remained, like a missing tooth.

A wolf cried in the night, and the women stopped kneading the dough, listening. A chill ran down Joanna's spine.

Someday she would get the courage to ask Him why her miracle failed.

"Lord, Son of David, have mercy on me!" A woman's shrill scream made Joanna jump, knocking her wooden mixing bowl over. Mary lurched forward, catching it before it tipped the dough onto the dirt floor.

"Have mercy, Jesus! My daughter is suffering terribly from demon possession!"

Everyone ran outside, where the male disciples were awake, standing around a woman who looked very much like a Canaanite, judging by her cosmetics. Her eyebrows were heavily painted in kohl, and her eyeliner was applied under each eye in a harsh line as well. The woman had a mass of tangled brown hair, thick heavy bags under her haunted eyes, thin lips sucked in over gaps where teeth should have been. She looked to be close to Joanna's own age, but life had drained the marrow from her bones.

The woman burst past the disciples and into the house, with the strength of a legion of soldiers. Joanna ran quickly to see what she wanted.

"Oh, have mercy on me, Lord, Son of David!" the woman cried, falling at Jesus's feet. "My daughter is cruelly demon-possessed! You can heal her. Please, Lord, heal my daughter!"

"I was sent only to the lost sheep of the house of Israel," Jesus said. He must have also assumed that she was a Canaanite, an ancient enemy of His people.

"Lord, help me!" she reached for His feet and, hesitating only briefly, rested both hands on top of them, delicately, carefully, as if touching a nobleman of great worth and esteem. No one in Nazareth had spoken to Jesus with such humility. No one in Nazareth had treated Him with such honor and deference. No one there had acknowledged His power. Yet Nazareth had just as many sick children, just as many broken lives and bodies.

Jesus's face remained resolute. "Let the children be satisfied first; for it is not good to take the children's bread and throw it to the dogs."

The woman sat upright at once, a look of expectant joy on her face. Her eyes were focused on nothing else in the room but Jesus as she leaned forward, hands clasped like a child about to receive a present.

"Yes, Lord," she said, "but even the dogs under the table feed on the children's crumbs, which fall from the master's table." Her smile broadened. She looked at Him, her breath stopped, waiting. It was not important to her who she was, not in that moment...all that mattered to her was who Jesus was.

Jesus's eyebrows shot up in merriment as a wry smile curved His mouth. "O woman, your faith is great! Because of this answer it shall be done for you as you wish! Go; the demon has gone out of your daughter!"

Within moments, everyone who had stood astonished began to celebrate. Which meant, of course, everyone wanted to eat too. Had Joanna ever properly thanked the kitchen servants at the palace? She wished now she had. And yet the chaos around Jesus in these moments made every sore muscle worth it.

She spent the remainder of the evening cleaning up and trying to find any of the disciples who could explain the details of healing. How did Jesus heal those who were not present? It was dawn before Joanna realized His own disciples were as confused about His methods as she was. She lay down on a pallet on the roof just an hour or so before dawn and decided to ask Jesus about it in the morning.

The next morning, Jesus was gone.

Some of His followers were upset and bewildered. Joanna wasn't. She had searched for Him before and already knew how elusive He could be. Wherever He went, she just had to follow. He wasn't hiding. He was leading.

Within a few hours, she and the women had their donkeys loaded with provisions. Anything they lacked, Joanna and Mary could provide. Joanna was rich, but Mary was the businesswoman. Mary had been a great help in bartering, negotiating, and generally explaining how money worked.

"It's a little more complicated than snapping your fingers and having a servant bring you what you want," she had told Joanna, teasing.

"Do not be foolish," Joanna retorted. "I never snapped my fingers. I called every servant by name."

"Oh, that's right. I forgot, you even name your donkeys."

The other women giggled. "What will you name this one?" one asked her.

Joanna sat up primly on her donkey and patted him on the neck. "I haven't decided yet."

Constans trotted past on a donkey that was not weighted down with cookware or clothes. He shook his head when he saw the women's caravan. "Your donkey needs a donkey."

"You had better not mock us, or I will name this one after you!" Joanna called. The women exploded into laughter. It was really an outrageous new thing Jesus had done, creating a world where men and women could not only speak to each other in public, but could be friends.

Joanna nearly fell off her donkey with a sudden realization. Her family was now larger than she could ever have imagined. She had brothers and sisters as far as the eye could see. Martha had forgiven her for the unintended offense from their first meeting, and Constans treated her with kindness now. She turned side to side to see the group riding to find Jesus. She belonged to these people, and they belonged to her.

She belonged. A tear rolled down her cheek. In the past, she had been placed, given, offered…but this was the first time she had ever belonged.

Near Mount Hermon
Summer, 32 CE

Thomas was the most inquisitive, perhaps, but Peter was Joanna's favorite. He was plain spoken and quick to act. She appreciated that. If she needed help with a heavy jug of water, he was the first to jump up and assist her. If children got separated from their mothers in the crowds that followed Jesus, Peter would swing the children up to sit on his shoulders. He'd whinny like a horse and gallop to stop them from crying, and they'd forget their tears long enough to spur him with their ankles. Mothers usually ended up scolding Peter instead of thanking him—he did gallop too fast at times. All the fishermen in the group were incredibly strong.

She'd never spent time with men who worked for their living, so she did not realize how labor changed them. She marveled that the fishermen had callouses on their palms, the traders had wind-chafed cheeks, and the farmers had broad shoulders. Labor made the man. Life was far more fascinating and rewarding than when she had lived behind palace walls.

When Peter returned late one afternoon with the brothers James and John, he did not want to eat supper. Neither did the brothers. They were pale and talking quietly with each other. Joanna pulled Mary aside.

"What has disturbed the men?"

Mary shook her head. "I don't know. They went out with Jesus this morning."

Joanna watched the men talking. As they gestured to each other, their hands shook.

Mary raised an eyebrow. "I'll find out what I can. Discreetly."

Within the hour, Mary's face had that same pale look. She motioned for Joanna to go outside. The two women walked to the communal bread-baking oven at the center of the houses. It was late in the afternoon, so there was no one baking bread.

"The miracles were hard to believe, yes?" Mary asked.

Joanna nodded.

Mary bit her lip and exhaled. "This next story is harder to believe, and I don't want to believe it."

Joanna leaned in.

"The men went with Jesus to the top of the mountain, presumably for prayer, as He does. They said something miraculous happened that they can't talk about." She shrugged. "That is not unusual with Jesus. He tells many people to keep secret what He does for them." She looked over her shoulder. "But they did tell me something disturbing."

"Disturbing?" Joanna asked, too loudly.

Mary put a finger up to her lips then continued. "Jesus is telling them He's going to suffer and be killed."

Joanna threw up her hands in exasperation. "They misunderstood Him. Or they dreamed! He's healed every disease and infirmity that anyone has ever brought to Him. He has raised the dead! No, He cannot be killed. Even if someone tried, He would stop it. I love the disciples like brothers, but maybe they just do not know Jesus."

Two mornings later

"Why?" Joanna burst into the dining area.

The disciples were seated along the low wooden table, reclining, eating breakfast with Jesus. Another late night with crowds pressing in, seeking healing as Jesus taught and ministered, had left them all bleary-eyed and drained.

"Why are you taking us back south?" she demanded, fear making her heart pound in her ears. She had thought she was free. Now Jesus was leading her right back to the place of her greatest shame.

"Is it because of John?" she demanded. "You know, yes?"

"Leave us," Jesus said quietly to the disciples, who obliged. Jesus worked miracles, but women were still mysteries of the universe, after all.

"You know that I convinced Salome to dance when she did not want to," Joanna said, her breath becoming ragged through building tears. "If it was not for me, John would be alive. And now You are taking us back toward Herod and Chuza because

You want to parade me in these rags I am wearing right past the palace."

Jesus's expression remained calm and kind. "Finished?"

"Yes."

He waited a moment. "Isn't there more you want to ask of Me?"

"No!" She still didn't have the courage to ask.

"You believe in My goodness?" He asked.

"You know I do."

"But you do not believe in My goodness toward you?"

It was as if a rock had hit her in the chest. All air was punched out of her lungs, and her vision was white at the edges. He was right; she did not believe in His goodness toward her.

"If I was not fit for the palace," Joanna replied, swallowing back the pain in her throat, "then how could I be fit for Your kingdom?"

"I will give you every good thing, Joanna. Do not be afraid. Just believe."

Wordlessly, she retreated. The next day, they moved on to Bethsaida, then Caesara Philipi, and the crowds followed, growing at every town. The women ministering to other women were a shock to the religious leaders especially. Joanna wondered what they would do if they knew that the women also financed this group.

Constans watched over them closely, worried about the growing hostility from the religious leaders. He stayed closest to Joanna, making sure that no harm came to her.

CHAPTER SIXTEEN

Summer, 32 CE
The village of Capernaum

The disciples bickered all the way to Capernaum. Matthew probably regretted his generous offer to host the group at his spacious home. Only Thomas was not embroiled in the tense whispered arguments. A local boy, he was at ease now that Jesus and the disciples had returned to the region of Galilee. He liked the land, not the water, and spoke with fondness of his home. His parents grew figs and grapes, and his twin remained back at home with them even now. Thomas had been called by Jesus to become a disciple, but his twin had not.

Or maybe his twin had been called and had rejected Jesus. Joanna wished she could ask Thomas. She did not know him well enough to ask such personal questions.

So she asked Constans instead. She found him tending the animals, as usual, after the day's journey.

"I don't know," he said, brushing the donkey's back as it stood patiently eating its feed.

Mary joined them. "The disciples whispered all afternoon. What is going on?"

Constans rolled his eyes. "Jesus chose men who have never taken orders from a commander for a living. They don't understand power, how it works or how it is earned. They want to be given their power, not earn it. Look at Peter. He's got the worst temper of all of them, and he's just a fisherman!"

The women looked at each other. Peter did have a temper. Everyone knew to avoid him first thing in the morning. And when he was hungry. Or tired. Fortunately, they were staying at Matthew's house. Peter was easier to avoid with the large rooms and immense layout.

Matthew was wealthy, at least by the working men's standards. Having been a tax collector, he had a nicer home than the fishermen. None of the disciples seemed to resent that, although they were still afraid of breaking expensive water jugs or dropping fine goblets. Matthew found it amusing. Wealthy people had a completely different attitude toward possessions. Material things served them, while poorer people were in awe of nice things and served the possessions.

Secretly, Joanna appreciated the finer luxuries that she had been missing, including the even floors. The floor of Matthew's home was cobblestone, like most homes in Capernaum. But because Matthew was wealthy, the stones were well matched and easy on her ankles. She didn't trip or stub her toes as she walked from room to room. The walls were basalt stone, and stacked without mortar between them, so there were no gaps for insects or spiders to find their way through and no birds nested in the thatched roof. Joanna had almost gotten used to checking her sleeping mat before she lay down at night, making sure no insects or animals planned on joining her.

Peter burst past them, startling the donkey from its heavy-lidded revelry. The women and Constans looked at each other, but just moments later, Peter burst back out the door, laughing.

"What's going on?" Constans called.

Peter lifted a coin. It was a fat one, most likely a four-drachma. "Off to pay taxes. Funny, isn't it? Staying at a tax collector's house, and I have to go fishing to pay off our debts?"

Matthew appeared in the doorway. "I would have given it to you," he called, looking confused. "Why didn't you ask me for money?"

Joanna frowned, confused as well. She and Mary had plenty of money too. Why had Peter gone fishing to earn money to pay his tax debt?

"No need," Peter called, moving quickly down the path. "I found it in the mouth of a fish."

That made no sense. Which meant only one thing. Jesus. Jesus had done it.

Mary went inside to investigate, and Joanna went to sit beneath an olive tree and watch the sparkling waves in the distance. The next day many of the women would be leaving the group. Jesus had announced that He was sending people out, in pairs, into the cities ahead of Him on the journey. Each pair would minister to the people and prepare them for Jesus to arrive. Women would travel together and minister to women. Men would travel together and minister to men. Joanna and Mary would stay with the disciples and Jesus.

Jesus, she knew, was grieved over the cities He had visited. She couldn't offer Him any comfort. Who could explain the human heart? She certainly couldn't. People had seen great miracles but had not entrusted themselves to the God who was prepared to do greater things than these.

Mary came out to join her, and several other women followed. Soon, most of the women who traveled with Jesus sat beneath the trees, watching the sun set over the water. An ease settled over them. Weary from the day's labor, each woman was alone with her thoughts. Many had never traveled from their homes before.

They leaned against each other, patting each other's hands in quiet comfort or offering smiles and gentle nods.

Joanna stood and walked to the edge of the group. Facing the water, she lifted her head, soaking up the last of the day's sun. Capernaum's skies were the indigo blue of a weaver's loom, with billowing white clouds. The sky above was so saturated with color that it made the world beneath richer too. The trees seemed greener, the stones glistened with their white and yellow flecks, the rooftops glowed with thatched yellow stalks.

The city had no wall for defense. The lack of a wall seemed to set the mood for the entire city—all were welcome, no violence would ever await a tired traveler. The waters of the Galilee glistened at the far southern edge of the city. With plentiful water and sun, everything grew well here—grapes, olives, and figs. Fishing was good, trade was easy, and the weather was balmy.

Turning, Joanna looked toward the city. The homes were all one story, with stairs leading to the roofs. There was only one main street that ran through the town. This was a town she could live in forever, she realized. It was simple and easy in every way. Constans led a donkey past the women toward the stalls. Joanna quickly turned her back before he could catch her daydreaming like this.

When she was sure he had gone, she turned back around, her cheeks still warm. Why did she feel that flush of embarrassment when Constans walked past? She was not a child.

Jesus stood on the roof of Matthew's home, looking out at the water. Silhouetted against the brilliant blue sky, with the radiance of the clouds gathered around Him, He looked like the long-awaited Messiah. But what was He delivering the people from, exactly, besides sickness and infirmity?

And more important, what was He leading them to?

Early winter, 32 CE

It was a dark and cold month when Jesus announced that He wanted to return to Jerusalem. The Feast of Dedication would bring many faithful to its streets, and Jesus wanted to be among them. And so they went, and within hours, Joanna watched as He was confronted by angry religious leaders at the temple.

"If You're the Messiah," a rabbi snapped, "tell us plainly."

"I did!" Jesus replied. "You didn't believe Me. The miracles I do in My Father's name speak for Me, but you do not believe because you are not My sheep."

The rabbi and his companions, all rabbis as well, looked disgusted. Dressed in their finery and carrying their scrolls, they would certainly never be mistaken for sheep.

"I give My sheep eternal life," Jesus continued, "and they shall never perish. No one can snatch them out of My hand. My Father who has given them to Me, is greater than all. I and the Father are one."

The rabbis snapped their teeth. Joanna saw the gleam of delight in one rabbi's eyes, though. Jesus had handed them a reason they could accuse Him of breaking religious law—He had just equated Himself with Yahweh. At its heart, Jewish law was simple: revere God above all. What had Jesus just done?

Each leader rushed to find stones, gathering as many as he could and pelting Jesus. The disciples yelled and yelped, grabbing Jesus by the arms and dragging Him back into the crowd. Stones were raining down on everyone who even bore a vague resemblance to Jesus. The crowd scattered in a hundred directions.

A lone child sat crying in the dirt, her withered foot still visible peeking out from her robe. Joanna's heart broke for the girl. The leaders had stopped this girl from getting her miracle and had condemned her to a life of begging. Joanna exhaled the name, almost as if she was praying. *Jesus, help her.*

At once, something in her compelled her to look up, and she did, meeting Jesus's gaze through the melee. As if time stopped, and all grew still, His eyes were an ocean of peace as He seemed to hear her heart's cry for this little girl.

Looking back at the child, Joanna gasped. The foot was healed and healthy. The girl's mother rushed forward, scooping the girl up, out of danger, running away from the angry mob.

Joanna made her way through the confusion to the main street.

Constans appeared at Joanna's side and grabbed her arm, pulling her out of harm's way before a carriage ran her over.

Wincing, she rubbed her arm, but before she could decide whether to scold or thank him, a woman emerged from the carriage.

Aresh.

Covered with exotic, richly dyed linens with tassels of gold and silver threads, she sparkled in the sun like an ornament. She was pregnant again.

Children crowded the carriage, begging for alms. Aresh opened a leather bag and threw small coins into the crowd. Catching sight of Joanna's torn and bedraggled dress, she tossed a coin at her feet. Nothing in Aresh's flat, disinterested gaze hinted that she recognized Joanna. A palace guard stood very close to Aresh. His hand rested on her back as he escorted her through the crowds.

Joanna turned her face away, feeling the heat rise in her cheeks, the shame becoming unbearable. Was she covered in dirt or grime from the street? When was the last time she had a proper bath or put oil in her hair?

Joanna thought on the irony of being homeless and watching a servant girl ride away with her old life. And yet Joanna had a real family, one that could never be lost. So maybe that was miracle enough.

She was sitting by an open fire outside the home of Mary and Martha before dawn the next morning when Jesus approached, alone. He carried a fresh fish and a roasting fork.

"Breakfast?" He asked. She scooted over on the stone bench that Lazarus had built by the roasting pit.

"You saw Aresh yesterday," Jesus said, busying Himself with threading the fish onto the fork.

She nodded. It was pleasurable to sit with Jesus while looking at a crackling fire. The fire offered background noise and filled the silence with comfort.

He pushed the fork into the low flames. She marveled at the freshness of the fish and how the flames sparkled across the silver scales.

She struggled to find the courage to ask the question that had haunted her for so long—why her miracle had failed.

He turned the fish over, letting the flames roast the other side. It was a Musht fish, fresh from the Sea of Galilee. But Mary and Martha lived in Bethany. How had He gotten a fresh fish so far from the water?

The fire crackled, and an ember flew up into the darkness.

"In the morning," Jesus said, "we will be moving on. We have work to do in other villages." He pulled the fish from the flames and tested it with the tip of His finger. It was not quite done, so He pushed it back into the flames.

The disciples called to Jesus, needing His attention to a matter. They came to join them at the fire, so Joanna stood to take her leave.

"Joanna?"

She stopped and looked at Him.

"You used to love to walk in the gardens at Herod's palace," he said. "I know you miss that."

She nodded. How had He known that?

"You know the scriptures? The story of life beginning in a garden?"

She nodded again. "Eve was banished, though. A little bit like my story, I suppose." She tried to smile.

"I wanted to tell you that one day, you will walk in a garden again. One day you will walk in a garden and know a joy that surpasses that of Eve. One day, in a garden, all of life will begin again."

The disciples reached them and crowded around. Joanna, mystified, walked back to the house, pondering His words. He said nothing else on the matter, and she did not bring it up. What a strange prophecy, she thought.

Weeks passed as they traveled from town to town, healing and teaching. Joanna did not grow tired of seeing healing and miracles, but she saw clearly now how the people's greed for miracles saddened Jesus. She felt sad for her own greed too, having followed Him in the beginning only for the promise of a child.

She tried to believe she was glad she hadn't confessed her doubts to Him, but the doubts only grew deeper and troubled her.

January, 33 CE
Galilee

The third month on the road after the conversation at the fire, Joanna walked into the bedroom to find Mary packing up all the clothes and personal belongings of the disciples.

"We have to go back to Bethany," Mary said.

Another interruption to the plans, but Jesus dealt with those every day. His was a ministry of interruptions. He never scolded anyone for them either.

"Why? What is in Bethany?" Joanna asked. A disciple's voice from the other room answered the question.

"It's Lazarus," a disciple's raised voice carried to her. "My Lord, he is near death!"

Joanna peeked out into the main room of the home. Jesus was surrounded by the disciples, many of whom were frowning in concern and near-outrage.

"We can't go back to that region!" one snapped. "They tried to stone Jesus there! We'll all be killed this time."

The disciples were fighting, but Jesus remained calm. Mary continued to pack, so apparently she knew what the disciples did not. Of course, though, Lazarus was one of Jesus's good friends. Jesus would never heal total strangers and then just let a good friend suffer. Of course Jesus would use His power to help a friend.

Thomas shrugged. "If they want to stone Jesus, let them come through me. I'm not afraid."

Joanna shook her head. He always was the brave one. Peter was a hothead, but Thomas was like a bull, stubborn and fierce.

"We're not leaving," Jesus said softly. The room fell quiet. Jesus was probably going to speak a word of healing, and Lazarus would be healed from here.

But Jesus did not.

"Lazarus is sick, my Lord," John said, as if Jesus hadn't understood the situation the first dozen times it had been explained.

"This sickness will not end in death," Jesus said.

The men looked at each other, questioning the news reports they had received, questioning their willingness to entrust their friend's life to Jesus's word. At last, Thomas stepped forward.

"That's it, then. We're not going."

And they didn't. For two days, Joanna and Mary tended to other matters, ministered to women who needed Jesus but could not, or would not, approach Him directly. Joanna felt like a fraud, more so with every passing day. How could she convince women to trust Jesus with their deepest shame and doubts when she had been unwilling to do so?

And then word came.

Lazarus was dead.

CHAPTER SEVENTEEN

No one spoke on the journey to Bethany. Dust stirred beneath their feet as the sun shone harsh, blinding rays.

Jesus had given His word! Lazarus would not die. That's what He had said, wasn't it?

No, Joanna reminded herself. Jesus promised that the sickness would not end in death. But it had.

It had.

Streets were quiet. Women on the path stepped aside, watching with wary eyes as they passed, pulling their children to their sides.

Everyone knew. Jesus had let one of His closest friends die.

Joanna heard the whispers of confusion and suspicion, and the derision on men's faces when they caught sight of her, a woman. A woman traveling without her husband.

"Don't let them unnerve you," Constans said, walking beside her. As he approached, the man with the sour face looked away. "You're used to crowds following us," he reminded her and the other women who listened.

"This is the first time the crowd doesn't seek a miracle," Mary Magdalene said. "When they don't need anything from Him, look how they treat Him."

"Us," a woman corrected her. "Look how they treat us."

"Everyone needs a miracle," Constans said. "Even if they do not know it. Be kind."

The street stones were uneven, and Joanna stumbled. Constans caught her, patting her on the back as she righted herself. Thanking him, embarrassed to be so clumsy in his presence, she knew she needed to rest. Overhead, a bird circled, crying.

One by one, homeowners lit torches as the sun fell. They approached the city, and Martha ran out to meet them.

Joanna saw Martha's grief. The same confusion and pain that Joanna had carried for so long was now etched on her friend's face. The same painful, impossible question: *Why? Why did this happen?*

For the first time that day, Jesus spoke. He spoke in quiet, hushed tones, to Martha only, and she was not comforted. Whatever He had said, it was not enough.

And so, for that reason, Joanna broke from the crowd. She left. She had to be alone with her pain, with her doubts, and could not bear to see the face of her Lord. His words had brought no comfort. He did not heal in time. What good was a savior who arrived too late?

In the early morning hours

Joanna's back ached from the weight of the water jug she carried. She would bring water to the house before dawn, to save the grieving sisters a trip to the well this morning. She knew how exhausting grief was. She felt foolish, and more than a little guilty, for abandoning them when the group had entered the village yesterday afternoon. Perhaps this would make up for it.

All was silent as she entered the home. They should be awake by now, fixing breakfast, she thought. Baking the bread, setting out water for washing faces and hands. Oh, poor Martha, poor Mary. They must be too exhausted to even wake up.

Joanna would bake the bread herself. It felt good to be useful. She imagined the women's faces when they saw her in the kitchen, preparing their food, serving them as she had seen them do so often.

Then a dead man walked in.

Joanna screamed, dropping a crock of water on the floor, shattering it.

"You're supposed to be dead!" she shouted.

"I'm sorry," Lazarus said, throwing his hands up in apology, stumbling backward. Disciples came stumbling into the kitchen from all directions. Peter already had his sword drawn, as did Constans.

"What is it?" Peter snapped.

"Where is he?" Constans yelled.

Shocked, Joanna pointed to Lazarus.

"He lives here." Peter frowned in confusion. "Why are you screaming?"

Joanna looked from face to face in confusion. "Lazarus? Lazarus is dead."

Lazarus stood, healthy and whole, his mouth open as if he was trying to explain something. "I was dead. I did die," he said, struggling for the words. "You're right. I'm sorry. I should be dead."

Joanna struggled to catch her breath just as Martha stumbled into the kitchen, quickly surmising what had happened. "Quit apologizing, brother. Peter, get me a towel. I've got to pick the shards up before anyone cuts their feet."

Joanna spoke over Martha. "Lazarus, I am glad you are not dead."

Jesus walked into the kitchen, apparently roused from sleep by the commotion.

Martha held out a hand, stopping Him from coming too close to the broken pottery. She was worried about the Son of God getting a cut on His foot. Joanna thought her mind might burst from the insanity of the situation.

"You raised Lazarus from the dead?" Joanna asked Him. "But he'd already been dead for days!"

The words sounded foolish to her as she said them, but they made sense. Saving someone from death made sense. Bringing someone back from death seconds after they died, that made sense too. But bringing someone back days after they were gone was simply impossible. She'd seen what happened to a body.

Jesus looked at her, His head tilted to one side. "If you believe, you will see the glory of God. Nothing is impossible, Joanna."

"But—"

Everything she should have said that night by the fire got stuck in her throat. If only she had trusted Him enough then to say those things, to confess her doubt! Why had she held on to her doubt? Why hadn't she just told Him the truth about what she was struggling with? Why had she let a little sliver of doubt rob her of witnessing a miracle?

Impossible should be her new favorite word.

"Oh, Joanna, you should have seen it," Martha said, and told her the story, start to finish. The women wept as she relived the details.

Joanna wanted to kick herself. A donkey was smarter than she was, and far less stubborn! She had held on to her private sorrows for far too long. The problem with hanging on to even one little *why?*, she realized, was that it had robbed her of a miracle. Her accusation against Jesus had now changed into an even bigger accusation against herself.

"Come with Me," Jesus said. He took her by the arm, leading her away from the women. "I'll show you the tomb."

As they walked on the dirt path toward the tombs, she finally worked up the courage to ask the question that had worked itself like a splinter into her heart.

"Why did You not heal me?"

Jesus spoke at the same time.

"I didn't have to," He said.

While Joanna was asking the question, Jesus had answered it. She paused, trying to understand.

"Your body was not the reason you were barren," He said. "Chuza's body was. Chuza cannot father children."

"Why did You not tell me?"

"You asked to bear a child, and someday you will."

"I have no husband!" *How could that ever come to pass now?*

Jesus rested His hand on her shoulder. "If I'd told you what I knew about Chuza, it would have put your life in danger. His pride has made him reckless."

"No," she argued. "He is a wise man."

"He was. Once," Jesus agreed. "But his pride and fear have grown unchecked for years. They drive him now. He would never have admitted any weakness in front of Herod. He would have blamed you. In the end, you would have been murdered. Herodias would have seen to that."

He nodded toward the tomb ahead. The stone had been rolled to one side.

"There is nothing to fear, Joanna. Death cannot have you. Sin cannot keep you. Your enemies cannot ruin you. Just trust Me. Trust Me when darkness falls and the final stone has been rolled into place. Trust Me when you think all hope is lost. Trust Me when you think the end has been written."

She peered into the empty darkness of the tomb.

"Will you do that?" He asked.

She looked up at Him, tears filling her eyes.

"Will you trust Me at the very end?" He asked again, urgency in His voice.

She nodded, confusion clouding her mind. "Yes, Lord."

Jesus exhaled, then grinned broadly, seeming to cast a heavy weight off His heart. "Then let's celebrate with Martha and Mary tonight. We will trust God with tomorrow."

Early spring, 33 CE

The wind howled at the door. Joanna shrank back. Why did Jesus want to leave for Jerusalem today? Why could He not wait for the heavy rains to pass by? He seemed to operate on a different schedule now, counting His hours by a measurement known only to Himself.

He spoke to the disciples in the next room. "Yes, it is as I said. We will go to Jerusalem for the Passover. There, I'm going to be betrayed and killed by the religious leaders and teachers of the law."

Constans broke away from the group, going into the kitchen. She followed him there.

"Why does He speak of death? He frightens me," she whispered.

Constans sighed. "His mood has changed of late. He says He will be betrayed and murdered."

"But why should that worry Him?" Joanna asked. "He can do anything, can't He? He knows what people are thinking. He knows what they're planning. He can create miracles and control nature. He can avoid death too."

"I don't know," Constans admitted. "No one knows. We're all willing to fight, but He's walking willingly straight toward it. And He could stop it with a mere word." He paused. "Can I ask you a question?"

She nodded.

"If it comes to that, should I stop Him? Should any of us? If He's not going to defend Himself, His enemies will end His reign before it even begins. Some of us wonder if we need to hold Him hostage, from Himself, I mean. Just until the threat is over."

"Keep Him safe until He's done with Passover and out of Jerusalem?" she asked.

Constans glanced out at the men talking to Jesus in the next room. Peter and Thomas sat together, their shoulders touching. Peter looked up, catching Constans's eye, nodding solemnly.

"I want to say yes," Joanna replied, "but…"

"But you think we should trust His plan?" Constans asked. "He doesn't have one, Joanna. If He does, He hasn't explained it. He's planning on dying in Jerusalem." Constans raised his voice enough that several disciples turned and looked at him.

She'd never heard Constans angry with her like this.

He leaned in, his voice barely above a whisper. "He is going to His death. You need to decide whether you can bear to have that on your conscience. You have a tender heart, Joanna. I don't think you can do this." Constans stood back. "I don't want to see you hurt. Ever again."

Wind shook the roof and bits of straw fluttered down as the sound of rain increased.

"The flowers will be beautiful this year," she murmured. "It will be a beautiful spring."

Constans looked at her, worry in his eyes. "If we can endure what's coming."

Andrew and Matthew whispered to each other, appearing to be in total agreement. Joanna busied herself with her sash, pretending to tighten it as she walked behind them. She wanted to hear every word.

"He fed five thousand men with nothing but a little boy's lunch, remember?" Andrew asked. "It's no coincidence why He chose that number."

Matthew shrugged. "I don't quite see it."

Andrew raised his voice in earnest. "Five? The number of our holy books. And there were twelve baskets left over. Twelve tribes! And the number of men was five thousand. That's a legion of Roman soldiers! Jesus is sending a secret signal to the Israelites."

"But then Jesus sent everyone home," Matthew countered.

"But then He did it again, and most everyone was a Gentile. Four thousand men were fed. Seven loaves. Seven baskets of leftovers."

"So, He was communicating to the Gentiles? In code?" Matthew asked.

Andrew sighed. "I don't know. You're the numbers man. What do the numbers mean to a Gentile? What is Jesus trying to tell them, and us? I don't want to just ask Him."

Joanna stifled a smile. She understood completely. Jesus spoke plainly, yet His stories could be difficult to interpret.

As the group passed by, a man sitting on the side of the road called out to them. He was covered in dust, caked in dried mud.

"What do you want?" Jesus called back.

"I want to see," the man replied.

Joanna gasped. What a strange reply. The man needed money, food, clothes. How could he possibly know that Jesus was near, or that Jesus would honor such a bold request?

"Go," Jesus said without hesitation. "Your faith has healed you."

The man blinked, slowly and heavily, then rapidly, his head whipping side to side. Tears welled in his eyes then cascaded down his cheeks, clearing a path through the brown debris that clung to his face. "My eyes!" he screamed, as his mouth flew open in astonishment. "I can see! I see everything!"

Joanna watched in amazement, not at the miracle, but at Jesus's pleasant attitude toward anyone who asked. Why was Jesus going to allow nearly everyone to have their way?

Oh my God, Joanna prayed, *please let me always want Your way, not mine. Because I think in the new kingdom that Your Son is bringing, we might get what we want. You might say yes to our requests, and we are such small-minded people, all of us.*

She fell to her knees, repenting, as the blind man fell to his knees rejoicing.

Jesus caught her eye, and a gentle peace washed over her.

Yes, He was pleased.

CHAPTER EIGHTEEN

Early spring, 33 CE

The poor had nothing to make a highway for their king.

As the traveling group approached the old city, people ran ahead to cut off branches from trees. Children screamed with delight, announcing the arrival of Jesus into Jerusalem once more. Branches and palm fronds were laid across the rough stone road. People even threw their cloaks down for the donkeys to walk upon.

These people needed their cloaks for shelter. They could offer them as a sign of discipleship, but a cloak was not just a garment. It was a mantle of spiritual authority, passed from father to son, and these they laid down for Jesus.

Joanna watched as the donkeys' long, thick, fringed eyelashes blinked at the commotion and shouts. The animals had never seen such excitement at their arrival.

The children were running and shouting as adults danced in the streets. A Son of David! A King! The children touched Jesus and patted His donkey, taking turns kissing both, making Jesus laugh at their giddiness.

Thomas was the first to mark the Roman guards' sour faces. "They think we are here to start an insurrection against Rome."

The Roman guards indeed remained passive and stoic. Their eyes shadowed by their helmets, they watched Jesus and the disciples with detached scorn.

"Aren't we?" Peter laughed.

Thomas glared at him. "Don't even joke about that out loud. None of us know why He's brought us here. He talks of death and resurrection, not empires."

"Hosanna! Hosanna!" the people cried.

The sun sparkled over the rooftops as the clop of donkey hooves and the swish of tree leaves and branches made a delicate song beneath the lyre and flutes. Women's scarves blowing in the breeze were like flags waving from the upper windows. Jerusalem had turned out in all her finery, and the city did not need wealth for that.

Jesus retreated for the night for food and rest. Huge crowds who saw or heard what He did for Lazarus followed, clamoring for a healing. The atmosphere was electric. Joanna wondered if anyone would sleep. What would be the next stage of Jesus's plan? She did not need to wonder long, for a messenger arrived within the hour.

"Who sent you?" she demanded for the second time.

The nervous young messenger rocked side to side, not wanting to answer. "A friend," he replied at last, shaking his head. "Chuza is ill. You must come to the palace at once. But do not enter through the main gate. Enter through the gardens and use the servants' hallway. Come to his chamber at night. He will be alone."

Why was the messenger so certain he would be alone? Aresh, his wife, did not come to his chambers at night? Poor Chuza. But why the secrecy?

"I am not welcome? I was once a member of the court," Joanna said.

The boy shook his head and left, unwilling to say more. Joanna quickly prepared to go to the palace in Galilee. Constans would accompany her, for security. He agreed to stay a safe distance away once they reached the palace grounds. As Joanna threw her extra robe and sandals into a satchel for the trip, Constans followed the messenger from a discreet distance. An hour later, he returned. "He rode a horse with the colors of the house of Herodias."

Herodias? "Salome!" Joanna cried. "God bless her. Her daughter sent for me. I once tried to be kind to her, and she now repays the debt."

Constans rested a hand on her forearm.

Her breath caught in her chest.

"What could Chuza possibly say that would make up for the past?" Constans asked, his eyes blazing. "You do not need him anymore."

Joanna searched her heart but found no bitterness there for Chuza. She had forgiven him long ago. Looking at Constans, though, she wondered why he had not. She placed her hand on top of his, a new understanding dawning. She promised herself that this time, she would not let soft words stay unspoken.

"I am not going to Chuza because he has something I need," she said quietly. Looking him in the eye, she smiled. "I am going there because I have already been given everything I will ever need. I am going there to let him know he has been forgiven."

Constans leaned forward and kissed her forehead.

"Come back safe," he whispered.

In the palace in Tiberius

Chuza's face was pale and thin, with a greenish cast, and a terrible odor reeked from his skin and breath. Shocked at his appearance, Joanna suspected something unnatural about his illness. He cried out in pain, shifting beneath the thin linen coverlet.

Sitting quietly beside him, she took his hand. "I'm here, Chuza."

His eyelids fluttered open, then closed again. His breathing became deeper and more rhythmic, as if seeing her settled his soul.

In the third watch of the night, she was awakened by his words. She must have drifted off. The journey had been a fast, difficult one.

"You must go, Joanna," he whispered, his voice strained. Everything in her body agreed with his command. The walls of the palace made her skin crawl with apprehension.

"You're awake," she said, forcing a gentle smile. Looking around the room for a bowl of water, she found none.

"Go." His voice was raspy and reed-thin. "She will send someone to see if I am dead yet. You cannot be here."

A chill slid down her spine. "Who has done this to you?" She caught herself. She believed he had been poisoned. But what good would that do to tell him? Could he fight? Have vengeance? No. There could only be peace now. That was all she could offer.

Without water or linens, she could not wipe his sweating brow. Instead, she tore a patch from the sleeve of her robe. It did not matter that she tore her robe. He himself had made the first tear. The bottom of her robe was so filthy now it was hard to complain about that, though. He wouldn't even recognize her if he saw her on the street, she thought. How wonderful that he still knew her face. He must have really loved her once.

She wiped his brow.

"Aresh is pregnant again," he said.

"Yes. You have one son already, and perhaps she will bear you another."

She waited for the words she needed, the admission that he had wronged her.

"I have hidden gold for you," he said. "When I am gone, the palace will no longer offer you any assistance. You can never return."

"Thank you." She choked out the words. She thought he would profess his regret, at least. Profess that a part of him still loved her.

He whispered the location of the gold, in a storekeeper's shop not far from the palace.

"That's all," he said. "Go."

She realized she was being dismissed. He did not know the truth about his new wife, about Aresh's infidelities, about the true paternity of the babies, about all he really lost when he sent her away.

She could tell him the truth. Telling the truth was not a sin, was it?

Didn't every man deserve to know the truth about his life before he died? Didn't she have the right to ask for an apology? He owed her an apology. If he died not knowing the truth, he would die without ever saying he was sorry. And he owed her that debt.

She did not know what to do.

A guard's footsteps in the hall hurried her decision.

CHAPTER NINETEEN

Joanna and Constans returned before the midday meal, anxious to rejoin the group. Constans split off from her as they approached the city gates. He wanted to go directly to the palace where Pilate was. He had business with the government. Joanna wanted to tell Jesus about making her final peace with Chuza, and that she had not revealed the secret she kept. Jesus would be pleased.

Passing the city gates, a crowd of angry protestors jostled her and the donkey. One man shoved her off the animal, grabbing the bridle, taking the beast for himself.

Before Joanna could protest, a hand grabbed her arm, pulling her into an alley.

"John!" She was startled to see one of the disciples. "What are you doing here?"

His face was drawn tight with anxiety. Flecks of dried blood crusted his cheeks. "The other women are desperate to find you. Come with me at once. And keep your face down. It won't be safe for people to recognize you."

"What's going on?"

John crept to the edge of the alley, looked both ways, then signaled her to follow.

"It's Jesus."

Her heart froze. What had He done now? Who had He angered?

John stopped, looking at the dirt at his feet as tears ran down his cheeks. "They're going to crucify Him. Judas betrayed us. Peter has fled. I don't know where the others are either."

Joanna could not move. The air around her became thick, choking off her next breath. Crucifixion was a Roman punishment, for crimes against the Roman government. Jesus was a Jewish citizen and had only been accused of religious improprieties. *Crucifixion was impossible.*

"He hasn't even had a trial!" she said. He couldn't have had one. A trial took days. Witnesses had to be called, plus the judges had to take a full day after the witnesses to deliberate.

"He's had six already today," John answered. "Three government, three Jewish." Joanna staggered back. That was impossible. How many times would that same word echo through her mind today? Never in the history of Rome, or in the history of Jewish law, had such a thing happened.

"Do you remember all the times when Jesus stopped the religious leaders from punishing a woman?" John asked.

Joanna nodded.

"Those punishments are inflicted on Him now. The crowd hurls abuse on Him as He carries His cross through the streets. It is not safe for women in the city. There's no savior to speak for them today. Stay close to me."

Joanna grabbed the sleeve of his garment, and they stepped into the crowd. She saw a palm frond coated in blood lying on the side of the road. The crowd had hailed Jesus as their King only days before. Now the tang of blood was in the air, the cry of the crowd was for vengeance.

Where had such evil sprung from, and so quickly? These people had been healed, fed, liberated from the tyranny of oppression. And now they demanded Rome kill Jesus as the worst of criminals?

She stopped, jerking John's arm back. "Send to Herod. We will demand a new Roman trial. In the capital. That will take days, at least."

"It's too late. They had a trial already."

"Impossible!" She gasped. She hated the word now. "Who testified?"

John's blank expression told her it was a rigged trial.

If only women could testify in court. Jesus had saved and healed so many of them that the court would have heard testimony for days.

A chill swept over her. This appetite for destruction would consume everything in its path, including her. She and John picked up the hems of their robes and ran through the streets.

She arrived at the Place of the Skull, the crucifixion hill, in time to see her Savior lifted on a rough wooden cross. He was unrecognizable. The torture inflicted on Him was so great, she had to look away for fear she would vomit. John led her swiftly to the other women.

Seconds later, she took Mary, the mother of Jesus, into her arms, shielding her from the horror. Joanna did not know her as well as the other women, but the other women had been with her since the predawn hours. They had seen things that left dark shadows beneath their eyes, mouths hanging open in trauma. Joanna was the only one remaining with the physical strength left to hold Mary and hold her ears closed from the dreadful sounds of her son's screams.

The agony of the poor woman was unimaginable. Joanna had once longed to give birth, and now her sacred job was to help a mother watch her child leave this world. His was a bloody departure. The women clung to one another through the hours of agony. Mary pleaded over and over to die alongside her son.

Each breath Mary took seemed to betray her breaking heart. She pleaded for it to be over. There was no way Jesus would live, so she wanted His death to be mercifully quick. Except that this was a crucifixion, and there was nothing merciful or quick about it.

The Jews did not teach about eternal torment, but they did not need to. Joanna knew now what it was, what it smelled and sounded like. She closed her eyes and prayed to be delivered from this place.

Mary travailed for long hours to deliver her son back into the arms of God. Joanna and the other women stayed at her side, midwives to her agony. They watched her, helpless, as she groaned and writhed in extraordinary pain, sweated and panted as her heart was ripped from her body, cried until her eyes were bloodshot and swollen.

At the last, the delirium of pain took Jesus to another place, where the whites of His eyes rolled back. His mother stayed at the edge, calling Him to come back, screaming to the heavens for a miracle that did not come. Dark clouds appeared on the horizon, swiftly churning. These were not storm clouds, nor the clouds of spring. These were clouds of wrath. Joanna felt a cold dread at the sight of their black race across the sky.

Suddenly, He looked at His mother, then at all of them. He called John over and committed His mother into his care.

As Jesus's final moments came, a wail arose from Mary that stopped everyone and all conversation.

In the hush that followed, Jesus spoke. "It is finished."

His body collapsed but was held to the cross by the nails. He was gone.

Mary, spent from grief, her body having given up her child for a second time, fainted as dark clouds rushed overhead, and the ground shook with rage. The birds took up her lament, the cry of all grieving mothers. A great earthquake began. The mute rocks had no voice, except to tremble, and so they did, the very ground shaking in mad fury. The earth split, its heart torn at the sight of the Creator crucified, the creation willing itself to die with Him.

Christ was dead.

CHAPTER TWENTY

After the crucifixion, John carried Jesus's mother home. Late in the evening she awoke. Mary Magdalene heated broth and spoon-fed her, insisting that she eat. The poor woman had not eaten or drunk since the day before, and the tears she had shed could surely have filled the Sea of Galilee.

Joanna was grateful that Mary Magdalene had such stamina. Joanna felt like she had been stoned with heavy boulders by an angry crowd. Every bone in her body hurt. Every muscle screamed. Her eyes were dry and scratchy.

But Mary Magdalene was a force of nature. Joanna watched her, grateful. Jesus had healed her of many demons, but Mary never talked about that other life much. She always preferred to talk about what Jesus was doing, not just what He had done. Joanna was so grateful for their differences at this moment, because Joanna did not know what to do. Even worse, she did not want to do anything.

Mary, Jesus's mother, caught her glance and patted the cushion next to her. She sat by the low dining table. Joanna stood and crossed the room to sit with her, ignoring her protesting body.

"Have I told you of His birth?" Mary asked.

"No. I have heard rumors. Only rumors," Joanna confessed.

"All of you, come closer," Mary said, her voice barely above a whisper. "I will tell you of the night an angel appeared to me."

"Do you have the strength, mother?" Mary Magdalene asked.

"No," Mary replied. "That is why I must. I need to survive this first night without my son, so I will tell a story. Stories of God are our strength. Let me tell you of a young, naive girl whose only thought was of the handsome boy she was soon to marry. That was me, many years ago. My heart was set on becoming a carpenter's wife, and I could imagine no greater honor…."

Joanna and the other women sat around Mary as she began the tale. Outside the window, the world was silent. No birds sang. No insects keened in the night. The wind did not rush past the trees. All was quiet except for the voice of a woman.

One by one, they told the story of how Jesus came into their lives.

No one could bear to think of a future without Jesus. Whenever the thought threatened to disrupt their peace, someone began a new story. They held on in the darkness together, in the long pause before dawn, between the worst of tragedies and the unfolding of grace. They held on to each other and were held together by their stories.

Before dawn on the third day

In the darkness of the kitchen, while the others were sleeping, Joanna checked the myrrh to be sure she had enough. The lid was tight on the jar, which was a good sign, and the myrrh inside was a sticky, thick golden-yellow resin. Mary Magdalene had bought the aloes and linen, and Constans had set fresh torches outside the door. The women would leave before dawn.

"His mother and aunt insist on coming with us," Joanna whispered to Mary, who padded softly in to join her. "I don't think that's a good idea. We need to go first. Make sure Joseph wrapped the body properly. His body was in such poor condition. We may need to rewrap the body before we let Mary see Him."

"I have already seen the worst," his mother replied.

With a start, Joanna turned. "I did not mean to offend you, mother. I am only trying to protect you."

"I know." Mary patted her on the arm. "But you cannot keep me from this. Let us go."

The cave was in a garden, and Joseph had sent word how to find it. As they approached the site, the scent of grass crushed underfoot rose to meet the women. Why, Joanna thought, did Joseph bury her Lord here, in a garden? Once, a garden had meant certain peace. A garden had been her one true refuge in the world, and once a sacred place is lost to a woman, who can restore that?

Joanna remembered Jesus's words to her. He had promised that life would begin again in a garden. How cruel His promises seemed right now! He promised life, and she was walking toward death. He promised that she would walk in a garden and find joy again, and yet here she was, carrying spices to anoint a corpse. Where was joy? Where was the promise now?

Mary, Jesus's mother, spoke softly as they walked. She said they should be pleased—Joseph bought a new tomb, one never used before. He had also applied his own burial spices to the body, so it had eased Mary's mind a little bit. What a mercy that Joseph had cared for the body properly. Crucified bodies were not permitted such graces, so Joseph must surely have bribed an official, or perhaps his good name had secured this unmerited favor.

Joanna did not understand how the woman found the strength to walk, much less to find things to be thankful for. She worried that Mary would never recover from seeing her son publicly tortured and killed.

Approaching the cave, Joanna felt weak with fear and dread at the thought of seeing Jesus's shredded, lifeless body. She had never seen a dead man in his tomb, and now she would handle one intimately, anointing and wrapping his broken, bloody limbs. She could not bear the thought of touching His face or His mouth.

His mother cried out first. "The stone!"

Looking up, Joanna saw it too. The stone that sealed the entrance to the cave had been moved. The cave stood open, exposed to the elements, to predators, thieves, and the disrespectful.

His mother sank to the ground with a cry of despair. "What have they done to You now, my son?"

Joanna lifted her, staggering to catch her balance. Mary Magdalene ran ahead.

Mary peered into the cave then turned back to face the women, color draining from her face. "They've taken His body," she said quietly. "I will go and tell the others." She lifted her face, surveying the garden in the quiet of the last dark moments before dawn. "Wait here for the men. The soldiers won't return to the tomb now that they've taken the body, but it won't be safe on the streets once daylight breaks."

Then she ran at once for the disciples.

Joanna looked side to side for a place to let Jesus's mother sit. Mary was limp with shock. Her sister fretted over her, but she was not able to help much, Joanna thought. Joanna didn't want Mary Magdalene to run back to the disciples, not now, not when Joanna needed her here.

Suddenly in the darkness two piercing white lights overwhelmed the women, one on each side. Gasping from the intensity of the white flames that burst suddenly to life beside them, the women dropped to the ground. Extending their hands into the blinding void, eyes squeezed tightly shut, they groaned in terror.

And a voice replied to them, cheerful as a sparrow's song in spring. "Why do you look for the living among the dead? He is not here; He has risen!"

The light receded. Blinking, their eyes watering and stinging, one by one the women sat up. Two men stood in front of them, their robes shimmering white. The men helped the women to stand.

"Remember how He told you," the man on the left said, "while He was still with you in Galilee: 'The Son of Man must be delivered over to the hands of sinners, be crucified, and on the third day be raised again.'"

A hush fell over the women.

Then Jesus's mother said three words. Three words that shocked Joanna's heart back to life, back into rhythm, and she hadn't even realized she had stopped breathing until that moment.

"He is risen," she gasped.

The angel on the right nodded, laughing. "He is risen indeed," he replied.

And the women cried out, but in joy, and the angels laughed. And in front of the empty grave, the women cried and clutched each other tightly, and danced, and the angels joined them too. In the brilliant light of dawn, a thousand flowers opened across the garden, and their fragrance was sweet.

Since that morning, many graves have been emptied, many angels have danced, and many women's shouts have echoed throughout eternity.

He is risen. He is risen, indeed.

FACTS BEHIND *the Fiction*

FIRST-CENTURY PALACE INTRIGUES

Herod Antipas, Jewish ruler of Galilee, divorced his wife so he could marry his half brother's wife, Herodias. And Herodias divorced her husband, Herod II (aka Herod Philip I), so she could marry Herod.

That was rude by any measure of etiquette. It was also illegal. Jewish law considered this marriage incestuous. "Do not have sexual relations with your brother's wife, for this would violate your brother" (Leviticus 18:16 NLT). Besides, "it is abhorrent" (Leviticus 20:21 NASB), and John the Baptist called Herod on it.

Herod's bride, Herodias, deeply offended by John's condemnation, made a call of her own—for "the head of John the Baptist" (Mark 6:24). It came on a platter, compliments of her daughter.

Herodias's daughter, Salome, danced at a birthday party for her stepfather Herod (reigned 4 BC–AD 39). He was pleased, and so, in front of the party crowd, he promised to grant her a wish. Before Salome responded to his offer, she consulted with her mother, hoping to please her. Herodias said what she wanted most was for Salome to ask for the head of John.

Herod didn't want to kill the popular prophet. But more than that, apparently, he didn't want to suggest to his guests that he was a king who couldn't keep a promise to his own stepdaughter. So John the Baptist was executed.

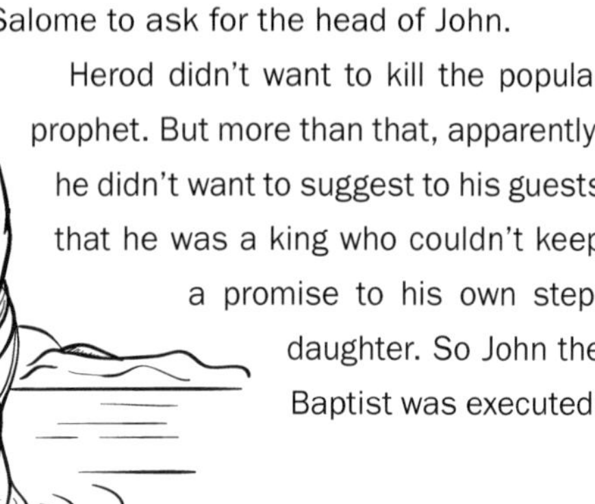

JOHN THE BAPTIST BAPTIZING JESUS

MORE PALACE INTRIGUE

Herod was supposed to be spending quality time with his half brother in Rome when he fell in love with his brother's wife. Secret divorce and wedding plans followed, but word got out and news made its way back home to Herod's lakeside palace in the city of Tiberias in Galilee. His soon-to-be ex, Phasaelis, packed her bags and went back to her father, Aretas, King of Rome's Arabia province.

That sprawling territory ran along the Arab side of the Jordan River, all the way down to the Red Sea. It dwarfed Herod's jurisdiction.

Both rulers sent their armies to fight over what they called a boundary dispute. But first-century Jewish historian, Josephus (AD 37–circa 100), said Aretas used this as an excuse to punish Herod for insulting him and his princess daughter. Herod lost the battle and much of his army.

HEROD ANTIPAS,
AS DEPICTED BY JAMES TISSOT

Josephus reported, "Some Jews thought God allowed Herod's army to be destroyed as a fair punishment for what Herod did to John, who was called the Baptist" (*Antiquities of the Jews*, Book 18, chapter 5).

A few years later, Herodias prodded her husband to write the new emperor, Caligula, and ask for a promotion from Herod's formal title of "tetrarch" to "king."

As it turned out, Herodias's own brother, Herod Agrippa I, was disgusted by her marriage. He grew up in Rome as a friend of Caligula, and he convinced Caligula that Herod's request was treasonous. Caligula fired Herod and exiled him to what is now France, and Herodias went with him.

COIN OF HEROD ANTIPAS

FIGS: THE FIRST FRUIT?

Figs have been a food staple since ancient days and would have been common fare in the time of Joanna and Chuza. Experts suggest that *Ficus carica,* the fig tree, is one of the earliest plants cultivated by humans, preceding even wheat and barley. The fig is mentioned in forty-four verses in Scripture, and is the third tree mentioned in the Bible, after the Tree of Life and the Tree of the Knowledge of Good and Evil. See Genesis 3:7, in which Adam and Eve sewed fig leaves together to cover their newly discovered nakedness. In other places, Scripture uses the fig to represent abundance (Deuteronomy 8:8-10), and safety and prosperity (1 Kings 4:25). The Bible also occasionally uses the fig as a symbol for Israel (for example, Joel 2:21-25). See Micah 7:1; Jeremiah 8:13; and Hosea 9:10-17, which refer to God searching Israel for early figs.

In the New Testament, Jesus talked about a budding fig tree (Matthew 24:32-35; Mark 13:28-31; Luke 21:29-33) as a symbol that the Kingdom of God was near, and about a barren tree (Luke 13:6-9). Jesus famously cursed a fig tree in Matthew 21:18-22 and Mark 11:12-20 in what some biblical scholars interpret as a visual parable about faithful prayer or a warning about not bearing spiritual fruit.

FIG LEAVES AND FRUIT

JOHN THE BAPTIST IN A ROMAN HISTORY BOOK

John the Baptist is one of the few Bible characters who is mentioned in a Roman history book.

First-century historian Josephus had this to say about John, who was beheaded a few years before Josephus was born:

"John was a good man. He taught the Jews to live as good human beings, both in the way they treated one another and in the reverence they showed toward God.

"He told the people to get baptized. He said that washing would purify their bodies and make them acceptable to God. He presumed they had already purified their souls and were living lives devoted to God.

"Crowds of people gathered around him, and what he taught them moved them deeply" (*Antiquities of the Jews*, Book 18, chapter 5).

Josephus went on to report the execution of John, but he offers a different version than the Bible does. Perhaps he drew on sources other than ones the Gospel writers used.

Bible writers said Herod executed John reluctantly, after Herod promised to grant a wish for his stepdaughter, who wished for "the head of John the Baptist on a tray!" (Matthew 14:8 NLT).

Josephus said Herod felt threatened by John's popularity. "He was afraid John might use his influence over the people to provoke a rebellion. It certainly looked to Herod as though the people would do anything John asked. Herod decided that his best course of action would be to execute John, to keep him from causing any trouble."

Indeed, Matthew reports that Herod wanted to kill John, but it adds that Herod was reluctant because "the people thought John was a prophet, and Herod was afraid of what they might do" (Matthew 14:5 CEV).

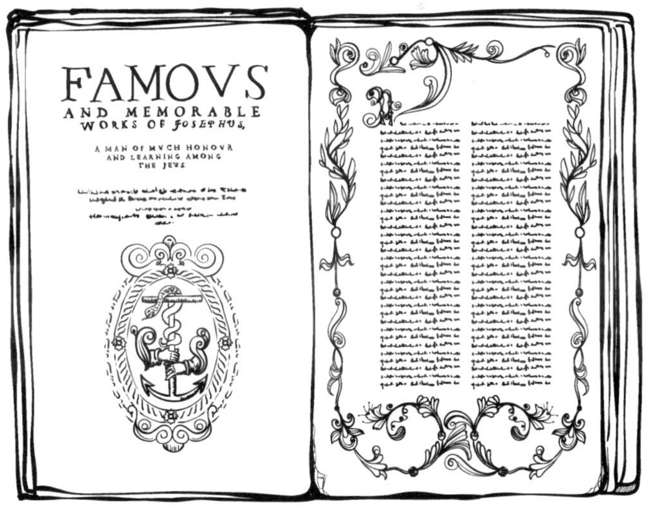

PAGES FROM FLAVIUS JOSEPHUS'S *ANTIQUITIES OF THE JEWS*

SALOME

Bible writers didn't tell us the name of the woman who demanded the head of John the Baptist. But she shows up in a Roman history book as Salome.

Gospels Matthew, Mark, and Luke simply identify her as the daughter of Herodias and stepdaughter of Herod Antipas:

"When Herod's birthday came, the daughter of Herodias danced for the guests. She pleased Herod so much that he swore to give her whatever she wanted. But the girl's mother told her to say, 'Here on a platter I want the head of John the Baptist!'" (Matthew 14:6–8 CEV).

Josephus said Salome married a man well placed in society. She married her stepfather's brother, Philip the Tetrarch (also known as Herod Philip II), her uncle. He was one of the sons of Herod the Great. Rome had appointed him tetrarch, the same title Antipas carried. That title was one step below a king.

Philip ruled three provinces north and east of Galilee, in what are now parts of Israel, Lebanon, and Syria. He died childless. Salome then married one of Herod's great-grandsons: her cousin, Aristobulus of Chalcis. Aristobulus, until about AD 92, ruled as tetrarch of Chalcis, a region along the northeastern border of Israel. The couple had three boys and gave them family names: Herod, Agrippa, and Aristobulus.

Queen Salome's picture appears on coins from her husband's kingdom, which expanded into eastern Turkey and Armenia, where Mount Ararat lies among the Armenian Highlands.

SALOME ON A COIN

So what if Herod Antipas divorced his first wife, princess Phasaelis? some would argue. Jewish law said he could: Moses said if a man considered his wife and "discovered something wrong with her" all he had to do to divorce her was to write her a note. Essentially, "We're divorced. You are free to remarry." Appropriately, this note is called a *get*. It is not a Hebrew word. Scholars guess the Jews may have picked it up during an earlier nationwide exile to what is now Iraq. It's similar to the Sumerian and the Akkadian words for a written document: *gidda* and *gittu*.

"He writes a document of divorce, hands it to her, and sends her away" (Deuteronomy 24:1 NLT).

There's no indication Herod followed Jewish protocol, certainly not in remarrying his sister-in-law Herodias—something Moses outlawed as incest. In addition, Jewish law didn't allow a woman to divorce her husband for any reason, though Herodias divorced her Jewish husband. By Roman standards, though, Herod and Herodias were properly divorced and married.

To divorce, all a Roman citizen had to do was find the nearest door and leave. Romans considered it good form to tell the ex about the divorce—and to tell a group of witnesses. First-century Roman historian Valerius Maximus reported that friends of a nobleman got upset with him for divorcing without telling them and without considering how the divorce would affect their network of friends.

A woman left a marriage with whatever dowry of assets she brought into it, unless she committed adultery. In this case, the ex-wife could get half. If the husband committed adultery, there was no penalty. Men wrote the rules in first-century Rome.

The reason it was so easy for Romans to divorce was because marriage wasn't legally binding. Marriage was simply a couple agreeing to live together. Because it was so easy to divorce, lots of Romans did it. The upper classes were most prone to divorce, often because they were looking for ways to climb higher and get richer. Herodias probably considered Herod an upgrade, until the emperor charged him with treason, fired him, and banished him to what is now France.

Parents often arranged the marriage, looking for an angle to elevate the family status. Families orchestrated a formal wedding ceremony in which the couple exchanged vows and then sealed those promises with a kiss. But the event was just an agreement to live together. Romans called it *affectio maritalis*, "marital affection"—their version of "matrimony," the state of being married.

Marriage was an affectionate agreement that lasted as long as the affection.

RELIEF OF FIRST-CENTURY COUPLE'S WEDDING SCENE

Roman fathers of the bride generally contributed a dowry to the marriage. It went to the groom, as a gift the bride could take back if the couple divorced.

The bigger the dowry, the more power the woman brought to the marriage, because the harder it would be for the husband to divorce her.

Here's a marriage agreement from about 13 BC in Roman-occupied Egypt. The couple was Thermion, bride, and Apollonius, groom. Think of them as Joanna and Chuza from our story. Here is what their marriage agreement might well have looked like. (We've filled in some numbers that didn't survive the years.)

Joanna and Chuza today agree that they will live together. Chuza confirms that he has received from Joanna's father a dowry of one pair of gold earrings weighing 48 grams [1.6 ounces], along with 3,000 silver drachmas [about 10 years of salary for a typical worker]. From this day on, Chuza promises to clothe Joanna

FIRST-CENTURY GOLD EARRINGS

and provide her with all other necessities of life. He promises not to mistreat her, abandon her, or marry another woman. If he does [any of those things], he agrees to return one and a half times the value of her dowry. Joanna agrees to do her duty as a wife. And she promises not to leave the house for a day or overnight without Chuza's consent. She promises, also, not to hurt their marriage or become romantically or physically involved with another man. If she breaks this promise, she agrees to forfeit her dowry and pay the designated fine [in some cases, a third of her personal property].

Fiction Author
GINGER GARRETT

Ginger graduated from SMU in Dallas, Texas, with a degree in theatre arts and a focus on playwriting. Although she applied to the CIA to become an international master of espionage, she had to settle for selling pharmaceuticals for a large corporation. She eventually traveled the world on her own dime and without a disguise.

Ginger now lives in Atlanta with her husband, three children, and two rescue dogs. She spends her time baking gluten-free goodness for her friends and family and mentors middle school students who want to become working writers. Passionate about science, history, and women's studies, Ginger loves exploring new ideas and old secrets. She especially loves good books read late at night.

Ginger is a popular speaker and a frequent radio and television guest. She has been featured by media across the country.

Nonfiction Author
STEPHEN M. MILLER

Stephen M. Miller is an award-winning, best-selling Christian author of easy-reading books about the Bible and Christianity. His books have sold over 1.9 million copies.

Miller lives in the suburbs of Kansas City with his wife, Linda, a registered nurse. They have two married children who live nearby.

THE LAST DROP OF OIL: ADALIAH'S STORY

by Virginia Smith

Dawn broke before Adaliah was ready. The lightening eastern sky crept over the dark silhouette of the distant hills with surprising speed. She fumbled with the rope as she pulled the jug from the depths of the well. Itthobaal would be awake, dressed, and waiting for her when she returned to their house. An image of his face—eyes narrowed with impatience, lips drawn tight—rose before her, and she nearly lost her grip on the rope.

"Pay attention," the woman next to her snapped. Her arm shot out to grab the rope before the jug fell back into the well. "You'll break the jug with your clumsiness."

Adaliah kept her gaze on the woman's hands, but from the corner of her eye she saw the smirk the woman turned on the others who waited their turn to draw water.

"Maybe that's her aim." The second in line wore a blue scarf over her dark hair. Her voice took on a sneer. "Then her husband could sell the village a new one at a fat profit."

"No, Keprea, the new well jug would come from your husband's kiln." Though the first woman spoke to her friend, her taunting gaze remained fixed on Adaliah. "Why give profit to the husband of one so inept at the simplest of tasks, like drawing water?"

The barb struck home, and Adaliah shut her eyes against the sting. Inept. The word was one she heard often at home. Her cooking was inferior to that of Itthobaal's first wife. Her stitching was not as fine. Adaliah's patch of garden produced an inadequate harvest in comparison to the bounty of Maresheh's. If Adaliah had dared to argue, she could have pointed out that the drought that gripped the land had squeezed every drop of life from any vegetables she might have been able to coax from the dry soil. But an argument would only earn her a slap, so she held her tongue. Besides, it might launch another long tribute to the incomparable merits of his first wife.

Indeed, Maresheh must have had the blood of gods running through her veins, for every task she performed had been done to perfection, according to Itthobaal and his daughter.

Every task except the most important. An inner smile accompanied the thought of Danel, the beautiful son she had born Itthobaal four years ago.

Aware that the women watched her closely, Adaliah kept her face a stoic mask. She hauled the clay jug over the lip of the well and filled her jar with clear, fresh water, then set the jug down on the stone with excessive care. Without meeting anyone's eye, she hefted her container to her shoulder and left the well. The murmur of their whispers faded behind her.

A western breeze carried the salty scent of the Great Sea through the nearly silent village. An increasing glow behind the hills illuminated the horizon, but the sun's fingers had yet to spread into the sky. Perhaps fortune would be with her, and Itthobaal would not yet have emerged from the bedchamber they shared. She might yet be able to assemble the morning meal of bread, olives, and cheese before he became aware of her lateness. She increased her pace, careful not to slosh precious water from the jar, her sandals kicking up dust on the village's main street.

When she rounded the corner, her hopes shrank. The curtain on the ground floor window of Itthobaal's house stood open, and the light of a lamp flickered inside. An invisible hand constricted her stomach. He had awakened, and she had not been there with his morning meal.

Steeling herself with a deep breath, she pushed open the door.

"*Imma!*"

Her son flung himself toward her, arms thrown wide. Adaliah braced herself in the seconds before he crashed into her and wrapped her legs in a fierce hug. Even so, water sloshed over the rim of the jar and spilled down her back.

"Watch out, woman," Itthobaal growled from across the room. "That's one of my finest pieces. If you break it…"

He left the threat hanging, and Adaliah had no trouble filling the gap. In the almost five years since her wedding she'd learned what could happen when she angered Itthobaal.

Danel released her and threw his head back to fix dark eyes on her face. "I woke up, and I looked for you."

"I was at the well. The task took longer than expected," she told the child, with a glance toward her husband. "There was a crowd at the well."

His nostril curled in a sneer. "Get there earlier tomorrow."

Nodding, she disengaged herself from Danel and unwrapped her linen scarf from her head and neck. When it hung on its peg by the door, she hurried to the sturdy worktable in the corner. If the only punishment for her tardiness was a scolding, Itthobaal was in a good mood. That boded well for the day.

She filled two cups with the milk she had gotten from their goat before her trip to the well and set them on the thick mat that served as their table. Both Itthobaal and Danel sank onto their cushions. Itthobaal raised his cup as she hurried to assemble the rest of the meal.

"Do you see this, boy?" He held the item aloft between them. "That's fine work at the wheel. Some men think all they have to do is slap on a lump of clay and give the wheel a few kicks. But a piece like this takes skill. Look how thin the sides are, and not a flaw anywhere. Why, King Ethbaal himself would be proud to have a piece like this on his table."

Danel nodded, his eyes round.

Adaliah took a large bowl from a shelf and removed the oiled cloth covering a lump of creamy goat cheese. This bowl was another of Itthobaal's pieces, and a fine one. The glaze with which it had been finished matched that of the water jar she'd filled, a crystalline sea-green with the faintest hint of copper, a blend of Itthobaal's making. The words of the women came back to her. Though he would be quick to turn a profit given the chance, no one could doubt that Itthobaal's pottery was among the most beautiful produced by anyone in Zarephath.

"Will you show me how to make a cup like yours, *Abba*?"

The admiration in the child's tone brought a smile to her face. Danel looked up to his father, and the realization never failed to soothe even the foulest of Itthobaal's moods.

Adaliah set the platter containing their meal on the mat and sank onto her own cushion.

"What is this?" Itthobaal picked up an olive and held it between his thumb and forefinger. "I'm sick to death of olives. Where are the dates?"

"There were none in the market." She worked hard to keep her tone even. "Nor grapes either. The drought has frightened people. Instead of selling what they have, they hold it close."

Disgusted, he tossed the olive back onto the platter and snatched up a cake of barley bread. He smeared on a thick layer of cheese. "When Maresheh set a meal before me there were always dates." He lifted the bread and cheese to his mouth and paused to eye her over it. "She knew my likes. After nearly five years, I'd think you would have learned."

Adaliah lowered her gaze and bit her tongue. Had she not just told him there were no dates to be found in all of Zarephath? She picked up an olive and bit into it. They may not be Itthobaal's favorite, but they grew in abundance in the area around Zarephath. She'd become adept at curing and seasoning them, and she relished the salty, slightly bitter taste that invaded her mouth. Next time a bit more coriander, if she could find some.

Across the mat, Itthobaal munched his bread and focused his attention on Danel. "Yes, I will certainly teach you to make cups, and pots and bowls and jars as well. One day you will run my kiln."

"I will?" The boy's eyes grew round. "When?"

Itthobaal chuckled at the eager question. "When I'm too old to kick the wheel."

At the unexpected show of mirth, Adaliah dared to lift her eyes. The pride on his face as he gazed at his son stirred her heart. Danel could always make his father smile like none other. Her gaze strayed to a crumb nestled in his beard, which was more gray than black these days. His hair too was heavy with silver. When he had first come to Sidon to claim her as his bride, her spirits had fallen when she saw that her new husband's hair had more gray than her own father's had. She'd hoped to marry a younger man, someone kind and handsome, for whom she could make a happy home. Within hours, that hope lay dead on the floor of her bridal chamber.

Yet the union had brought her the most prized blessing of all.

Danel picked up his own cup and gazed at it, dark eyes full of wonder. "One day I will make even better cups than this."

Her breath caught in her chest. Would Itthobaal take the childish comment as an implied insult? Had she voiced it he surely would have.

But he threw back his head and laughed, clearly delighted with the boy's enthusiasm. "To be sure. But not for a long time, my eager son. You have much to learn." He popped an olive into his mouth. "Would you like to begin today?"

Danel's face lit. "I may go with you to the kiln today?"

"Yes. It is time you learn the trade."

The child's delighted gaze flew to Adaliah. "Will Imma come too?"

The question elicited a scornful blast. "To my kiln?"

Danel looked at her, concerned. "But you will be alone all day."

She had no chance to reply.

"She will stay here and try to make a decent evening meal for our return." Itthobaal's tone underwent a change when directed toward her. "I expect something other than olives. And at least an attempt at good bread." He tossed a crust onto the platter. "I almost cracked a tooth biting into an unground kernel. After nearly five years I would think you could manage a better cake of bread."

Though the rebuke stung, such a look of worry covered Danel's face that she pasted on a smile. "I have plenty of work to fill my time," she told him. "And I'll visit the market to see if any of the sellers will part with a few dates." Her smile deepened. "Or perhaps an apple."

The mention of his favorite fruit brightened the boy's expression. She left the platter on the mat and tied Danel's sandals. He had yet to master tying, his small fingers awkward with the thin leather strips. He watched the procedure intently, always eager to learn. In that way he was more like her than his father, who bristled at any change to his everyday routine. She kept her movements slow so he could see. Then she helped him don his outer tunic.

When she straightened, Itthobaal grabbed her upper arm in a fierce grip and jerked her face close to his, his eyes glittering.

"I give you coin to buy food, since you can't seem to grow any on your own." His breath stank of last night's wine. "If I see no better return for my money than that"—he jerked his chin toward the dining mat— "maybe I will pay Tanytha to cook my meals."

He released her with a shove that sent her stumbling backward as he stomped out the doorway. The threat of inviting his daughter, whom he clearly considered as capable as her late mother, sent a cold shiver down Adaliah's spine. Tanytha would love nothing better than to announce Adaliah's ineptitude to the entire village.

Danel came close and tilted his head to look up at her. He gestured for her to bend close to him and when she did, he whispered, "I like olives."

Then they were gone. She stared after them, rubbing her arm, where a bruise would surely appear by evening.

Adaliah dribbled a bit of water over a wilting potato plant. The time to harvest lay weeks away still, but from the looks of the pitiful plant the yield would be meager. In years past her small courtyard garden had produced a generous array of potatoes, carrots, cucumbers, and celery that had made her chest swell with pride, even though Itthobaal insisted that Maresheh's garden had always proven more bountiful. Now the sandy soil was dry and cracked, without enough moisture to properly nourish even an onion.

The priests who served at the gods' temple placed the blame for this drought on a Hebrew prophet who commanded the skies to subdue the rain and the ground to hold back the dew. His reason, they said, was to force King Ahab to put aside his wife, Jezebel, because she lived a life completely devoted to Baal. They pronounced elaborate curses on all prophets of the Hebrew God and claimed victory when they announced that the queen's guards had unearthed yet another hiding place and put the false prophets to the sword. And yet the drought continued.

Adaliah let a few more drops of water fall from her jug onto a sadly drooping carrot plant. Sightings of the princess—now Ahab's queen—had been a regular occurrence during her childhood. Princess Jezebel had enjoyed frequent excursions into various parts of Sidon, always accompanied by a full complement of palace soldiers. When the trumpeters announced the advancing royal party, Adaliah and her friends would race to the roof of whatever house was closest, eager for an unimpeded view of the beautiful princess. For the next several days their conversations focused on the princess's shining raven hair, her silken gowns, the gemstones set in gold that adorned her fingers, wrists, and neck.

A loud bleating drew Adaliah's attention to the small olive tree, where their goat Boz was tied. She straightened, massaging an ache from the small of her back, careful not to spill a drop of the precious water. Boz bleated again, the sound reminiscent of Danel's cries when he was an infant.

"You wouldn't have to be tied up if you could be trusted not to eat the vegetables," she told the unhappy animal.

As if the drought wasn't devastating enough on her garden, Boz's taste for vegetables had destroyed her cucumbers when he escaped his pen a few weeks ago. Itthobaal had come home to find Adaliah weeping and a fretful Danel trying to comfort her. He became so enraged he aimed a series of kicks at the poor animal, until Danel threw his spindly arms around Boz's neck to protect her. Instead Itthobaal loosed his wrath on the small pen, which still lay in a pile of splinters. Then he pointed an accusing finger at Adaliah for her inability to manage her household as a good wife should.

She shuddered at the memory. That had not been a good night.

"I know you're hungry, but we need these potatoes," she told the goat.

She covered the distance between them and poured water into the urn she kept beneath the tree for Boz. The goat drank it dry and then looked up, her expression hopeful. Adaliah placed a hand on the animal's head and scratched the coarse hair between the horns. Boz had grown thinner in recent weeks and her milk less plentiful, ever since the shepherd charged with taking a small flock into the plains had declared that steps must be taken to ration the dwindling grasses there. The village leaders had responded by limiting the flock's grazing to half days in an effort to prolong the inevitable.

"I'll go to the cistern tonight," she promised Boz.

Water collected in the giant pit was deemed useful for animals, on which the clear well water should not be wasted. Zarephath's cisterns were being emptied at an alarming rate, and no new rain had fallen to refill them. Before long, there would be no water for the animals at all, and then…

She turned her head to look toward the house, where the statue of Baal stood near the doorway leading into the main floor of the house. When she arrived in Zarephath as a bride, Itthobaal told her the idol had been crafted by his father's own hands and baked in the kiln that had provided his family's livelihood since his grandfather's day. Privately she thought it a grotesque depiction of the god, with horns protruding from its head and its arms thrown wide. In one hand it held a thunderbolt in the shape of a spearhead. The expression on its bull-shaped face was one of cruelty, and it never failed to send a shiver down Adaliah's spine. She much preferred the statue she'd brought from her father's home in Sidon, which stood on a shelf in their bedchamber. That image of the god's face had no features, and its body was formed of graceful curves as suited the god of fertility.

Of course, Baal was also the god of storms and rain, was he not? She lifted her gaze to where the afternoon sun glittered in a clear blue sky. He wasn't attending to his chores lately. Or maybe the God that Hebrew prophet served had bested the mighty Baal in the matter of rain and dew.

Shocked by the irreverent thought, she gave Boz's head a final scrub and hurried toward the house. When she passed the god's image, she averted her eyes lest he see the blasphemous thoughts in them.

She entered the living chamber to find Tanytha standing at her worktable, peeking beneath the oiled cloth that covered the remains of the goat cheese. The woman snatched her hand back, guilt flashing onto her face. A moment later the expression disappeared, replaced with one of haughty arrogance that reminded Adaliah sharply of her father.

"Tending to that pitiful patch of garden, were you?" Even the woman's voice held the same snide tone as Itthobaal's.

In the past five years Adaliah had become adept at hiding her emotions behind a cool mask of pleasant indifference. "The past months have not been kind to my garden," she admitted. "Though I'm sure your harvest will be as plentiful as your mother's always was."

Tanytha's eyes narrowed as though trying to decide whether to take the comment as a compliment or an insult. Apparently, she settled on the former. "Baal has gifted me with my mother's way with plants."

Adaliah bit back a comment to the effect that the god had better begin spreading that gift around, else he would have no worshippers left. Instead she carried the empty water jug across the room and set it beside the door, ready to be filled this evening when the sun's fierce rays were hidden behind the Great Sea.

"Abba and the boy paid me a visit on their way to the shop."

Tanytha's refusal to refer to Danel by name always set Adaliah's teeth on edge. The woman had hated Adaliah even before her arrival in Zarephath, and that feeling only intensified when Adaliah confided her pregnancy a short time later. At first Adaliah made excuses for Tanytha's intense dislike of her. How difficult it must be to welcome a stepmother into the home when her dear mother had been gone for only a few months. And with Danel's birth, how humiliating to see the father she adored transfer his affections from his only daughter to his newborn son.

Adaliah had cherished hopes that the enmity between them might pass when Tanytha wed Resheph, the handsome son of a maker of purple dye. But as the months, and then years, passed without a child of her own, Tanytha's dislike had deepened. Now, four years after her wedding night, the woman's waist was still as slim as a maiden's. She was barely civil to Danel, and only rarely to Adaliah.

"Did they?" Adaliah forced an agreeable expression. "That must have been pleasant."

Tanytha snorted. "Abba asked me if it was true that there were no dates to be found in the marketplace." She half turned toward the worktable and picked up a wrapped bundle Adaliah hadn't noticed before. "I told him I had no trouble finding dates and offered to bring some for his evening meal."

Now Adaliah did have trouble suppressing a grimace. When Itthobaal returned he would accuse her of lying.

"How kind of you," she managed to say. "From whom did you buy them? I've asked everywhere in the market."

"What do you expect? You're an outsider in Zarephath." Tanytha straightened her shoulders. "I'm one of them, something you will never be."

The statement slapped Adaliah. It was true. She didn't have a single friend in the entire village, thanks, she suspected, to the vicious tongue of the woman standing in front of her. The memory of Maresheh cast a deep, dark shadow in which Adaliah was completely hidden from view. She was an outsider in the village, just as she was an outsider in her own home.

She drew a slow breath into her chest and let it out silently before she dared speak. "Thank you for your gift for our table."

Tanytha's mouth hardened into a brittle line. "The gift is for Abba and no one else. Don't think for a minute that I won't know if he is robbed of a single date."

She slammed the bundle back on the worktable and stormed out of the house.

In the silence that followed, Adaliah stared at nothing and battled fearsome thoughts. Without a doubt, Itthobaal would point out Tanytha's success in procuring his favorite fruit, with an emphasis on Adaliah's failure. What he might say didn't worry her.

But oh! How she feared what he might do.

A NOTE FROM THE EDITORS

We hope you enjoyed another volume in the Ordinary Women of the Bible series, created by Guideposts. For over seventy-five years, Guideposts, a nonprofit organization, has been driven by a vision of a world filled with hope. We aspire to be the voice of a trusted friend, a friend who makes you feel more hopeful and connected.

By making a purchase from Guideposts, you join our community in touching millions of lives, inspiring them to believe that all things are possible through faith, hope, and prayer. Your continued support allows us to provide uplifting resources to those in need. Whether through our communities, websites, apps, or publications, we inspire our audiences, bring them together, and comfort, uplift, entertain, and guide them. Visit us at guideposts.org to learn more.

We would love to hear from you. Write us at Guideposts, P.O.Box 5815, Harlan, Iowa 51593 or call us at (800) 932-2145. Did you love *An Unlikely Witness: Joanna's Story*? Leave a review for this product on guideposts.org/shop. Your feedback helps others in our community find relevant products.

Find inspiration, find faith, find Guideposts.

Shop our best sellers and favorites at
guideposts.org/shop

Or scan the QR code to go directly to our Shop

Find more inspiring stories in these best-loved Guideposts fiction series!

Mysteries of Lancaster County

Follow the Classen sisters as they unravel clues and uncover hidden secrets in Mysteries of Lancaster County. As you get to know these women and their friends, you'll see how God brings each of them together for a fresh start in life.

Secrets of Wayfarers Inn

Retired schoolteachers find themselves owners of an old warehouse-turned-inn that is filled with hidden passages, buried secrets, and stunning surprises that will set them on a course to puzzling mysteries from the Underground Railroad.

Tearoom Mysteries Series

Mix one stately Victorian home, a charming lakeside town in Maine, and two adventurous cousins with a passion for tea and hospitality. Add a large scoop of intriguing mystery, and sprinkle generously with faith, family, and friends, and you have the recipe for *Tearoom Mysteries*.

Ordinary Women of the Bible

Richly imagined stories—based on facts from the Bible—have all the plot twists and suspense of a great mystery, while bringing you fascinating insights on what it was like to be a woman living in the ancient world.

To learn more about these books, visit Guideposts.org/Shop

Printed in the United States
by Baker & Taylor Publisher Services